CONFESSIONS OF A RELUCTANT PSYCHIC

CONFESSIONS
of a
Reluctant
Psychic

JOCELYN SMALLEY

AONIAN PRESS
JAMES A. ROCK & COMPANY, PUBLISHERS
ROCKVILLE • MARYLAND

Confessions of a Reluctant Psychic by Jocelyn Smalley

is an imprint of JAMES A. ROCK & CO., PUBLISHERS

Confessions of a Reluctant Psychic copyright ©2008 by Jocelyn Smalley

Special contents of this edition copyright ©2008
by James A. Rock & Co., Publishers

Cover Artwork by Sam Casados.

All applicable copyrights and other rights reserved worldwide. No part of this publication may be reproduced, in any form or by any means, for any purpose, except as provided by the U.S. Copyright Law, without the express, written permission of the publisher.

This book is a work of fiction. Any resemblance of the characters in this book to actual persons, living or dead, is coincidental and beyond the intent of either the author or the publisher.

Note: Product names, logos, brands, and other trademarks occurring or referred to within this work are the property of their respective trademark holders.

Address comments and inquiries to:
AONIAN PRESS
James A. Rock & Company, Publishers
9710 Traville Gateway Drive, #305
Rockville, MD 20850

E-mail:
jrock@rockpublishing.com   lrock@rockpublishing.com
Internet URL: www.rockpublishing.com

ISBN: 978-1-59663-541-8

Library of Congress Control Number: 2007923713

Printed in the United States of America

First Edition: 2008

To my dear friend

Patricia Paullus

ACKNOWLEDGMENTS

Special thanks to Pat Paullus for countless hours spent reading my material, and for loving my characters almost as much as I do. You always seem to know exactly when and where I need a (gentle) push. I truly mean it when I say that I couldn't have done it without you.

Thanks also to Sam Casados for the original cover art. Not just anyone would have been able to so exactly capture the design I had in my head. Your art is an inspiration.

Someday this *will be your past life.*

Act accordingly.

The Past Comes Back to Haunt Me

People are probably disappointed when they meet me. I'm not spacey, I rarely wear scarves or flowing skirts, I can't abide the smell of incense, and you will absolutely never catch me chanting or playing drum. The truth is, I seem pretty much like everyone else. Which could be my life's mission, actually, to prove that I am just like everybody else. Or better yet, that everybody else is just like me.

For most of my life I went about quietly—reading, cooking, taking beach walks with friends. Let's face it, I was boring. But that was the old days, before Detective Jonah Haley came into my life and before I helped solve a single, messy case and got just a little bit known for it. I'd blame it on Jonah if I didn't know better, but the truth is, it was meant to be.

Maybe if I'd never picked up that refrigerator magnet ...

I got the call at my desk, which was piled higher than usual with an assortment of client files, psych journals I'd never get around to reading, and yellow stickies with notes scribbled in a hand I could barely decipher—my own.

"Elizabeth?" I couldn't quite place the voice at first. "It's Frank. Frank, from school."

I reviewed my college days, what I could remember of them, went back further to junior high where I'd first met him, zoomed back to high school, senior year, where we'd almost gone all the way.

"Frank Emerson?"

He laughed. I always loved the way he laughed, full out, like there was no stopping him. I was smiling now, a good, fine memory.

"Can we talk?" Had his voice always been this satisfying, this deep?

"Sure, but isn't that what we're doing?"

"I meant over lunch," he said. "Unless your husband would object."

"Unlikely, considering we're divorced."

I heard a satisfied sound from the other end of the line.

"How about the Beach Grille," I said happily. "Like old times."

I love the Grille and I'll use any excuse to eat there. They have the best clam chowder in town. It's the perennial favorite at the chowder cook-off, served with thick slices of buttery garlic bread and coffee that's always perfection. The walls are old faded brick with picture windows that look out over the bay. There's a courtyard filled with wooden tubs of geraniums and round white plastic tables unfettered by tablecloths, and the waitresses there have proudly seen better days. It's not fancy; it's solid and old, like the waitresses, a reminder to me of many things, some painful, but all of them precious after all this time.

Parking can be a problem. Starting in early spring and lasting till late in the fall, the town fills up with tourists, mostly from the San Joaquin Valley. Smart locals make themselves scarce except when playing escort to out of town guests and the streets fill up with surfer types, loud families with kids and dogs, and middle-aged couples wearing those awful matching tees.

Still, I was determined to meet Frank on home ground—old home ground. I stepped into the café, made my way out to the patio, and saw him stand to greet me, still so dark-haired and striking to look at, his smile pleasantly familiar after all these years. As he reached out to envelop me in his arms, however, I had a strange sensation that something was definitely wrong. I realized what it was when he finally let go of me. Inches from his neck, I saw it, the pure horror of it—he was wearing a clerical collar and he was dressed in black. I stepped back violently. I had been hugging a priest.

He caught my look, but said nothing, pulling out a chair for me. I gratefully sat down. The waitress plopped paper place mats and plastic menus in front of us and I nodded to her, speechless, as she offered coffee. I took a big drink, nearly scalding myself, and set the cup down with a bang, slopping coffee all over my *Scenic Map of the Area* place mat.

Frank jumped into action, dabbing at the spill with his napkin. Then he sat back and grinned. "Gave you a bit of a start, didn't I?"

I was going to protest, but the look in his eyes stopped me. They were still so … blue.

I swallowed hard and tried for nonchalant. "So, Frank, what's new?"

He reached for my hand, but I pulled it back, glancing furtively at the other diners. It would hardly do to hold hands with a priest, even if he was an old high school running buddy.

"When did you ... uh ..."

He toyed with his silverware. "It's not what you think, Elizabeth."

"Okay. So this is what? Your Halloween costume? You've turned to acting and you're just really getting into the part?"

"I guess I didn't realize how much it would impact you."

The waitress was waiting impatiently at my side. I ordered clam chowder and coleslaw. Frank went for the barbecued beef and onions on sourdough, just like he used to do, while I struggled with what to say next. "So, while I was getting divorced, you were getting ... What? Sort of married?"

Frank looked puzzled. "I'm not married." He suddenly got it. "Oh, you mean ..."

"The vows," I said solemnly.

To my great surprise, he started to laugh. "I'm a priest, Elizabeth."

"Yeah, I got that."

"You were brought up as an Episcopalian, right?"

I nodded.

"Well, if you'll remember—although we didn't spend a whole lot of time in church, you and I," he said, causing my face to turn inordinately pink, "I was raised Episcopalian, too. I'm an Episcopal priest."

"Not Catholic." I breathed my relief.

At first it seemed infinitely better until I remembered again that summer we spent so much time down by the creek and the way his eyes were then, just the same as they were now.

"I've been assigned to St. Alban's, which means I'm back to stay awhile."

I nodded, trying to process this, whether it was good or bad. Either way, I could suddenly think of nothing more to say. We sat silently for some time, me staring out the window at the way the sun sparkled on the sand; he, I am quite certain, staring at me.

"Well, I don't really go to church anymore," I said when the silence got to be too much for me. "Actually, the last time ... Oh, God, it must have been when I got married."

"Oh, yeah?"

"Yeah. And they've since burned that church down and put up a savings and loan."

We shared a smile over that, but, oddly, it was true.

"So, anyway, I don't know, I get more of a feeling of connection if I just go out and take a beach walk than if I sit in some ... pew somewhere." He was looking thoughtful, so I blathered on. "Sitting in a church, it just doesn't cut it for me."

He smiled and nodded. "Both work."

"Exactly." Why was I feeling such a need to justify? Still, I couldn't seem to stop myself. "And then, I meditate sometimes. That works really well. Or just sitting quietly."

He nodded again, looking like the wise father.

"So, I just don't go to church anymore."

He reached out and took my hand. "Well sure," he said, softer than he'd planned. "But maybe you'll start in again."

I let him keep my hand, but I couldn't look at him. *Father Frank*. It didn't compute. I remembered the time my folks had to pay big bucks to the plumber after he stuffed my brother's algebra homework down the toilet, the afternoons we ditched class and went to the lake, the way he could unhook my bra with only one hand. Even I couldn't do that. Now.

"So, then, what should I call you?" My silliness suddenly kicked in. "His High Holiness?"

He squeezed my hand, and I had to look at him at last. "How about … Frank," he said.

After lunch I went down to the beach, took off my fashionably uncomfortable shoes, and kicked around in the clear cold water as it bubbled up along the sand. I had almost asked Frank to come, but I couldn't quite get my mind around him walking barefoot in the sand, dressed to his neck in black. I've always cared for Frank, but I never really felt like I was in love with him. Oh, sure, the adolescent idea of marriage and romance had crossed my mind back then, at seventeen, and again at twenty-one when I married someone else instead and wondered *What if.* And now, what was he doing back in my life? And what would he think of me and who I'd now become?

I threw a broken sand dollar into the sea and turned back towards town. An hour with Frank, and I'd already agreed to go to church next Sunday, just to see.

On my way back to the car, I stopped in at the Shell Shocked Shoppe. I love cheap, tacky tourist junk in the worst way, and there is probably no place on earth better for finding it than at the Shell Shocked Shoppe. I was in my element, happily choosing between the salt and pepper set made to look like clams with beady eyes, and the fake coral night light with the faux diamond trim, when my eye was caught by the ultimate refrigerator magnet. Large by any standards, and set off with gaudy colored glass jewels, it featured a sea lion dressed in old-fashioned striped bathing trunks and sported the words, *Life is a beach*. Needless to say, it was soon mine.

Happy as, dare I say, *a clam*, I exited the shop and ran straight into Jonah Haley. I mean literally. I ran into his comfortingly solid chest, stumbled back, and was caught and held by him.

"You okay?" He set me back on my feet but kept hold of my shoulders as if he thought I might topple on over.

I was as dazed by seeing him there as I was by having run into him. It was the second time that day that I'd been thoroughly surprised.

"What are you doing here?" I finally managed to say.

"Looking for you." He let go of me at last.

"Okay, but how did you know to look here?" I stopped him as he started to speak. "And don't say, because I'm a detective."

"Your office said you came down this way for lunch."

I made a face. "I need to have a talk with those people."

He grinned. "So, how've you been, Libby?"

We started along the sidewalk together, looking in the shop windows. "It's Elizabeth," I said shortly, "and I've got to get back to my office soon. I have a 2 o'clock appointment."

"Then I'll get right to it."

"I was afraid of that." I was afraid of that. And I was having a great deal of trouble holding onto my joy over that glorious refrigerator magnet now half-forgotten in my purse.

"I guess I could have been nicer when we worked together last spring," he said.

"Is that what we did? Worked together?" I opened the door to Kite Heaven and sailed in, Jonah in my wake. He waited while I picked through the merchandise and finally chose an orange and gold box kite. It was beautifully simple.

"Nice kite," Jonah said, which from what little I know of him is a lot of conversation.

I smiled my agreement. "For my niece."

I paid for the purchase and waited for the shop girl to wrap it while Jonah paced in the background. As I headed for the door, he jumped ahead to open it for me, then caught up with me as I hurried along the walk.

"Look, Elizabeth ..." He said my full name as if it pained him. "Bottom line—I need your help."

I looked at him triumphantly. I knew that all along, but it took him a damn long time to spit it out. "If it's got anything to do with a crime, Detective, I'm just not interested."

He nodded, but I could tell he wasn't going anywhere. When we got to Tilly, my sweet cherry of a VW Bug, he wasn't about to let me in. "I suppose you've heard about that Janet Packard case?" He sounded so casual.

"The murder case splashed all over the news for the past two months? Yeah, I think I did hear something about that."

I reached for the door handle, but he stopped me. Being a lot bigger than me, he could do that. "It's not a murder case. Not technically."

"Only because you haven't found the body yet."

He relented and stepped back so I could get in my car. "It isn't the easiest thing for me, asking," he said, shutting the door for me.

It had to be true. Cops don't like to admit they need psychics. Hell, they don't even like to admit we exist. I rolled down the window so we could talk.

He looked at me with eyes like a sad Dalmatian. "She's only twenty-eight," he said. "She's got two beautiful little girls, four and six. You want to see their pictures?"

He was offering them to me.

I waved him off. "Finding a missing person was one thing, but getting involved in a murder case …"

"Maybe you could just think of her as a missing person, then."

I gave him a long, hard look.

"You know something?" He looked hopeful.

"It's just that if she's been missing this long …" I started the car. "Besides, you don't realize what you're asking."

"You don't have to get real involved or anything."

"It doesn't work like that."

"Then you don't know anything?"

"It's not that I don't know anything …" Was that another hopeful look? I had to wipe it off his face quickly. "It's that I don't want to know anything."

He stepped back, frowning.

I looked up at him, shading my eyes against the bright sun. "Since when do you even believe in this stuff?"

He shrugged. "Maybe I don't."

I started to roll up my window.

"If you should get any … ideas," he said. And then he walked away.

So there I was on a perfectly fine afternoon suddenly weighed down with a burden I didn't want, a burden Jonah had handed off to me, probably without realizing it; a burden that could be hard to shake. He'd planted a seed, and now, no matter what I felt about the whole thing, or what I wanted to feel, I was involved; the energy was with me, and it would most likely follow me around.

It's not that I see dead people. I don't. It's not part of my gift, and trust me, I'm grateful. But I can and do hear them and feel them there. It's been that way all my life, although I did my best to ignore it until things really broke through for me a few years back and I could no longer pretend it wasn't going on. I've learned first hand, sometimes the hard way, that there are endless levels of existence, even though most of us only seem to experience one. People like me, for whatever reason, experience more of them. I realize the idea of unseen beings might creep some people out, but for me it's become part of my daily life, my reality. Hollywood wants us to think being psychic is about scary dead people and high crimes (they sell more tickets that way), but it's about so much more than that—the joy you get from feeling a direct connection, a sense of inner peace like nothing else. It's a wonderful thing, really, when you get to know it, because it means that love really does exist and that we are truly not alone.

When I first met Jonah Haley he was spitting nails. It was late April, during a thunderstorm, and he had just had it out with one of his superiors. Something to do with missing evidence, I understand. Not his mistake, but he was the one having to pay for it. A particularly important piece of evidence on a particularly important case had been misplaced, and he was not happy about it. So I'd have to say he wasn't all that thrilled to see me when I arrived, unexpected and soaking wet.

The cop at the front counter led me down a short hall and into a room full of mismatched desks and file cabinets. In the far corner, behind a desk piled with binders and papers of all sizes and description, Jonah Haley sat hunched over his phone, athletic in build, his light brown hair falling over his forehead unnoticed by him—noticed by me. It was thick and lovely.

I sat down carefully, ready to beat a hasty retreat.

He slammed down the phone and growled in my direction when the cop introduced me. "Elizabeth Brown," he said, glancing at the paper where he'd hastily scrawled my name. Tapping his pencil impatiently against the desk, he looked at me directly with dark eyes that were obviously used to scrutinizing suspects. Not used to being scrutinized myself, I looked away.

"What's this about a missing person's report?" He was in a hurry.

"Not a report, exactly ..." In trying for a firm, clear voice, I managed only a small one. "I have some ... information."

His brow raised, his doubt was evident.

"About the little girl."

His gaze narrowed in on me again. "You related?"

I shook my head. It was all I could do to speak, but I knew I had to do it anyway. The urge had been strong in me for almost a week and the signs were everywhere. It was as if the little girl had come looking for me, and she was not about to leave me alone. It had never happened to me before, and I wasn't at all happy it was happening to me now, but there it was.

"I ... uh, had a dream." I waited for the mocking response and found it in his eyes. "Sometimes I'm able to see things," I said, knowing I couldn't stop now. "And, the thing is, I keep seeing her. She's alive but she's really, really scared. She's with people she doesn't know. Two people, I think. Up near the lake."

He looked pained.

"In a campground. In an RV."

"Well, that narrows it down." He was right; there were at least eight or nine campgrounds up there, and hundreds of camping sites.

I knew I had to ignore his sarcasm if I wanted to get anything done. I played my trump card. "If you'll take me up there, I think I can find it."

"Give me the address. I'll send somebody to check it out."

"But that's just it. I don't know the address."

"Let me get this straight," he said. "You want me to chauffeur you around the country while you try to find somebody you had a dream about?"

Ready to bolt, I struggled to stand my ground. "I know this sounds crazy to you, I realize that, but ... Look, being here is not exactly my idea of a good time, okay? I'm sorry. It's just that I can't eat or sleep the last couple days, I'm so plagued by her need to be found."

He sat back in his chair and stared at me. "Maybe you should get some medical attention."

Enough was enough. I stood up. But then the little girl's face popped back into my inner vision. With a heavy heart, I sat back down.

"I just don't think I should go up there alone."

"Nobody's going anywhere," he thundered, just as the storm outside renewed its assault.

Half an hour later we were on our way. I'm not pushy, but I know when I'm right. Besides, it was meant to be.

We forged an uneasy peace that day, made stronger when we actually did find the little girl, alone and very frightened, locked in the closet of a battered fifth-wheel that was parked in a remote corner of the second campground we looked. The couple who'd taken her had gone to town, leaving her bound and gagged, but she was okay and I'll never forget the relief in her bright eyes when she finally understood who we were and that she was safe. The local cops picked up the perpetrators at the mini mart where they were buying, coincidentally, mini-marshmallows and beer. Since they made a deal with the D.A. before the case ever got to court I never had to see them face to face, except for their mug shots in the newspaper. That was scary enough.

Jonah softened up a bit on the way home. Unable to explain my ability to pinpoint the place, he was never the less very grateful to have solved the case. He bought me dinner—okay, it was Jack In The Box, questioned me about my abilities, danced around the idea of there being anything to it, and then we went our separate ways. And though the family met with me later and thanked me profusely and the local paper put a story about the whole thing on the front page, giving me publicity I really didn't want, I hadn't seen Jonah again in over five months. And now here he was, dropping a puzzle in my lap and walking away.

* * *

The first thing I did when I got home that night was find display space for my new magnet. I had to relocate the plastic Kokopelli to the side of the refrigerator and move the pink fuzzy dice from Vegas down almost to the floor. I finally settled on just the right spot for my fashion victim sea lion right next to a 3D cutout of Marilyn Monroe in *that dress*, circa 1955. One thing for sure, I needed a bigger refrigerator.

My cat, Peeps, took up the next half-hour, first with feeding, and then with his ever-insistent need to have his ears rubbed. You can try doing something else when Peeps is pushing his head against your hand, but you won't be successful. He's like a heat seeking missile; he'll find you wherever you go. I sat down on the couch and really got into it. So did Peeps.

The phone rang too suddenly. I let it pick up.

"Lizbeth? It's Jonah Haley. You there?"

I considered my options. He was a cop. Would he somehow know I was sitting right there?

"If you're there ..." He hesitated. "I've got some new information."

He wasn't going away. I picked up. "It's Elizabeth," I said, "and I'm off duty."

"But dedicated." I could tell he was smiling.

Peeps was now rubbing his chin against my ankle. "My cat doesn't think so."

"What?"

I picked Peeps up and made him happy again. "Never mind. What makes you think I'm interested in information, new or otherwise?"

He made me wait a few seconds. "Can I come over?"

"Now?"

Peeps looked offended.

"Wanted to show you something."

"I haven't eaten yet," I said, looking longingly towards the kitchen.

"I'll bring pizza." The man had an answer for everything.

I thought about my refrigerator again. The outside was great, nicely decorated, but inside was a bottle of soda, some stale lettuce, a bag of old oranges, and a partial can of tuna even Peeps would reject.

"Make it Canadian bacon," I said, "with pineapple."

By the time Jonah arrived forty-five minutes later I was ready to eat the box. Peeps nearly tripped him as he came in, taking a deep sniff at his sneakers, then turning up his nose and prancing away.

"Your cat?" Jonah set the pizza box and a six-pack of soda on the kitchen counter.

"You mean, you didn't bring him?"

Jonah grinned. "You always like this when you're nervous?"

"I'm not nervous," I said nervously. I pulled a tray of ice cubes out of the freezer, shutting the door so hard that my new magnet fell to the floor.

Before I could pick it up, Jonah grabbed it, checking it out carefully. As he put it back up, he stopped in wonderment, dazzled by the collection before him. "Good God," he whistled. Then he carefully surveyed the rest of the room.

I may have a weakness for tacky tourist junk, but I keep it contained to my refrigerator, and, admittedly, a few cupboards and drawers. The rest of the house may not be *In Style Magazine* but it is close to *Woman's Day*, with soft, cozy colors, and rooms that are warm and bright.

"Looks normal enough," Jonah said.

I let the jab pass, setting glasses and plates on the table. As we sat down, it suddenly hit me that I was going to have to eat pizza in front of a guy I really didn't know. I have a long-standing policy about that— never eat pizza on a first date. Not that this was a date, but still ... Pizza may be the number one food choice of most Americans, but it has got to be one of the most embarrassing foods on the planet to eat. Who among us can feel sophisticated or wise with mozzarella stringing out of our mouths?

The wonder was that Jonah didn't seem to care. Ignoring my eating habits, he dug into his pizza like a man possessed, finishing three pieces in the time it took me to delicately nibble on one. I could see I was going to have to speed up if I wanted anything much to eat. When I caught him slipping tidbits to Peeps, I knew I was okay. The man might be trouble, but at least he accepted the possibility of cats.

What do you want from me? I so wanted to ask.

He looked up as if he'd heard me. "You want the last piece?"

"You and Peeps can fight over it."

Jonah divided the pizza, breaking off a small, especially cheesy bite, and setting it on the floor. "Great cat," he said, and I almost think he meant it.

He wolfed down his remaining pizza before Peeps could wolf down his own, took a last swallow of Coke, and looked at me so directly I knew the time had come.

I tried to put it off. "Coffee?"

He shook his head, got up, and dumped the empty pizza box in the recycle while I put the plates and glasses in the sink. Then he followed me into the living room.

"This psychic business ..." He sounded uncertain. "You ever do anything like talk to relatives?"

I turned to see if he was joking. It was hard to tell. "You mean like a dead aunt?" I sat on the couch, ready for the inquisition.

He sat, too, rifling through my *Marie Claire*, stopping to stare at a very hot model in a tiny black dress, while I tried to imagine him dressed in black, with a clerical collar. Nope, it just wouldn't do. I pictured him more easily in faded out jeans and a flannel shirt, which, funny thing, was just what he was wearing.

"I've heard all the jokes," I said, "but I understand you have to make them."

Jonah closed the magazine, laying it back on the coffee table.

"Really. I'm used to it. Take your best shot." Sometimes a preemptive strike was best.

He smiled at me, a very nice smile. "Libby ..."

"Please. I'm just not the nickname type."

He nodded, but didn't look convinced.

I felt suddenly, inexplicably impatient. "Is this ... work time?"

He looked startled.

"I mean, are you on duty? Do you always work evenings?"

He shook his head. "My wife says when I get like this I'm *on a mission*."

"Oh, your wife ..."

"Ex."

I suddenly felt more satisfied.

"Obsessed," he said.

"With your wife?"

"My work. With my work. Which is just one of the reasons she's now my ex, I guess."

I spoke before thinking. "Oh, but it's not very recent."

He frowned.

"I'm sorry," I said hastily. "It's none of my business." But I could feel it, feel that he wasn't in pain anymore, so, obviously, it wasn't very recent.

"What else do you know about me?"

"You're a detective. That's it. I swear."

"I got divorced about two years ago," he said. "I have a seven-year old daughter, Amy, but she's with her mom right now in Sacramento. I'll see her at Thanksgiving. Anything else you want to know?"

Uncomfortable, I decided it was time to get back to work. "How about that new information?"

He seemed to relax, settle back a bit. Fishing in his shirt pocket, he pulled out a worn leather watch. "Janet Packard's ex-husband came by the station this afternoon. Said he was worried about her, wanted to know how he could help, but ... Something just didn't click."

"So you stole his watch?"

"Borrowed it."

"And that's the new information?"

"I was hoping you could tell me. You know, from the watch." He seemed a little worried about my reaction, and when I didn't speak, he said, "I saw something like that on TV once. This guy could read people's stuff."

I was surprised at his request.

"Can you do things like that?"

I nodded reluctantly. "Sometimes."

He offered me the watch, but instead of taking it, I sat back further on the couch.

"Now I've made you mad."

I shook my head. "I'm just not all that eager to dive in." Touching something like that watch could throw me into a place I didn't want to be, somewhere hard to get out of. "It's just that there's energy in it, you know? There's energy in everything, and once you touch something, well, it might be ... Who knows? Dark, unpleasant."

For a fleeting moment I considered telling him about the time an ancient and angry spirit followed me home from a Native American ceremonial site, but then thought better of it. The neighbors might wonder if a detective ran out screaming into the night.

Jonah said nothing for a few moments, and then, almost under his breath, "The thing is, I thought maybe we could save her life."

Now the guilt trip.

"I've always had such a fear of getting involved in things like this," I said, "which is one reason I really don't want people even knowing about it, you know?"

"But you're the one who came to me the first time. With the little girl, I mean. If you didn't want to get involved, then why?"

He'd cornered me and I had to say it. "Because, I just kept thinking maybe we could ... save her life."

"Bingo."

I held out my hand. He took hold of it and with his other hand, pressed the watch gently into my palm. I felt this zing, this absolutely delightful and unexpected energy that arched between us, more like a rainbow than a lightening bolt. It was a long moment before he let go of my hand. I closed my eyes, trying to avoid looking into his, but I was too late. They had already told me what I didn't want to know, and after that, I was going to find it very hard to focus.

I jumped up and started pacing the room, concentrating on my breathing, trying to recite the Gettysburg Address, trying to remember my own name. It was little use. All I could feel was him.

"Give me a minute," I said without looking at him, though I wondered desperately what he was doing, what he was feeling. I sank down in a chair, the farthest I could get away from him and still be in the same room. Mentally I pushed him back. Gradually, gradually, I began to feel less surrounded by him, more myself.

I focused on the watch and tried letting go. Closing my eyes, I saw deep purple, which has come to be a sign to me that I'm connected into my guides. Instantly I felt the comfort of them there; old friends, love and light. I don't know how long it was after that before I finally spoke.

"It's not something he enjoys, telling time," I heard myself say. "It had something to do with their break up, actually. Not telling time, but having to be on time, and having to be structured rather than free, closed rather than open."

"Who was the closed one?"

"Not him."

I sat with the watch awhile, grateful Jonah was saying nothing.

"It does seem like he has some sad feelings over her loss, but it's not so much about losing her specifically as about the actual fact of losing ... someone, anyone. About failure and what it signifies. Losing someone is failure to him. Divorce is failure, so he can't ever be a success now." And then a rush of feeling: "His mother gave him this watch, or some close, powerful female relative. Somebody who thought he wasn't good enough. He wears it because he should wear it, not because he wants to. It symbolizes everything he doesn't like."

"He doesn't like women?" Jonah sounded hopeful, like he'd found a clue.

"Being told what to do. Being told ... anything at all. He doesn't feel all that ... hateful, though."

"Plenty of murders happen without hate. A motive, sure, but hate? Not necessary."

I sat with my inner silence a few more minutes, then opened my eyes slowly, still in a sort of haze. I closed my eyes again, a little woozy, then began to slowly will myself back into the room. It took awhile—I'd been way out there. Or way in. I'm never sure which. "So, anyway," I said finally, rubbing the back of my neck, "I'd be surprised if he was involved."

I opened my eyes fully at last to find Jonah looking at me, a rather bemused expression on his face. "Thanks," he said quietly, and then, "Is there anything else you want to tell me?" He sounded so content.

Lord yes, but it was way too soon to even formulate the thoughts.

His beeper went off, breaking whatever spell had been stealing over us. I pointed toward the kitchen. "You can use the phone in there."

I stood up slowly, stretching myself back to life, then followed him, dropping the watch next to him on the kitchen table. It was the coward's way out, giving it back to him without actually touching him again. Part of me was just a little bit disappointed I wasn't going to get that chance.

I wandered back to the living room to give him some privacy. Peeps, still sleepy from his post pizza nap, tailed me eagerly to the couch and crawled onto my lap, planting his front paws on my chest. I petted him lazily while he purred his little heart out, staring up at me with wide yellow eyes that spoke of something grand.

Jonah came to stand in my kitchen door, his height filling it. "Sorry," he said, twirling the watch. "I've got to go. Trouble in paradise."

I started to move Peeps.

"Don't." Jonah smiled at one, or both, of us. "I can let myself out." He seemed uncertain what to say next. "Sorry if I ruined your nice quiet evening."

"It's okay. Really."

He nodded. "I'll ... see you, then. Thanks again."

He gave me one last look before heading out the front door, leaving me to wonder when and where I would see him again, because yes, he had definitely ruined my quiet evening. And it had very little to do with that old leather watch.

* * *

I work in this absolutely crazy place; a sort of cooperative, a jumble of small offices stuffed together in an old warehouse, each office unique, each occupant even more so. We have a psychologist, two MFCC's, an

LCSW (me), a paralegal, and an eating disorder clinic, which I avoid like the plague, especially around the holidays.

My office is about twenty feet square, with high, narrow windows that look out on two different, yet stunning views of the parking lot. I have an entry door that would be far too narrow for some of the eating disorder clients and far too wide for others, and a wood floor I've partially covered with a colorful braided rug because I'm way too lazy to refinish it. Clients tell me they feel cozy there, even safe, but sometimes, I swear it's claustrophobic.

When you come into the entry hall of our building the first thing you notice is Rita's curiously beady eyes peering at you over a tall Formica covered counter, like a little child who can just barely see over the edge. Even then, she has to have a step stool, but only the staff knows about it—she's very touchy about her size. Along the hall are a few straight plastic chairs, an overgrown philodendron, and a wicker wastebasket. We like to call that our waiting area. Rita directs traffic, routes calls, and takes messages, and I suspect it was her who told Jonah how to find me at the beach. Married twenty years, none of it happily, she seems to feel it's her sacred duty to get me into something like that, too. She'll do anything to achieve that end.

I was humming when I crossed the threshold the next morning and Rita grabbed onto that and held on. "Nice evening?"

"Nice morning," I said lightly, not wanting to give her anything at all. "Sun's shining, birds are singing ..."

But she wasn't about to be deterred. I could tell she'd stepped off her stool, because she disappeared for a second, then came around the end of the counter and peered up at me. "So, did he find you?" She hadn't been at her post yesterday afternoon when I'd returned from lunch, so it was her first chance to grill me.

"Who?"

She grinned.

"He's a cop, Rita. It was business."

Rita nodded happily. "You hate cops."

"I hate one particular cop." But that had been over a year ago.

I think I heard her humming "Fools Rush In" as I headed off down the hall.

Once in my office I collapsed in my chair, grateful no appointments were due till at least ten. I had a lot of things on my mind, a lot to think through. It was time to come clean. There actually was that one other time I had run into the detective. It's just that I'm so confused about what happened that night, I usually try not to think about it. Somehow it always feels too dangerous.

I was at a club. Well, truth be told, in our little town we have lots of bars, but nothing glamorous enough to qualify as a club. However, it is called the Club Contempo, so I guess I can legitimately refer to it as that. It's actually a few worn booths, a twelve by twelve dance floor, and an "L" shaped bar that seats maybe ten. Music comes from an old time jukebox that plays "Smoke Gets In Your Eyes" (the original) alongside the Back Street Boys and Eminem.

It was a Tuesday night, and Tuesdays, I have always felt, are far worse than Mondays because nothing defines them. Mondays, at least everybody commiserates and Wednesdays you're halfway home, but Tuesdays? Stuck in the middle of nowhere, they're horribly mundane. Kind of like watching baseball on TV. Invite me to a Giants game and I'm there, willing to sit in bone chilling fog for hours, pay exorbitant prices for hot dogs and dodge the spilled beer from the drunken guy who inevitably sits behind me. But, baseball on TV?

My friend, Lindsay, had just lost another one—another seemingly perfect, but ultimately flawed boyfriend. Needing to drown herself in something that particular Tuesday night, she had chosen to do it with cheap wine. Lucky me, I got to go along for the ride.

I was having just a little bit of fun group dancing with her and a shaggy-haired guy we'd met earlier that night at the Burger King. I was dating a regular guy at the time, or should I say I was dating a guy regularly, but he wasn't able to go with us that night. Probably watching baseball on TV.

We were in the middle of the bunny hop, and the song, if I recall, was naturally some kind of hip-hop, when my bladder got the best of me. Heading down the dark hall at a fast clip, I rounded the corner and there he was—Jonah. I hadn't seen him since the day we found the little girl and in my slightly altered state of grace it was hard to place him right away.

"Hey," he said softly.

"Hey." I was happily playing for time. He looked good, even in the dark, and he was smiling as if he was glad to see me. How could I forget who he was?

"Jonah Haley," he said, holding out his hand. "The detective."

I took it and held on, almost forgetting to let go.

He grinned. "So you do remember me."

In my embarrassment I embarrassed myself even more, mumbling something about urgent needs, and heading into the restroom. Coming out, he seemed to have disappeared, but about an hour later, just when I was thinking of leaving, he was suddenly at my side.

"Dance?"

He didn't wait for an answer, but pulled me onto the tiny overcrowded dance floor. As it happened to be a slow dance, he took me into his arms. My sudden dizziness might have been from the Long Island Iced Tea I'd just finished, but seemed more connected to the arm around my waist. When Lindsay gave me an exaggerated wink from across the floor, I was just drunk enough to giggle.

Jonah looked down at me. "Am I that bad?"

And then something happened, the very something that makes me wonder if I dreamed it all, or should have dreamed it. And it makes me confused, in a nice romantic way, but still, confused. He looked down at me like it was the most natural thing in the world that we should be together, and we just sort of locked onto each other. Maybe he was a little drunk too, and maybe it wouldn't have happened otherwise, but whatever it was, it was like, at that moment, we might go on forever, me in his arms, our eyes and bodies seriously and intimately entwined. Nothing else needed. Ever.

The song ended and we stepped apart like we'd never been together, awkward to know what to say, so we said nothing. I drifted back to my friends and he to wherever he was going. For such a small place, it was easy to get lost in when it was full. Lindsay told me later that I seemed out of it for the rest of the night, and I remember nothing past that time, that eternal time, when I looked at him and saw myself.

Running into Jonah yesterday had brought it all up again, stirred a pot I'd rather have left alone. How do you work with a guy like that when you're still wondering what it all meant, or if it ever really even happened? If he never brought it up, could I? And what if he did bring it up, what could I say? I decided there was only one thing I could do. I would go and talk to God.

***

Sunday morning seemed early even at eleven o'clock. I usually get up around eight on Sunday and putter around in my nightgown until noon, so wearing panty hose and carrying my purse seemed really odd. And church had changed. I guess God no longer has a dress code because most of the people hadn't even bothered to dress up; some wore jeans and tees. Even one of the altar boys had jeans sticking out below his robe. Feeling ready to run, I positioned myself in the very last row, miserably out of place. Once again, I had managed to wear the wrong thing, even to church.

When the service began, Father Frank spotted me right away. I could see his pleased reaction and then it seemed as if he had to force himself to *not* look at me, though once in awhile I thought I saw him sneak a peek. I wondered if anybody else noticed. The sermon was quite something—sin and forgiveness and the power of prayer all rolled into one, and this from a man I once did some remarkably heavy petting with down by the creek. He certainly had a way with words I'd never been privy to before.

I sat out communion. It had been far too long, and although I could still recall the way the wafer used to feel on my tongue, my memory of what to do after that was pretty foggy. I had to fight a wild desire to skip out early rather than face my old friend in his new environment. He was a different animal now and I didn't have a clue how to deal with him.

I stood in line to shake his hand and congratulate him on his insightful sermon but when it was finally my turn, I could only nod my head and grin.

"Wait for me, Elizabeth," he said in a low voice.

I stood back, watching the old ladies gurgle over him (at least they still dressed up), as well as some of the younger ones. When his groupies finally thinned out, Frank beckoned me to follow him, and we went back into the church. A blonde woman was taking down flowers from the altar. About twenty-five, with a short, tight skirt and a body more suited to Hooters than St. Albans, she smiled and waved at Frank as if he was the best thing she'd seen in a month of Sundays.

"Whoa, Frank, " I said, "the Altar Society has changed. They didn't make them like that when I was a girl."

Frank looked embarrassed. "She's a little ... eager." With a token nod in her direction, he took my hand and led me into his office. "It's the funniest thing," he said. "Something about the robes, I guess? Maybe it's like being in uniform. Since I've been a priest, there seems to be this constant, unrelenting interest in me."

"You're complaining about that?"

"Well, no, I'm still a guy. I still have an ego, but ... I'm not exactly in a position where I can date around a lot, you know?"

"Like being married," I said. 'When you're single, it's hard to meet eligible men, but while you're married, they're all over the place."

"God's little joke," Frank said, smiling.

I watched as he removed his vestments. At least I think that's what they're called. Being a lapsed Episcopalian, I'm not really sure.

Frank hung the garments up carefully. "First church I was at, one of my parishioners kept trying to set me up with her seventeen year-old daughter. Seventeen!"

"Well, a priest does make a good catch."

He looked at me closely.

"I mean from a mother's point of view." I perched on the corner of his desk, finding it hard to settle, ready to fly.

"So, what did you think of the service?"

"Good." I stumbled over the word. "I thought you were really … good."

He looked at me, head tilted, questioning.

"You've very … verbal." I wasn't getting any better. "Really, it was great. I'm just not used to you being like this, I guess. How'd you get into it, anyway? Last I heard, you were living with Annie and teaching math to seventh graders."

"And that's enough to make anybody turn to Jesus," he said, grinning. And then more seriously, "What can I say? I wanted something more for a long time, I just didn't know what it was. I loved the kids, but I needed … Well, I didn't know what I needed." He stared off into space, thinking, then looked back at me. "Then one day I just happened to run into a guy," he said. "Former teacher, going to the seminary. Everything just fell into place all of a sudden and then I felt like it was where I was supposed to be. Like I should have known it all along."

"So it really is like a calling?"

"Yeah. Only Annie didn't think so."

"I'm sorry, Frank."

He nodded. "Well, things work out the way they should, I guess." He came to me and took both my hands in his. "It's just so good to see you, Elizabeth." He leaned down and kissed me on the nose. No, I'm not kidding. He kissed me on the nose, then pulled back to look down at me benevolently. I swear he was beaming. Had I just been blessed?

"You think you might start coming on Sundays?"

I made a face without thinking about it, then tried hard to retract.

"Once in awhile, then?" He squeezed my hands hopefully.

I thought about it more carefully this time. "I'll try." I pulled my hands free and got up from the desk. "It's just … This takes some getting used to, Frank. You know, with our personal history and all."

"That was a long time ago." I looked up at him to find his blue eyes sparkling. "Although it almost seems like yesterday. I may be a man of God, Elizabeth, but I'm still a man."

I could feel my face warming. Had somebody turned up the thermostat?

"It's okay, you know. It's allowed."

"I guess I've just never been close friends with a priest before," I said. "For that matter, I've never known one who wasn't married."

"I'm working on that," he said.

It was right about then that I decided I had a pressing engagement somewhere and really had to fly.

Messages from the Other Side

Jonah didn't even realize he was in trouble until his sister called to ask him to a barbecue. "Bring Helen," she said. "Haven't seen her in awhile."

Neither had he, but he managed to avoid the inevitable sisterly lecture about commitment phobia by making a more general excuse. "Helen's in New York," he said. "Some kind of work thing."

At least she'd been going there the last time they talked, and that was over two months ago. He then tried, unsuccessfully, to get out of the invitation himself, but Ruby, being Ruby, was way ahead of him.

"C'mon, Jonah. Saturday's Ben's forty-first."

"You know how I feel about parties, Ruby."

"Yeah, so? The folks are still out of town. Nobody else from the family will be here. You have to come, represent the family. Besides, it's just gonna be a few of our closest friends."

Which meant the movers and the shakers. He hated the movers and the shakers.

Jonah hung up the phone thinking about Elizabeth. He walked clear into his small kitchen, had a big drink of water and set the empty glass on the sea blue tile before it even dawned on him that it was odd, him thinking about Elizabeth. But ever since he'd seen her the other night, on her own home ground, he had this sense she was always somewhere in the back of his head, maybe always had been.

He went out for a long run along the cliffs. By the third mile he had hit his stride nicely and was toying with the notion of asking Libby to the barbecue. By the fifth, he almost tripped over a rock sticking up dead center in the path, a rock he'd never had a problem with before. At that point he could clearly see Ruby questioning Helen about her career, her back almost literally against the wall. The poor woman had made him swear later that he'd never, ever make her be around Ruby again. It wasn't why they'd drifted apart, but still ... He loved Ruby, but she could be such a shit when she took a dislike to someone.

In the last mile or so, when all the good feelings of the run had kicked in, when he felt, at least temporarily, that he could run on smoothly and forever, something totally unexpected happened—memories of the night he'd seen Elizabeth at the Club Contempo rushed in. One minute he was enjoying the view of the bay and the fresh, salty bite of the breeze off the ocean, and the next he was seeing instead the look in her eyes that night, and feeling that connection when she'd slipped into his arms so perfectly he'd never wanted it to end.

He slowed to a jog, then a fast walk and kept that pace awhile, trying to banish the look of her, the feel of her. Not one to waste time on things he didn't understand, he'd pushed thoughts of that night far away, but today, try as he might, he couldn't stop them.

He went through his stretching routine on autopilot, his mind and feelings somewhere else. He simply couldn't get the memories to leave him alone.

When he got home, he called her, then hung up without leaving a message when her recorder picked up. Congratulating himself on a narrow escape, he jumped into the shower, but she was waiting for him even there.

Jonah didn't do relationships, not well, anyway, and he wasn't exactly itching to start another one, especially with some weird psychic chick. He didn't even like the word *chick*— in fact, he hated it, but it somehow seemed to fit in this particular case. She was weird ... Hell, she was downright cheeky when she wanted to be. And he never had figured out how she'd found that little girl, never come up with a satisfactory explanation anyway. He and the Chief had decided to do a background check just to be sure she hadn't somehow been involved in the kidnapping, but he'd discovered no clues, nothing at all suspicious, nothing but glowing reports, and now here he was asking her for help again.

He stepped out of the shower and grabbed a towel. He knew the real reason he'd contacted her again. Sure he wanted to find that missing woman, but the real reason he'd asked Elizabeth for help was something else entirely—just being near her set off some kind of silent alarm. Her voice, her body, her attitude, turned him on like nobody had for a very long time. He'd noticed it the first day they met, and he noticed it now. Maybe he would ask her to the barbecue.

His phone rang just as he finished drying off. He wrapped the towel around his waist and went to answer the call.

"Oh, hi. Jonah? This is Elizabeth Brown."

He nearly dropped the phone.

"Sorry to bother you at home, but I had this sort of ... feeling, I guess you'd call it. So I thought maybe I'd better talk to you about it right away."

"A feeling?" His heart was beating fast. Why the hell would she call now, just when he'd been obsessing about her?

"About that missing woman." She hesitated, sounding uncertain. "Sort of a knowing, really. You ever have things like that, where you just sort of know something?"

"I don't think so." He walked to the window, staring out at the neighbor's perfect green lawn, frowning at his own, imperfect one.

"Well, it's hard to describe, but basically ..." She seemed to be lost in thought, then finally continued. "It's like you suddenly just know something, and there's no doubt, like it springs up inside of you, full blown." A hesitation, and then, "So, anyway, the thing is, I think she's still alive."

"Janet Packard?"

"Yeah."

"You're kidding." And when there was no response, "What makes you think that?"

"The feeling." She was matter-of-fact.

He perched on the end of his couch. "That's it?"

"Pretty much. Anyway, I thought I'd better at least mention it to you."

"It's not a lot to go on."

"No, but ... um, look ... It's just really very strong."

"Like with the little girl?"

"Yes."

"All right. Thanks."

"I'll let you know if I get anything more, okay?"

"Okay."

She was hanging up.

"No, wait."

She did.

"You wouldn't want to go to a barbecue this Saturday, would you?"

"Oh," she said softly.

"Mostly my sister's friends. I'd understand if you didn't want to."

"Well ..."

He waited for what seemed like an inevitable *no*.

"It's not a work thing?"

He stood up and started walking the room, smiling. "Nothing to do with a crime," he said lightly.

"Okay."

"Okay?"

There was a tentative sound of agreement from the other end.

"Great. Then I'll pick you up around three."

He hung up, amazed at what he'd just done. And the fact she'd said okay. It almost felt like some larger force was at work, except Jonah didn't believe in a larger force. He smiled to himself as he headed into the bedroom to get dressed, remembering how she'd looked when he'd seen her the other day. Her dark brown hair was thick and wavy in a way that made him want to bury his hands in it. The soft curves of her body made him want to do even more.

Maybe he was headed for trouble, maybe not. Maybe she was just really good at reading people and her "gift" was nothing more than that. Only time would tell, and hopefully, he'd have a really good time finding out.

Living in the Now. Again

There wasn't much point in staring at the phone. It didn't seem to be giving me any answers. I sat back in the chair, uncertain. I had called Jonah with the express purpose of ... What was it I had called him for again? Certainly not in regards to a date, but inviting me to a family barbecue? Wasn't that a date? I was suddenly aware that my whole body seemed to be shaking.

My phone rang and it was Rita telling me Sandy Roget had finally arrived. With a standing ten a.m. appointment every Wednesday, she always manages to be exactly seventeen minutes late, on the dot. Since I now plan it into my schedule, this meant she was actually right on time. I got up to meet her as she came in the door.

"Well, aren't you looking swell?" Sandy is twenty-five, but scavenges her vocabulary from the dustbins of our lives. Partial to soft skirts, leather boots, and long sweaters, she came into the room with her usual swish and settled delicately on the couch, crossing one leg over the other.

"Smoke?" She was offering me a cigarette.

I just looked at her.

She put them away with a sigh. Every week, she tries.

I waited for her to begin. With most people, it takes some gentle conversation first, maybe even talk of the weather, but Sandy always just launches in when she's good and ready.

She leaned forward, intent. "Jimmy says this is making me worse."

"This? You mean the counseling?" We'd been working together for about eight weeks.

"Yeah. He says I'm becoming a ... *man hater*." She used her fingers to put quotes around the term.

"In what way?"

"Well, he says ... And get this, he's so hoity-toity himself, you wouldn't believe it ... He says I'm parading around the house like I own the place."

"Don't you both own it?"

"Yeah, but he says I think I'm Princess Grace on her high horse."

"What do you think?"

She looked a bit grim. "He's just flummoxed 'cause I don't cow tow to him like I used to. I don't bow down." She illustrated, making a mock bow.

"And this is because of our sessions?"

"Well, that's what he thinks."

"And you?"

"God's honest truth? He's the problem. We've been married less than two years and he doesn't even want to do the deed anymore."

"You mean, have sex?"

She suddenly looked near tears. "Does he think I'm made of stone?"

I handed her a tissue. "You haven't mentioned this before, Sandy."

She sniffed and nodded, then blew loudly into the Kleenex.

"Is this a recent change?"

"About a week and a half, I guess."

"Did something happen?"

She looked a bit hesitant. "I bit him on the shoulder." And to my surprised look, "It sounded like such a good idea. I read about it in *101 Ways to Make Your Man Moan*."

"Oh."

"Have you read it?"

"No, I don't think so."

"It's number 34. It's a real bitchin' book," she said earnestly. "Tells you how to really turn guys on. Unless he's a slug-a-bug like Jimmy." She stopped to blow her nose again, then sat back and crossed her arms almost angrily. "I may have bit a little too hard. I don't know. I was just trying to ... You know ... Light his fire." She pulled out her cigarettes, then checked herself and put them back in her purse. "Last night he said I was trying to be like those women who yell at the wolves."

"It's *run* with the wolves, Sandy."

"Well, whatever. How can I be one when I don't even know what that is?"

I waited for her to go on, but for once she was waiting for me. Since she was looking so serious, I had to try hard to suppress my smile. "It's always best if you explore new things with your partner before you try them, Sandy. Talk things over. You know, feel him out first."

She giggled nervously at that.

"Both of you, you need to talk things like that over before you try them. And it's your chance to let him know what you'd like, too. Which is really important. You can't expect a guy to just know." I had a fleeting memory of Erica Jong's *Fear of Flying* and her memorable description of a "zipless fuck." Wouldn't that be nice?

My phone rang. Since Rita has strict instructions never to call me during a session, it had to be an emergency. Apologizing to Sandy first, I picked up. Before I could speak, Rita did. "There's a man here asking for you."

"Rita, I'm in session."

Rita was practically whispering into the phone. "I know that, Elizabeth, but he's a priest." Being a dedicated Catholic, Rita could only imagine it was important.

I smiled apologetically at Sandy as I spoke into the phone. "Tall, dark, and handsome?"

"Blue eyes better than Sinatra's," Rita breathed. "Why is it the church gets all the good ones?"

I had to smile at that. "He's a friend, Rita. He can wait, or I can call him later."

"Okay," she said, "but you have got to tell me what is going on."

Later, when I walked Sandy out, Frank was sitting in the reception area, dressed in his usual black, with the collar, of course. Maybe that outfit gets him in the door. Rita was conveniently watering the philodendron, even though I was pretty sure I had seen her water it the day before.

Frank stood and kissed me warmly on the cheek. Ushering him back to my office, I could feel Rita's eyes on us as we went down the hall.

He spoke as soon as we stepped inside. "I just really needed to see you." He was standing so close that I had to fight the urge to move back. He reached out and took me by the shoulders. I started to speak, but before I could say a word he pulled me into him, kissing me almost fiercely on the mouth.

I pulled back, flummoxed, as Sandy would have said.

"I can't stop thinking about you, Elizabeth. Ever since I saw you on Sunday ..." He slid his large hands down my arms as he spoke, taking hold of my smaller hands when he got to them.

"But, Frank ..."

"I feel like a teenager again. I can barely eat or sleep. And the dreams ..."

"Don't tell me about the dreams," I said quickly.

He grinned. "Seriously, Elizabeth, I'm beginning to wonder if that's why I'm here."

"The dreams?"

"No," he said, giving my hands a squeeze. "I mean, maybe that's why I'm back in town. Maybe God called me to the church and I got sent back here because all along we were supposed to be together."

I pulled away from him and sat down in the chair in front of my desk almost without realizing it. I needed to put some space between us, take some time. Besides, I had just discovered an awful truth—Frank Emerson may look like Adonis, but he kisses like a fish. Stiff lips, cold somehow. Kind of like a halibut.

Meanwhile, he stood there smiling down at me like he'd just discovered the meaning of life.

"I think you'd better sit, Frank," I said.

With a grin, he settled into my rocker, the one I keep to make clients feel more at home, more relaxed. I couldn't help but notice that his lovely, long fingers immediately started caressing the arms of the chair.

I tried to focus. "So, what you're saying is that God's giving us another chance."

He nodded. "Something like that."

Now I know that sounds romantic, but it's the kind of logic that can get you into some serious trouble. More often than not it's as much an attempt to justify your rash behavior as anything else. Sometimes what seems the perfect set up, may be just that—a set up. And, our chance to sit back and realize what's really going on and just say no.

"If God fixes things so people will meet and get together, how do you explain all the divorces, Frank? What about battered women?"

Frank looked pained. "Well, of course." He sounded a bit dejected. "I know it's not that simple, but in our case ... We're old friends, Elizabeth. I already know you."

"You knew the high school me."

"You're still the same."

"God, I hope not."

"I mean, you're still funny, witty. Outspoken, I always liked that." He rested his chin on his hand, his elbow on the arm of the chair. "You're still the same pretty little ..."

"Little, Frank? I'm five-seven. And I weigh ... Oh, probably fifteen pounds more than I should." It's actually more like twenty, but honesty in this area should only go so far. I may not be plus-sized, but I am a little plush.

"You look fine to me," he said, earning my eternal gratitude. "Besides, there's just something about you, Elizabeth. You've got that ... look."

I felt a sudden tingle of response, never mind where I was feeling it. "Men want to hold you."

Speaking of looks, we sat there looking at each other, blue eyes to brown.

He patted his knee and said, teasingly, "Why don't you come over here?"

The playful look in his eyes had heated and changed. I felt my body respond in kind, talking me into it, throwing caution out those two narrow windows right into the parking lot. Hadn't I regretted not letting him be the first and wondered what it would have been like to be with him? So what if he was a priest? So what if I was conflicted? And as for the kissing thing, maybe he was just out of practice. We could work on that.

I launched myself in his direction and let him pull me down on his lap, but instead of kissing me again, he guided my head to his shoulder and started rocking me, his warm breath on my neck. I prayed no one would open my door just then, because the priest was rocking the social worker.

He kissed my neck and this time I felt his tongue there, too, ever so lightly. Okay, that was warmer, better. He nuzzled my ear. Then he stopped, which of course only made me want more. I snuggled in to him. Nothing. I looked up at him—looked him straight in the eyes, hoping to spur on another round of kissing, but he didn't take the bait. Instead, he tucked my head back under his chin and started stroking my hair.

"I know I can't just suddenly appear back in your life and expect you to drop everything," he said softly. "You probably already have a guy." Now the halibut was fishing for information.

"Nobody, really," I said, as visions of Jonah popped, unbidden, into my head. "No commitments, anyway."

Was that Peeps purring? Or was it Frank making his happy sound?

A knock on the door brought me up straight. "Your next appointment's here," Rita called sweetly from the other side of the door. Damn her, she came to the door to knock like that, she used the phone. I heard her spike heels tap, tap away.

I gave Frank a rueful smile, then got up reluctantly, feeling a bit light headed. From behind me, he slipped his arms around my waist and pulled me back against him. "Pity," he said softly. He held me there for a moment or so while I closed my eyes and let my imagination take me all the places I didn't have time to go right then. I turned in his arms and kissed him, but only lightly. No chance to check the fishing report.

He finally let go of me. "Will I see you Sunday?" And when I nodded, he said, "Come to the 11:00 o'clock. That way, after the service we can have lunch."

He exited out the door, leaving me limp and wanting more. After nearly fifteen years away from the church, it had come to this. I was now attending regularly, but for all the wrong reasons.

* * *

The problem with being psychic, if there is one, is that it isn't always convenient. For the most part, you can pick and choose the times you want to tune in, but there are those other times when it just comes right at you. You could be in the middle of the supermarket or driving your car, and there it is—a sentence in your head, a strong sense of urgency, or a sense you need to be somewhere or remember something. Like on AOL, *You've got mail.*

After a while you learn that ignoring that mail, those messages, can be a very bad idea. For instance, you feel a strong urge to take a certain route to work, ignore it, and end up in a massive traffic jam. On the other hand, if you listen to your gut, everything goes smoothly, but you have no idea what would have happened because you never run into that traffic jam. After a few false steps, some large and some small, you pretty much follow those urges.

But what was my urge regarding Frank and Jonah? Okay, I know what some of my urges are—I'm not that naïve. I was suddenly feeling ripe with possibilities, and just possibly overwhelmed by them. Experience has taught me that men can look so good at first and then end up being nothing more than mirages on the horizon. It would be a while before I knew for sure if the sheltering palm trees and the crystal clear springs were really there.

* * *

Saturday morning the clouds started rolling in, and by noon, rain was looking like a definite maybe. Not a normal thing for us this early in the fall on the Central Coast, but this was, after all, supposed to be an El Nino year—anything could happen. I found myself hoping the barbecue would be cancelled. Of all things, going to a private party with a guy I barely knew, when he would of course know everyone there, was starting to sound like a really bad idea. Going to a barbecue where it might be pouring rain sounded even worse.

I picked endlessly through my clothing choices, finally settling on my favorite good jeans and a pink top that my best friend, Lindsay, insists makes me look *hot*. Though looking hot is pretty much something I do only after the thermometer has hit at least eighty degrees, I needed all the confidence I could muster.

When Jonah arrived about five past three, the ground was still dry, but only through some kind of miracle, as the clouds had grown and thickened. When I answered the door I didn't even know him well enough to know what to say, so I just smiled.

"Elizabeth," he said. There was something so nice about the way he said my name.

I glanced at the sky. "I think I'll just get my umbrella."

When I returned, he was standing on the porch examining the weather for himself. "I don't think it would dare rain on one of Ruby's parties," he said. He watched me as I locked the door, and I swear I saw pleasant warmth in his eyes when I turned to face him.

"I wonder if I should have brought something," I said as we went down the steps.

He shook his head. "Ruby likes to ... control the menu. Anyway, I brought a bottle of their favorite wine."

When we got to his SUV, he actually opened the door for me, which threw me. I couldn't remember the last time someone had done that for me.

Once we were on our way, I asked him about the one thing we had in common. I asked him about the case.

"Not much happening." He sounded down about it. "But we have pretty much ruled out the ex. Looks like you were right about that."

"So, then, what happens next?"

He drove for so long before answering that I was beginning to wonder if he'd heard the question. "Just keep doing what we're doing," he said finally. "Hope for a break. The leads we've had so far haven't gone much of anywhere."

He fiddled with the radio, finally settling on jazz. I hate jazz.

"I still feel she's alive," I said. I was just going to add that nothing else had come to me, when a strong, clear image popped into my head. "Oh, wait a minute ... Does she have some kind of Florida connection?" And to Jonah's odd look, "It's just that I'm seeing this kind of country where there's water going everywhere. Sort of like canals. I thought maybe the Everglades." I hesitated, experiencing the vision further. "No. No. There isn't much growth, hardly any trees."

"What about the Back Bay? It's laced with canals."

I thought about it, then shook my head. "It's more ... inland than that." The picture was fading from my head. "There are a lot of birds there," I said lamely.

He was having trouble hiding his frustration. "Birds?"

I sighed. "I'm not trying to be difficult. I'm only getting bits and pieces. Not the whole thing." I sat back in my seat, discouraged.

We drove quietly for a few minutes, then Jonah spoke. "Can't you speed it up? Expand it or something?"

"You mean the vision?"

He nodded, looking uncomfortable at my choice of terms.

"It's not really up to me."

"Then, who ...?" He stopped me before I could speak. "Never mind, I don't think I want to know."

Another few minutes and then, "So, that's what it's like, being psychic? You get these ...ideas?"

"It's not exactly ideas."

He gave me a curious look.

"I don't mean to sound mysterious. It's just hard to ... put into words."

"Doesn't seem like you like it very much."

"Oh, but I do," I said, hastily. "It's pretty wonderful, actually. It opens you up to this sense of knowing ..." My voice trailed off. I wasn't used to putting myself out there like that with somebody like him. "It teaches you first hand that there's this love there. This ... eternal love that truly never dies." Now I was just starting to sound hokey. "Words fail me," I said, trying to joke.

He glanced at me, but said nothing.

"Actually, I hate talking about it. People have all these assumptions."

He nodded.

"I read this newspaper column once where the writer was making fun of something, I forget what. But whatever it was, he said it was about as rare as an unemployed psychic. You know, his joke was that psychics are such money grubbing fakes, they'd never be out of work, out of money." I waited a moment to give it more import. "The thing is, I was out of work at the time."

Jonah gave me a questioning smile. "Like a lot of things in life, people put a label on you and lump you in with everybody else."

"Exactly. And the judgement can be really harsh."

We pulled into an expansive circular driveway and parked in front of a large, austere home that looked more suited for a plantation in Alabama than an upscale neighborhood on the California coast. The house must have looked good on paper but it had landed in the wrong spot, an uncomfortable and alien presence. I felt sorry for it.

"Home sweet home," Jonah said.

As we went up the broad steps together, he said, "One of these days I want to hear more about what you do, okay?"

I liked the way he looked when he said it, so I nodded my head.

And for once I didn't even feel the need to explain to him that it's not what I do, it's who I am.

The door was open, so we went in. We made our way through a perfectly white, perfectly coifed home and out very tall French doors onto a large terrace that stepped down to an equally large redwood deck that was partially covered by an awning. A curved stone area beyond the deck held a huge built-in barbecue, and out from there was a Godzilla-sized pool, covered now for fall. There was an abundance of plush patio furniture, the kind you'd never buy on sale.

There were maybe eight couples lounging around, all of whom suddenly seemed to be looking directly at us. "Jonah," someone called, and Jonah raised a hand in general greeting. "Hey, everybody," he said. I want you to meet … Elizabeth." I could tell he was still having a hard time using my full name.

"Hi." I tried gamely to make eye contact with everyone at once.

Behind us I heard someone exit the house in a hurry.

"Jonah, you rascal!"

I turned just in time to see Jonah being bear-hugged by a woman nearly as tall as he was. She was dressed in sleek black pants and a sort of caftan sweater thing in a very bold red. Words fail me in describing it. I'm no fashion expert, but it screamed *designer* all the way. With hair the exact color of Jonah's (sort of a honey wheat color, I think) she was slender and delicate almost to the point of being frail. But she had the voice of a truck driver. A big one.

She was now zeroing in on me. "So, Jonah, who's this?" She shot him a look of pleased surprise as he turned to introduce us, then shook my hand like she was finalizing a very satisfactory business deal. Her eyes were all over me. For the first time in my life I felt too small.

Someone named Ben slapped me on the back and handed me a cold Pacifico. I don't like beer any more than I like jazz, but I started sipping it gratefully. Just as it started to rain.

"Ah, it's just a sprinkle," Ruby said. "C'mon over everybody. Come meet Jonah's new girl."

Nobody seemed to hear my disclaimers, though they were really pretty loud.

Hands were extended and shaken. One younger gentleman (I use the word loosely) squeezed my arm and at the same time brushed his leg against mine with all the finesse of a rutting bull. Must have been my hot pink top. A high-maintenance brunette in a tight black denim skirt and a low cut tank confided in a silky voice, "Better keep an eye on him, Elizabeth. We'd all like a piece of him, if you know what I mean." I did.

Just when I thought the ordeal was about to end, Ruby intervened, taking me firmly by the arm and commandeering me to an empty table under the awning. She handed me another beer and I was surprised to realize I'd actually finished the first one. Scanning desperately for Jonah, I spotted him too far away to rescue me. He was talking with Ben at the barbecue, no doubt doing that man thing where they fiddle endlessly with the fire and the meat. If women spent that much time cooking, we'd probably all starve.

"Time for some girl talk," Ruby said matter-of-factly. "Let's get to know each other, shall we?" She grabbed a bowl of Kettle Chips from a nearby table and plunked it between us, then sat back grandly and smiled at me as she munched on a particularly big one. "You sure beat the hell out of that Helen person," she said.

"Thanks."

"You should have seen her." She shook her head in disbelief. "Well, hopefully, you never will. Where does Jonah find these people?"

She looked at me as if she expected an answer, then went on ahead. "One thing for sure. That woman had a bee up her butt."

She selected another chip and frowned when it crumbled onto her chest. "It was all Helen could do to even force a smile," she said, brushing the crumbs off her sweater.

I forced a smile.

"So, where'd he find you?"

I didn't really want to answer that. "Through work," I said carefully.

"Good lord, you're not a cop, are you?" She looked alarmed.

"I'm a therapist."

She slapped her hand on the table. "My little brother's getting therapy?"

Right. I'm counseling him and dating him at the same time. Out loud I said, "No, no, I didn't mean that. I'm involved in some ... police work with him."

"Oh." She settled down, crunching a chip lazily, swinging her sandal-clad foot to some unheard beat. I noticed that her toenails were painted a deep red to complement her top. She somehow managed to wiggle her big toe independently of the rest of her foot, which I found strangely fascinating.

"How long you known him?"

I had to force myself to pull my gaze away from those dancing piggies and back to her face. "Not long."

She nodded. "Well, watch out. He can be kind of slippery." But I could hear the affection in her voice. "He's a good guy. Speaking of which ..."

Bless him, Jonah was making his way towards our table. I saw the concern in his eyes and felt a rush of gratitude that he was feeling it. He swung a chair out from the table and sat down next to me. It was all I could do to keep from grabbing onto him for moral support.

"Ruby been giving you the third degree?" He was smiling, but serious, and I could see that his sister knew it, too.

"Ah, she's gonna do fine." Ruby reached over to pat my hand. "She's a good sport. A box of Cracker Jacks."

I felt suddenly acceptable, though I knew not why.

All of us had to crowd under the awning to eat, as the sprinkle had defied Ruby to the point of becoming a steady rain. Fortunately, it was a warm storm. I met maybe two other people I liked; a couple, as it turned out, and since Jonah and I were seated next to them, mealtime wasn't too bad. We feasted on shrimp and steak, grilled vegetables, and salad. White wine replaced the beer, allowing me to slip into a more comfortable place. In fact, by the time we left, I had slipped quite a ways.

In the car, I leaned back against the seat, grateful the party was over.

"I never should have done that to you," Jonah said. "I don't know what I was thinking."

"It was ... fun."

He fastened his seat belt, giving me a dubious look.

"It was okay. Really." The wine made me smile. "Your sister is ..."

"A piranha?"

I started giggling. It's a curse for me, giggling.

Jonah looked relieved, and somehow pleased. "I'm glad you can laugh about it. Some people ..."

"You mean, like Helen?"

I could see I'd surprised him. Something inside me said I should stop, but I plunged ahead anyway, entertaining myself. "Ruby said ... Well, Ruby said that Helen ..." I was grinning so much that I couldn't quite spit it out. "That Helen had a ... A bee ... Up her ..." I melted hopelessly into giggles.

"I think I know the rest." His smile was so indulgent, I felt warmed by it. I was instantly aware of our isolated little world in the car, the rain pounding down around us. It felt like there was nobody else in the world and, at the moment, I was fine with that.

"I'm kind of surprised you're still talking to me," Jonah said.

Without thinking, I leaned over and kissed him on the cheek. As I started to move away, he caught me and held me close to him, then kissed me softly on the lips.

I think I may have whispered something profound like *That felt nice.* And when he kissed me again I slipped my arms around his neck and kissed him back, in kind. With maybe a little extra something thrown in for good luck.

He looked down at me and I could see the sparkle in his eyes. "You're a little drunk, Libby." His voice was so warm and deep I wanted to crawl into it and stay awhile. One last sweet kiss and then he let go of me. I sank back in my seat in some kind of happy stupor, the misery of the party fading from my existence.

* * *

The first thing I remembered when I woke up the next morning was those sweet kisses, in the car, in the middle of the driving rain. I stretched happily and closed my eyes, not wanting to lose the immediacy that I still felt. For a little while I managed to pretend I was still there in the car, in the rain.

The rest of the evening returned slowly—the party, the great food. Ruby. I had made fun of her in the car, and of Helen. Oh, Lord, I'd made fun of his sister and his ex-girlfriend. At least I hoped she was an ex. I had been drunk, at least a little, while Jonah had limited himself to one or two beers, designated driver. I reacted in horror, knowing from experience what it's like to be sober to somebody else's drunk. You think you're hysterically funny, so witty, while the sober person just thinks you're drunk.

When we got to my place, he did his usual door opening routine. Probably thought I'd fall flat on my face on the sidewalk if he didn't. The rain was lighter by then, so he carried my umbrella in one hand, and—Oh, glory—I remember it now, put his other arm around my shoulder as we went up the walk. On the porch he let me fumble with the keys, then took over and found the right one for me, letting me gently into my own house. Peeps met us at the door, giving him a happy greeting, but ignoring my existence. Peeps does that sometimes if I leave him alone longer than he thinks I should.

We stood face to face inside the entryway. "Do you want to come in?" I looked around. "Oops, I guess we already are in."

He smiled down at me. "Good night, Libby." He gave me a soft kiss on the lips, then turned and headed out the door.

* * *

I was just settling down with a cup of coffee, and Peeps was just settling down on the comics I had spread out to read, when I glanced at the clock and realized it was Sunday—Sunday morning, ten o'clock. No longer a lazy, relaxing time of the week, Sunday had now become something else and I had exactly forty-five minutes to shower, dress, and do something with my ungodly hair before I had to leave for church. With much groaning and grumbling I dumped Peeps off my lap and headed into the shower. Peeps, I am sure, headed over to the potted palm. When truly perturbed, I can count on him to deposit a little something for me there.

I made it to church at the last possible moment, slinking into a nearly empty pew near the door, my hair limp, my attitude equally deflated. I had forgotten to rinse the crème rinse out of my hair and it was not a pretty sight. Being a woman, my hair can really set me off anyway. If it's looking good, I feel like I could run a company or a marathon. If it's bad, I feel weak and useless, like leftover coffee.

Glancing down, I was dismayed to discover a large hole in my panty hose, strategically placed over my big toe. Wiggling and writhing, I tried surreptitiously to twist the panty hose around so the hole would be under my foot. I was only partially successful.

The four-year-old sitting with her parents at the other end of the pew was staring at me, obviously fascinated. I gave her a silly smile and a wink, hoping to defuse the situation, but no, she grabbed onto her mother's elbow and said in that high, piercing voice that only a preschooler can manage, "What's wrong with that lady, Mommy?"

The organ music ended and Frank made his entry, stage right, looking particularly solemn and thoroughly priestly. On him, it looked good. Since coming to my office last Wednesday, he'd left two rather intimate messages on my recorder. Seeing how fine he looked in front of his congregation made me regret that I hadn't returned his calls.

He once again managed to pull off a stunning sermon. He had the congregation in the palm of his hands by the third sentence. He rhapsodized about the power of love, both human and celestial, and I got the distinct impression he was talking directly to me, especially when he said that humans can express God's love by loving one another very well. I wondered exactly what he meant by that.

After the service, I noticed that some of the regulars were now keeping one eye on me, knitting two and two together. They'd already seen me with Frank last week, and now here I was again. Not only could I now count on being dinner conversation for Ruby and her friends, I could also anticipate being fodder for gossip at the Altar Society.

I went through the line just for the hell of it.

"Stunning sermon." I shook Frank's hand with vigor as he did a second take. "You really ought to think about starting a TV ministry."

The old woman next in line winked at me. "He's a keeper, alright."

I nodded to her. "I'd put him up against that crying lady with the big pink hair any day."

She grinned her agreement, then moved in to shake his hand. "I know I'd watch, Father Frank."

I noticed Frank looked almost relieved that we were moving on. I waited for him in what was fast becoming an old familiar haunt, the vestibule. As there was no Altar Society vixen to ogle today, I read the bulletin board. There was a large snapshot of Frank being welcomed into the flock at St. Alban's, another of the children's choir at Christmas. Hadn't anyone else noticed the little blonde kid in the second row giving the boy in front of him devil horns?

Frank finally came to find me, leading me into his office. "Are you okay this morning, Elizabeth?" A concerned look from his baby blues.

Without waiting for an answer, he led me out the side door to the small house next to the church. As we entered the old fashioned kitchen, I realized we must be in the rectory. I stopped to stare at the neat little room. Gingham curtains? I didn't know you could get them anymore. The table was set for two with Blue Willow.

"Very homey," I said, picking up a plate to read the back. It was an original.

I had assumed we'd go out to eat, but apparently Frank had other plans. Right now, for example, he was trying to gather me in his arms.

"Frank, we just came from church."

"So?"

"You just ... administered the holy sacrament."

He pulled me closer. "And finished two services back to back. And I'll probably spend at least a couple hours this afternoon visiting the hospitals. Right now, though, I've got some free time."

It did feel good in his arms.

"All I could think about in church was coming over here and touching you," he said.

I pulled back a bit.

"What?" He looked puzzled.

"You gave a sermon and all the while you were thinking about sex?"

He laughed a rather sensual laugh. "I didn't say anything about sex, Elizabeth. Were you thinking about it?"

I let out a nervous little giggle. He kissed it away—several times, then relented and let me go just when I wanted him to hang on. Why did he keep doing that to me?

Feeling awkward, I explored the kitchen. The cabinets had leaded glass doors and inside, neatly arranged, was a wonderful collection of glassware and china.

"It belongs to the church, " Frank said. "All this stuff belongs to the church."

"It's a really nice little place, Frank." I turned to look at him.

"It gets lonely." He was looking at me directly, like it ought to mean something.

I changed the subject, or at least I thought I did. "Where's your housekeeper? I thought priests had housekeepers."

"Catholic ones do."

"Oh, right."

"Episcopal priests have wives."

So much for romance. Talking about the utilitarian purpose for having a wife wasn't right up there on my list of sweet talk. I suddenly saw myself, the good little preacher's wife, faithfully finishing up the church bulletin at 2 a.m., teaching Sunday school to snotty-nosed four-year-olds, and cleaning up the church after a particularly messy wedding.

Frank dug into the refrigerator, pulled out a bowl of pasta salad and handed it to me. In my panic I pulled the plastic wrap off the salad with such vigor that the bowl spun precariously to the edge of the table.

Frank caught it just in time. "You really are out of it this morning," he said, but he sounded affectionate when he said it. He set the bowl safely in the middle of the table, then handed me a loaf of French bread and a bread knife. "You want to slice it? Think you can handle it without slicing yourself?"

While I did that, he cut up some apples and pears. "This feels nice," he said, "working together."

I nodded, only sure of one feeling at the moment—hunger.

Frank set out butter and poured bottled water into our glasses. We sat together quietly for a few moments and then, of course, he said grace.

* * *

"Basically, men are jerks." Lindsay illustrated her point by stabbing her lettuce with her fork.

"Not all of them." I couldn't help myself.

"I just stopped seeing Alan because he said he wanted to take my breath away."

"That sounds kind of romantic, if you ask me."

"Yeah, except I think he meant it literally." She slashed her cherry tomato till its little guts squished out on her plate. "Seriously, E., I bet that there are bodies buried in his basement."

I gave her my best sympathy look, which she returned with a look of curious appraisal. "Wait a minute ... No rants on men, no eager commiseration?" She narrowed her eyes and examined my face carefully. "What have you done with Elizabeth?"

I sat there grinning like an idiot.

She leaned back in her chair so she could get a better look at me. "I think you'd better spill," she said.

Twenty minutes later we had not only finished our salads, I had also spilled the beans.

"Let me get this straight," Lindsay said. "Two guys? Two guys." She recorded it on her napkin as Lindsay—"0," Elizabeth—"2."

"It's not a contest."

"Easy to say when you're winning."

"Don't you think you should give yourself points for Walter?"

"Walter's just a friend."

"And Clinton didn't inhale."

She grinned. We'd had this conversation before. About Walter, not Clinton.

"Come on, Lindsay, Walter's a guy, not a fall back position. A very nice guy. You treat him like he'll always be there, no matter what." As I said it, I knew it was true. He'd always be there. No matter what.

"He is a good guy," she said, but I could see that her mind was already off to someplace else. She sat back, playing with her fork, considering, then finally said, "Sounds like this Frank, the priest guy, is pretty hot under the collar for you, E."

I grinned and got into it. "Okay, then what about Jonah? The cop guy?"

She pretended to seriously think it through, then smiled triumphantly. "That's easy. He wants to ... collar you." She giggled, something we have in common.

"I'm not so sure what he wants."

"Then why did he ask you to that party?"

"Afraid to face his sister alone. She's a ... piranha." I smiled a secret smile, remembering the night he'd used those words. And then I sailed right back into that night, remembering the rain, the kissing ...

"E." Lindsay tapped her fingers on the table to bring me back to her. "Don't go all gooey on me. I need facts, details."

"He's a great kisser," I said dreamily.

"That makes me feel so much better."

"On the other hand, Father Frank kisses like a fish." (Though he was certainly improving with practice.)

She erupted with laughter, spraying the water she'd been sipping out over the table. When she stopped coughing and choking, she carefully took her pen and changed the "2" beside my name to "1.5." The "0" she'd recorded for herself, became a "1."

* * *

At my age I'm still perfectly capable of panic when a guy doesn't call. And when two guys don't call? The sixteen-year-old Elizabeth popped out of me like the creature in *Aliens*, and took control. I paced the room, got mad at Peeps for no reason, and sprawled endlessly on my bed silently beseeching my phone to ring. And yes, there were a couple times when I actually did lift up the receiver to be sure that it was working. It was like women's lib had never really happened. Like I never really grew up. Maybe women really are the weaker sex after all.

Days dragged by without a single call. Well, at least three days dragged by. When I'd left Frank he'd mentioned he had an especially busy week, but still ... Wasn't he thinking of me as his future better half? Couldn't he spare a moment for her?

And Jonah? I had to think my performance of Saturday night had sent him packing. I convinced myself I could live just fine if I never saw him again, except for one thing—Janet Packard. How could a woman I'd never met be so persistently in my thoughts? She had gradually pushed her way into my energy, baggage and all, and it felt like we were now sharing a condo in my head. Evicting her was not an option and I knew that her unwanted presence would eventually have to lead me back to him.

Monday night, I had a dream. I was sitting alone in Frank's kitchen, looking at one of the Blue Willow plates. The sun was shining through the window over the sink so brightly that it nearly blinded me. Looking up, I saw the outline of a face watching me at the window. I knew I should go see who it was, but I was frozen in place by my fear. I heard a voice say, "It's not death you need to be afraid of." And then the face was gone. I thought it might have been Janet.

The next day Lindsay dropped by my office so we talked about it, that dream. Lindsay isn't psychic and she doesn't want to be, but she lets me be that way without making a fuss about it, and even draws on my help now and then when something is really troubling her. And more than once, she's stuck up for me, reaffirmed her belief in me at even the suggestion of someone else's doubt. I don't ask that of her. She just gives it to me.

"Sounds like a nightmare, all right." Lindsay was sitting in the rocker and I was having the worst time blocking out memories of Frank holding me on his lap there. "Maybe you should have just gotten up and gone over to that window."

"That would have really freaked me out."

"Yeah, but at least you might have figured out what was going on."

She had a point there.

"What about that missing woman, though, Elizabeth? Everybody says she's dead. Even the police."

"I just don't think she is," I said slowly. "Otherwise, I wouldn't be having this dream. I feel like she's trying to tell me something."

"Yuck." Lindsay jumped up from the rocker and went to look out the door into the hall. She could only stand so much of this kind of thing. She had her limits. "You really need new floor coverings. I can't believe you guys still have that green linoleum out there." Lindsay isn't a decorator; she works as a sales manager in dental supplies. But she has an eye for color, as she likes to say.

She came back into the room. "So, how are the boys?"

"I haven't heard."

"Figures," she said.

"Well, they're both busy men."

"And you're a busy woman."

"Then the point could be made that I should call them."

"It's not the same. I don't care what people say, it's just not the same." She grabbed her purse and slung it over her shoulder, then gave me a quick hug. "I've got to run, E., but keep me posted, okay? I hate to see you like this, having scary dreams and mooning around."

"I'm not mooning around. And besides, it's only been a couple of days," I said, but she had already exited, leaving me to moon around.

That night I dreamed the dream again. Only this time, the voice definitely came directly from the face at the window. And it was her face, her voice. I answered back, "I am not afraid of death." But I was still too frozen with fear to go to the window, and the face again disappeared.

The next morning I still felt consumed by it. Jonah had started it all by bringing it to me, and now Jonah was happily somewhere doing whatever it is that Jonah does, and I was left to deal with the consequences. Last week, I might have called him to complain. This week, after sharing a personal evening with him, I didn't feel I could call him at all.

I determined to set aside some time, tune in, and deal with things directly. I tend to go off on my daily journey and ignore the psychic stuff. Sometimes it's easier that way. But if I wait too long to check back in, something comes around to remind me it's there and I really ought to call on it for help. This was one of those times. First, though, it was Wednesday morning, 10:17 a.m. I would have to deal with Sandy Roget.

She was wearing a huge gold bangle bracelet. Fourteen carat, I'm sure. She flashed it at me as she sat down and took out her cigarettes. I put up my hand to stop her, and she silently put them away. Then she sat back, narrowed her eyes and surveyed me slowly. "You look ... tuckered out this morning."

"Excuse me?" Was I a charity case? And, worst of all, was I that transparent? I tried planting a firm, but professional smile on my face.

"I only meant ..." She stopped, obviously embarrassed. "Uh ... Maybe you didn't get much shut eye?"

"I'm fine."

"Good, because I really thought ..."

"Sandy?"

"Uh huh?"

"I appreciate your concern, Sandy, I really do, but as you know, we're here to talk about you."

"Oh, right. Sure."

She looked down at her lap for a moment, as if to reconstruct her thoughts. When she looked up again, she was all smiles. She held out her arm, displaying her bracelet, jangling it loudly. "So, what do you think? It's from Jimbo."

"It's very ... large."

"So's Jimbo." She gave me a suggestive look.

"I take it things have taken a turn for the better."

"Well, sort of, I guess. At least he bought me jewelry. I did what you suggested. We had a pow wow, him and me, a little summit meeting."

"Apparently he was appreciative."

"Or afraid. Maybe he thinks I'll get a roving eye if he doesn't, you know ... put out."

"He's still not interested?"

She shook her head. "We're smooching on the porch, but he still doesn't want to go for the gold."

Mixed metaphor. Her laughter broke my train of thought. "When I really want to get him, I just snap my teeth." She demonstrated. She has very large, very white teeth.

"Do you think that's wise?"

"I don't know, but it sure is fun."

"But maybe that's why he's still not interested in the Olympics," I said. Oh, God, I was beginning to sound like Sandy.

* * *

I had a two-hour break till my next appointment so I drove down to the beach, found a small private sand dune tucked back against the state park campground border, and settled in. There is no place else like the beach for me. Thoughts come more easily there, I can feel things more freely, remember things more clearly, and most of all, tune into my guidance at the drop of a hat.

Over the years, through time and experience, I've learned to trust my guidance, but I have never stopped questioning it. I never surrender my experience, my control. It's my life, after all, and I'm responsible for it, for making decisions and for living with the consequences. Otherwise, whose life would it be?

Sitting down, I dug my hands into the sand beside me and let the warmth, the deep energy of it, sink into me, soothing me both physically and psychically. I was well aware I hadn't been consciously connecting much of late and it felt like old home week to be doing it again now. Like regaining my balance, my core. I let go happily, feeling myself melting into the landscape, the sound of the waves across the sand like a distant bell that calls from somewhere far away.

Frank popped into my head, only to be followed by Jonah and several other people. Rita stopped by to tap her way across my vision in her high, high heels. The talk I'd had with Lindsay intruded and then drifted on, and I began to experience the familiar soft peace; a peace that seems both inner and outer at the same time. There was an immediate sense of something coming that would be hard to deal with, something that felt very big. Something I didn't want to see. Something the peace could help me see. The words *a rough patch* came into my head, and I saw a stormy sea followed by a clear day.

I opened my eyes. The sand around me was sparkling white. The beach before me was clean, flat, and nearly empty of people. The waves beyond were large, rolling, and beautifully gray-green, the sign of a storm far out to sea. Here where I was sitting it was calm and bright, but the roughness of the waves spoke of something else, somewhere yet to be seen.

I went back to my office knowing things I wasn't ready yet to express.

That night, I had the dream again. I was back in the same kitchen, the sun was once again shining in my eyes. I looked for the face in the window, determined this time to take some kind of action, but the face wasn't there. It was then I realized with horror that someone was standing right next to me, a dark shape, and it was as if they were talking to me without words; telepathically. I tried to move, but couldn't. I tried to scream but nothing came out.

I woke in a panic, the unspoken words ringing in my head. Though I couldn't remember them exactly, I knew that they were hard words, violent and destructive. I switched on the light on the bedside table and lay there trying to calm myself. Flashes of another dream I'd had somewhere in the night started coming back to me. There were birds flying low over a marshy landscape—all of them moving swiftly past me, as if I myself was moving very, very fast.

More Messages...

Jonah was in such a deep sleep that when the phone rang so loudly, so unexpectedly, it took him several seconds to orient himself to what was going on. Realizing where the sound was coming from at last, he grabbed the receiver. It slipped through his hands, but he caught it again just before it touched the floor.

"Yeah?" His voice sounded groggy, even to him.

"Jonah?" It was a woman, sounding shaky.

He rubbed his eyes, trying to come back to life.

"I'm sorry to call so late," the voice said hesitantly.

His clock radio showed 2:23 a.m. "Who is this?"

"Elizabeth."

Jonah sat up, suddenly more awake. "What's wrong? Are you okay?"

A pause while she decided how to answer. "Actually, I had this ... dream ..."

It occurred to Jonah that he ought to be more upset. She was waking him in the middle of the night to babble on about some dream. But he wasn't upset. All he could think about was how soft her voice sounded, how vulnerable. The artifice was stripped away and he had the sense that he was hearing the real Elizabeth for the first time.

"You probably think I'm crazy," she said.

"No, I don't." Her voice was making him want to hold her. He glanced at the empty bed beside him, imagining her there.

"I didn't intend to call. I just ... Things got a little weird, and ... God, I'm sorry I woke you."

"It's okay."

Silence while he kept the phone close to his ear because it was the closest he could get to her.

Finally, she spoke. "I know this sounds stupid, but I'm afraid to go back to sleep. I thought maybe talking ..."

"Go ahead." He stretched out on his side on the bed. He could think of all kinds of things he'd like to say.

"Sometimes dreams are more than dreams for me." She cleared her throat. "I mean they can be very ... immediate." And then, very softly, "I can't seem to shake this one."

"Elizabeth, do you want me to come over?"

"No." The answer was quick, definite. "I just need to ... you know, settle down a little."

"If there's anything I can do to help ..." And he meant *anything*.

Another long silence and then, "Have you gotten anything new on Janet?"

Now she and the missing woman were on a first name basis?

"No. Have you?"

He heard a heavy sigh, then the sound of a chair being moved around.

"Hold on," she said. "I'm just moving out into the living room."

He felt a stab of disappointment that she was no longer in bed. He heard sounds of her settling in. Then she came back on the line. "Somehow it feels a lot better out here."

"Good. So, tell me more about the dream."

She sounded reluctant. "The thing is, someone keeps talking to me about death."

"In the dream."

"Yes. At first I'd just see this face at the window and think it was Janet, but then tonight, there was this man standing beside me. I couldn't see who he was, but he ... threatened me."

"What did he say?"

She couldn't quite remember.

"You've had this dream before?"

"It seems to be becoming a regular thing."

Jonah's guilt was growing. After all, if he hadn't asked her to help ...

"I was thinking that maybe I just need to realize something or remember something. Then it might stop. Maybe if you described the suspects or told me more about Janet it might help me let go of this," Elizabeth said wearily. "Relax a little. Get some sleep."

He had an idea of how to help her do that, but instead he said, "I never should have dragged you into this."

"It was one thing seeing the face, but having him close by ..."

"I never should have dragged you into this," he said again.

"Well ..."

"Seriously, Elizabeth ..."

"Some things are meant to be."

"That sounds fatalistic."

"Or realistic."

He didn't quite know what to say to that.

"There was another dream, too, with all those birds I told you about. You remember? Or maybe it was part of the same dream. I'm not sure. The two dreams always seem to come together." A half-laugh. "Now you must really think I'm crazy."

"I think you're scared," Jonah said. "And I'm coming over." He hung up quickly, before she could tell him no.

Sole Mates?

I turned on the porch light, anxious about Jonah's arrival but also immensely relieved. I'd lived alone since my divorce but at the moment being alone in the night felt unbearable. Maybe Jonah would have some news, some bit of information that would help me make sense out of what I was dealing with. He wouldn't know what to do about the dream, but he might know something helpful about the case that would give me some relief.

The other part of me, the female part, wanted to curl up and die. If I was going to call someone, why not call Lindsay? But no, I had just called a guy in the middle of the night, a guy I barely knew, a guy who hadn't bothered to call me back after our semi-date last weekend. I felt needy, cloying. I geared myself up to act strong and invulnerable when he arrived, but when I saw him at the door it was all I could do to fight the urge to crumble against him. After all my relationships and all my formal training, it seems that I'm still hunting and pecking on the typewriter when it comes to men.

"You really didn't need to come," I said, all the while desperately happy that he was there, and rather pleased about the look he gave me as he came in the door, too. He followed me into the living room and I invited him to sit down as if it was normal—as if I always had callers in the middle of the night. Tucking my slippered feet under me, I pulled my oversized gray sweatshirt down over my bent knees, all the while wishing I'd at least have had the sense to change into a prettier color of sweats.

As Jonah sat on the couch, Peeps appeared from my bedroom where he'd been blissfully snoozing on the end of my bed. No bad dreams for Peeps. Seeing we had unexpected company, he meowed loudly, then landed with all fours on Jonah's lap.

"Peeps ..." My cat was embarrassing me again.

"No, he's okay." Jonah scratched him between the ears, something Peeps would gladly kill for. He butted his furry little head against Jonah's hand, purring loudly.

"I wrote down some names." Jonah fished a rumpled paper out of his shirt pocket and reached around Peeps to hand it to me. "If you can come by the station later, I can show you a few pictures, if you think that might help."

I nodded, still trying to look business like. I reviewed the names but none of them rang any bells. Besides, his handwriting was nearly as bad as mine.

"I had to fly to Cleveland this week," Jonah said. "They picked up a bank robbery suspect I've been looking for, so I had to go get him. Just got back a few hours ago."

I looked up and our eyes met. "I brought you something."

He moved a resistant Peeps off his lap and reached into his other shirt pocket. "This is for you." He leaned forward and placed something in my hand. I was delighted to see a refrigerator magnet—a bright green plastic guitar with the words, *Rock and Roll will never die* emblazoned in glittering rainbow colors.

"Didn't have time to get to the museum. Picked it up at the airport."

Suddenly, I was all smiles. Not only did he have a really good reason for not calling me all week, he'd brought me a present.

"I love it," I said. "Thank you."

He looked equally pleased. Peeps came over to check it out and I held it down so he could get a sniff. Even Peeps looked pleased.

Jonah sat back against the cushions again. "So, you want to tell me more about that guy?" His voice was careful, almost gentle.

"He was only a dark shape, really, probably not even a real person. Maybe it was just my fears." I proceeded to tell him in detail about my recurring dream, and then about how the birds and the swampland were flying past like some strange moving picture.

"The thing is, I feel like I've seen it before. Like it's someplace I've actually been to before." I shook my head, frustrated. "I could handle the voice at the window, but the one right beside me ..."

"And you still can't remember what was said?"

"No."

We talked about other things then, and I had the distinct impression he was sort of talking me down, helping me distance myself from what had happened, helping me to relax. After I had yawned for the second time he said, "Why don't you try to get some sleep? I'll stretch out here on your couch. That way you know I'm here if anything else should happen."

"I couldn't," I said. "I couldn't impose on you like that."

We talked a few more minutes or so and then I got him a blanket and pillow and tottered off to bed.

I woke up about 7 a.m., just as it was getting light outside. Remembering my guest and wondering if I might have dreamed him, I went into the living room to find out. Sure enough, he was still there, sound asleep, one arm over his eyes, Peeps curled happily between the bend of his legs and the back of the couch.

I had a sudden attack of the guilts. He'd gotten up in the middle of the night for me. Okay, part of me was quite pleased about that. Only a little part was actually guilt. After returning home from a long, stressful trip guarding a dangerous fugitive, he must have been exhausted. And he was way too tall for my couch; his feet were hanging off. Why hadn't I at least offered him my spare room? Sleeping on the daybed might be like sleeping on a slab of concrete, but surely it would have been better than this.

I gave my cat a stern look and slipped into the kitchen. I returned a few minutes later, leaned over the back of the couch to carefully extract Peeps, and was just ready to carry him off when Jonah stirred and woke up.

"Light sleeper," he said. "Did you get any?"

"A little," I lied. I had slept like a happy baby.

He was lying there looking up at me and there was something so enticing about him I couldn't seem to move away. I dropped Peeps to the floor and he trotted off to either his kitty box or the potted palm. At the moment, I didn't care.

"There's coffee," I said rather unevenly. I turned towards the kitchen, then stopped. "Towels in the bathroom."

I retreated to the kitchen without looking at him again and the next time I saw him he was standing in the doorway watching me fix breakfast. He came into the room in his bare feet.

"Smells good in here," he said. He poured himself coffee, added sugar, no cream, and stood near me, sipping from his cup.

I took the turkey bacon out of the pan, strip by strip, laying it out on paper towels to drain.

"You always go to this much trouble for breakfast?"

"It's the least I could do."

"Any more dreams last night?"

I shook my head.

"Good."

He watched me as I took some plates out of the cupboard.

"I've got some bad news," he said. But he was smiling.

"Oh?"

"Ruby really seems to like you."

"And that's bad news?"

"Means she's liable to invite you over again."

I pulled the eggs out of the refrigerator and grabbed a bowl to crack them into. I couldn't help but notice that Jonah was looking around my kitchen as if he liked what he saw. After a quick glance out my patio door into the back yard, he topped off his coffee cup and settled down at my kitchen table looking lazy and content. I didn't look at him again for awhile, but when I finally did he said, "Maybe it's time you and I went out on a real date. Elizabeth. What do you think?"

I fished the eggshell out of the bowl and nodded my agreement.

* * *

"Well, but no kissing?" Lindsay looked almost offended.

"It was an awkward situation."

"This guy you're crazy about sleeps over and nothing went on?" Apparently she couldn't get past this.

"I wouldn't say I'm crazy about him. Interested, maybe, but not crazy. Besides, we were talking about work stuff."

Lindsay could hardly contain herself. "Trust me, Elizabeth, he wasn't there to talk about work stuff. Guys don't come to your house in the middle of the night to talk about work. Surely you at least made out?"

I shook my head.

"Nothing?"

"Nada."

We were in T.J. Maxx trying on clothes. I was in a sudden mood for something new to wear, something pretty. Never mind the closet full of clothes at home, I needed something special for Saturday night.

Lindsay threw another top into the pile of clothes in the shopping cart. "Here you were having a nightmare, this guy comes over because he's so worried about you, wants to take care of you. You've got to admit it's the perfect set up."

I smiled. She was right. And yet, somehow, not doing anything had felt so much better. I examined a dress on the rack, but hung it back again because it was too long. "Why do they make them like that so they practically drag on the ground?"

"Either that or you can't sit down in them they're so short," Lindsay said eagerly. As usual, we were bonding over fashion's idiosyncrasies. The shared truth of being a woman in America today isn't so much about the great questions of life—it's more about the really, really small ones.

"I thought you said he was a great kisser."

"It's not always about sex, Lindsay."

She grinned. "It is for the guy."

"You really think so? You really believe that guys think about sex every few seconds how people say they do?"

"Based on observed behaviors ..."

"But, how would it work? I mean from a practical standpoint. How would they ever get anything done? Car repairs? Business deals?"

Lindsay shrugged. "No wonder the world's in the crapper."

"I mean, can they get through an entire sentence without thinking about it?"

"Sure. If it's short enough."

We laughed.

"Let's say a guy is trying to balance his checkbook."

"He probably gets overdrawn a lot."

We stood there shaking our heads, then Lindsay steered our overflowing cart towards the dressing room.

I followed, frowning. "Seriously, Lindsay, I want to know how it actually works. I've wondered about this for years."

She stopped to face me. "Who handled the checkbook when you were married?"

"I did. He was hopeless with numbers."

"Enough said."

We found an open dressing room and I went in, while Lindsay stood just outside doing the important work of coordinating the trying on and the judging of the outcome. It's difficult work. You've got to be honest enough to make it meaningful yet kind enough to make it bearable and remain friends.

She handed me a red dress, low cut, with a swingy little skirt.

"I didn't pick this out." I took it doubtfully and shut the door. "We aren't doing anything fancy."

"So?" She hung another dress, black and low cut, over the dressing room door.

"You've got it, you should flaunt it."

"We're just going out to eat." I slipped on the black dress and was entirely pleased with my reflection. If I wore it, there would be no question as to what Jonah had on his mind. But fifteen minutes later, after much debate, I chose a deep brown knit top with a square neckline and three-quarter length sleeves that I'd wear with some great khakis I already had. The low cut black dress would have to wait for another time. Feeling hopeful, I bought it, too.

We ate at the Bunch O' Lunch, Lindsay's current favorite place, as much due to a certain waiter as to the flavor of the food. As soon as he could he came over.

"Hi," he said.

"Hi." She was grinning like a schoolgirl, which fit, actually. He was only about twenty-three.

"Sorry I didn't have a table for you." He seemed to notice me for the first time. "I like to take good care of my customers."

It didn't sound to me like he was talking about the food. Finding our breadbasket empty, he picked it up, frowning. "I'll get you some more," he said, striding off towards the kitchen.

"He's really thoughtful, isn't he?" Lindsay said.

"A guy doesn't just come over to your table to get you bread sticks," I said, grinning.

He was back in record time with a full basket. "Later," he said, and zoomed off to his own tables across the room.

She offered me the basket, and when I opened the cloth to take out a breadstick, there was a note tucked inside. Without even looking at it, I handed it to her.

She read it eagerly. "God, how sweet. He wants to go out with me sometime." She showed me the note, which simply said, *Call me*, and included his phone number.

There was also a super sized question mark with a happy face drawn into it.

"Maybe he wants to take you to the prom."

"He's in college," she said huffily. "An art major."

"Hence the happy face," I said.

She giggled. "Good thing he'll have his waiter skills to fall back on."

We giggled some more but before long she got up and disappeared around the corner. Lindsay is legendary for choosing men who are one way or another absolutely wrong for her, men with whom she doesn't stand a fighting chance. Men to whom she, herself, would never want to commit. From the looks of things, it was happening again.

I had nearly finished the new basket of breadsticks by the time she returned.

※ ※ ※

We got to the police station about an hour later. Lindsay had insisted on going along. She said it was to give me moral support. I suspect a more pressing reason was getting to meet Jonah. I was grateful for her presence either way, as I was feeling a little shaky going in.

We had to wait a few minutes, sitting in a small area with several other people, all of whom looked suspiciously like criminals to us, even though they might have been lawyers, family members, or even people like us. We sat close together, and whenever a cop came anywhere near the front counter, Lindsay would whisper, "Is that him?" Since she was asking about guys in uniform, I had to set her straight.

"Oh," she said, "like in the movies. They wear designer suits."

About that time Jonah appeared at the counter.

"Not all of them," I said, as he nodded at me.

Lindsay didn't have time to whisper anything in my ear, so I don't know what she thought of him as a first impression. When I introduced them he seemed a bit surprised I'd brought a friend. We followed him back to a small, windowless room where he left us alone while he went to get the pictures.

Lindsay pointed to the wall with the glass you couldn't see through, then got up and pressed her face against it, trying to do just that. "Interrogation room," she said, sounding impressed. "Elizabeth, we're in a real, live interrogation room."

She came and sat beside me, but kept glancing back at the glass. Finally, she could resist it no more. "Who do they think they're fooling, anyway, with this one way mirror thing?" She got up, went over to the window, and started pounding her fists on it.

"Lindsay ..."

She grinned at me, then started in again.

"Lindsay ..."

She was now mumbling something like, "I'm innocent, I tell you. Innocent."

"Has it occurred to you that you may be giving some cop a real show?"

"Maybe I want to," she said. But she dropped her hands and came to sit down.

Jonah returned with a few pictures and an odd look on his face, especially when he looked at Lindsay. Finally he said, "I think maybe you'd better wait outside."

"Guess I'm busted," she said to me, so only I could hear, and then, louder, "Oh, right. Sure. I'll just wait out there with the felons." But she looked rather pleased with herself as she followed Jonah out the door.

When he returned, he sat beside me. "She seems ... nice." It was a bit of social conversation, nothing more. Lindsay's the kind of attractive, slender brunette men stop to watch, but I don't think he'd even looked at her, really. His mind was somewhere else. He set the pictures on the table. "How about you? You doing any better?"

I nodded. "You must be exhausted."

"I'll survive. How's ... Peeps?"

He couldn't have asked me a nicer question. Of course Peeps was fine; he was always fine. But to have him ask, to have him remember his name, and to have him smile at me like he was doing now—it felt so intimate. Right there in the middle of an interrogation room in the middle of the police department, it felt so good. It transported me back to my kitchen table where we'd sat and eaten breakfast together only a few hours earlier, talking about normal things, daily things, and feeling oddly content.

"Well," Jonah said finally, "Are you up to taking a look at these now?" He began laying out some photos, turning them over, but I stopped him.

"Uh ... Could we do this a little differently?"

He waited for me to explain.

"I know this sounds weird, but it might be easier for me if I could look at their energy first. Instead of actually looking at them." I wasn't quite ready to see their faces. In fact, at the moment, I was feeling petrified. Something I didn't want him to know.

"All right," he said. He pushed the pictures towards me and sat back to watch.

"Actually ... by myself might be best."

He stood up reluctantly.

"Give me half an hour or so, okay?"

He nodded. "I'll be right outside."

*　*　*

He was. It didn't bother me much when I was in the middle of my work, but as soon as I was finished, I was suddenly all too aware of that window with the dark glass. There might have been one person out there or a crowd, but I knew without a doubt someone was there. I was pretty sure it was Jonah. So I was not at all surprised when he almost immediately rejoined me in the room after I was done.

"Why don't we go somewhere more private?"

"Right," I said softly. "You never know who might be watching."

Looking a bit guilty, Jonah took me to a larger room with real windows that looked outside. He pulled out a chair for me, and we sat face to face rather than looking at the table. "So," he said, "Did you have any luck?"

I shrugged. "I'm not sure. I guess time will tell."

He nodded, and I could tell he was really curious.

I selected two photos and placed them side by side on the table. "I certainly got some things," I said, touching the two pictures. "These two—their pictures don't mean anything to me, but it's where the energy is strongest. That may mean they're involved, or it may just mean that Janet has a stronger emotional bond with them than the others. And the emotional bond could be anything—love, hate, fear. It's hard to say for sure."

Jonah started to speak, but I stopped him. "Let me tell you what I got from this first. Then, I'd like to hear what you know."

He nodded, leaning forward to listen.

I started with the man who had no hair. It was obviously a police photo, the kind you'd see in a book of suspects. Black and white and kind of grim. The man was young looking not to have hair—maybe thirty? He must have shaved it. "He has a very bad feeling," I said. "I mean, I have a very bad feeling about him, his picture. He's dark here ... and here." I illustrated his neck and the area in the center of his chest, between his breastbone. I sat back, wondering how far I should go. "The chakras," I said. "Have you ever heard of them?"

Jonah frowned.

"Okay ... Well ..." I tried to think of an easy place to start. "Okay, without getting in too deep, the chakras are the places in our bodies where energy connects into us. For example, from other levels of energy."

"Other ... levels?"

I had gone too far, but something urged me to continue. "What it shows me is that this man hasn't made much of a connection—any true connection, anyway, in the areas of communication and ..." I stopped, seeing his face. " ... and heart. You know, this is too much. Let's just start over. I just feel very strongly that he's really easily corrupted, maybe even to the point of being willing to kill. If it suited him."

Now Jonah seemed intrigued.

"And his relationship with Janet seems recent, maybe even ongoing. The energy feels very active there."

Jonah nodded.

"Now, this ... gentleman ..." I referred to a snapshot of a tanned man in white shorts and a bright blue and white Hawaiian shirt, sunglasses dangling casually from his hand. It wasn't that he was posing for a picture; it was more that someone had snapped him unaware. "How did you get this picture, anyway?"

A half-smile from Jonah. "Let's just say it's not the first time he's been tailed."

"Oh." I sat back and took a moment. "Well, anyway, this guy is obviously on vacation."

I was trying to joke but it took Jonah a couple seconds to get it. Why is it people think that psychic readings should always be completely serious? If there's one thing I've learned, it's that the universe, or

God, or All That Is (whatever you want to call it) has one hell of a sense of humor. Just look at the poor potato bug.

I got back to business, picking up the photo and looking at it again. "He's harder to read. Not so out there like Baldy. More like a snake in the grass."

Jonah smiled, and I wondered why.

"He feels very confident, very outgoing. The type who thinks he's got everything and everybody under control." I tapped the first picture, the man with no hair. "If I was him, though, this is the guy I'd be worried about. Baldy."

"You think they're connected?"

"I think they're connected."

"Interesting."

"It's where we should look, Jonah. It's where we should look." In my excitement, I reached out and touched his hand. "The other three—not so connected. Connected to her, but no active energy there between them." I pulled one man's picture out of the stack. "Even ex-hubby here."

"Wait a minute. How'd you know that was him?" Jonah sounded shocked.

I could have played with it awhile, but it hardly seemed worth it. "I saw his picture in the paper. Besides, I would have recognized that watch anywhere."

Jonah smiled and I recollected for a moment what a nice evening that first night at my house had actually turned out to be, even if it had led to those tiresome dreams.

Jonah pulled Baldy's picture over in front of him and stared at it. "My turn?" And when I nodded, "Jason Jakes. Used car dealer over in the valley. Out of business now. He got busted for selling stolen cars. Twice."

He picked up the second picture. "And this guy—Mr. Snake In the Grass, is just that. Lawyer. Not that they're all that way, but ... Known for taking the really ratty guys and getting them off on a technicality."

"And they both somehow know Janet?"

"Yeah. You might say that. The lawyer is Brad Hernandez. Janet's live-in boyfriend."

"Oh ..." It hit me hard. "But how did she know the other guy?"

"Hernandez was the lawyer who got him off. So she may have met him casually, at least. Neighbors said they saw him around the house a couple of times in the last month or so before Janet disappeared."

"So that's why he's on the suspect list? Because the neighbors saw him there?"

Jonah nodded. "Hernandez uses a home office on the weekends. Sometimes his clients come there."

"Wow." I sat back and considered the possibilities. "The car dealer—he feels very strong in her life, Jonah. A casual meeting now and then, I don't think it would account for that."

"We'll look into it," he said.

We walked back to the car together, talking of things I couldn't remember as soon as I'd said or heard them because I was too busy remembering how Jonah had looked asleep on my couch.

"See you Saturday, then," he said, shutting the door for me. He nodded briefly to Lindsay, gave me what felt like a heart-stopping smile and walked away.

Oh, sure, he's kind of cute," Lindsay said, starting the car. "The question is, can he take your breath away?"

* * *

That evening Frank called and we talked old times for over an hour, each recounting long ago stories to make the other laugh. I hung up remembering how close we'd been, how in sync, but thinking, also, that maybe he and I worked best when we stayed in the past. I knew him there; he knew me. It just seemed easier. Except that Frank, dear glorious man, kept trying to bring us back to the future.

"Maybe we could have a picnic after church this week," Frank said.

I had been planning on talking to him about church. Yes, I'd come sometimes, but that didn't mean our relationship could, or should revolve around it. If we were going to date, he needed to take me somewhere once in awhile or at least meet me on another day. Trying to mix church and a relationship was mixing me up, too. And there was Jonah to consider—I had no idea where that relationship was going yet. Having two men at once is a nice concept, but the reality is, as much as my ego likes all that attention, complications are bound to ensue. I told Frank cryptically that I might not be able to make it on Sunday.

The next day, he sent me flowers at work. The card looked suspiciously like it had been tampered with when Rita appeared in my office and plopped the huge bouquet on the desk in front of me. She waited impatiently for me to open the card and said, finally, "So, who are they from?"

"You tell me," I said, making obvious my examination of the envelope.

She looked offended. "I hope to God you aren't breaking any papal decrees, Elizabeth." She marched back out, her head held high. I decided right then and there never to tell her that Frank wasn't a Catholic priest. It was way too much fun the way it was.

I settled back in my chair and opened, or should I say reopened, the card:

> *Dearest Elizabeth,*
>   *I want to make new memories with you.*
> *Love,*
> *Frank*

I have to admit it made me go all soft and gooey. Guys send flowers for lots of reasons; usually more to do with guilt, regret, or apology, than anything else. When a guy sends flowers strictly *because*, well, it's more than I can do to overcome that. If more guys realized this, a lot more guys would be getting lucky.

I called Frank up, but got the church secretary. "He's on his way to a funeral," she said crisply. "Can I take a message?"

"Just tell him Elizabeth called."

"Concerning?"

"He'll know," I said softly, " He'll know."

I sat back and looked at my flowers. Not just red roses, but pink and white ones too. And some kind of exotic (or was it erotic) looking deep purple thing. All tucked nicely in a cut crystal vase.

I read the card through a couple more times. Flashes of Frank's face kept coming into view, the passion in him when he was speaking to the church, looking down at all of us from his perch. I love a man's eyes, the way he looks at me, but I don't think there's anything more attractive to me than a man who is totally passionate about his work.

I finally forced myself to go back to updating clients' charts. Just when I finally got into it, Sara and Arlene, the two therapists who run the eating disorder clinic came in, eyes wide to see the big bouquet and quiz me gently about its origin. For once, they didn't catch me munching on something. They must have wondered why.

After they had gushed and left, I got back to work, but within a few minutes it was all I could do to keep my eyes open as I finished another write up. I leaned back in my chair to rest but just as I was giving in to my Peeps urge to nap, I was roused by a tap on my open door. It was, of course, Frank.

I pulled myself together and quickly sat up. "Frank ..."

"You have a minute, Elizabeth?"

When I nodded, he came in and closed the door behind him. "Glad I caught you alone," he said. He did a quick visual check of the bouquet while I did a quick visual check of him. Yeah, just as I suspected, he was looking especially fine.

He sat down by my desk, looking earnest. "After we talked on the phone last night, I realized how right you were. Seeing each other just on Sundays isn't cutting it. It's too limiting. I've been so busy with work that it didn't dawn on me before. I've been trying to fit you into my schedule along with everything else. Foolish of me."

"It's okay. I know you're busy."

"It's not okay."

I got up and went to him. "You don't exactly have a nine to five job, Frank."

We were eye to eye and I thought we might end up doing the lap-sitting thing again. But then he stood, too. "It's time I got my priorities straight." Which apparently meant me. He took my face in his hands and I thought for sure he was going to kiss me but instead he butted his nose against mine. We were suddenly nose to nose, staring into each other's eyes so closely that it was disturbing. And blurry. I had to close my eyes.

Which was convenient for him. He started kissing my eyelids. "You're all I think about, Elizabeth," he said softly between kisses. "I want to make ... desperate love to you."

I opened my eyes. Wide.

"Let's not waste any more precious time."

"You mean ... here?" His lips were almost touching mine now and the near kiss was somehow more erotic than an actual one would be. It was clouding my mind.

"Anywhere, anytime, love," he said, letting his lips touch mine at last. But just as I let go and felt myself soften against him, he hesitated, pulled away. Looking tormented. Looking at his watch. "It's just that right now I have to ... Well ... be somewhere."

Oh, good God. The funeral.

"I can be back in a couple hours," he said hopefully.

What, after the eulogy?

"Maybe we should just go out on a date or something first, Frank."

He pulled me in to him again. "Maybe we should just go to bed." He kissed me like he meant to stay, then set me away from him with a sigh. "Just think about the possibility, Elizabeth. I know I will."

I stood there trying to think of reasons why we shouldn't do anything, but nothing came to mind. My afternoon was free. So, apparently, were my hormones.

"I'll be back as soon as I can," he said, "but right now ..."

"I know," I said, more sharply than I'd intended. "You have to be somewhere."

After he left, I sank down in my rocking chair remarkably out of breath. Fish don't kiss like that.

I spent the next half an hour arguing with myself about whether or not to have sex with Frank. Naturally it had been in the back of my mind already, more as a concept than a reality. Like imagining what it would feel like to float gracefully in a parachute as opposed to actually plummeting out of a plane. I might try it someday, but was I really ready to do it this soon?

Feeling sure that things would become clearer if I just stopped thinking about them so much, I dug out an article on multiple personalities I'd been meaning to read. I tried focusing on it but by the time another half an hour had passed, my personality seemed to be the one that was multiplying. My hormones and my imagination were getting the best of me. The journal I'd been reading was lying forgotten on my lap, my feet were propped up on my desk, and I was staring into space, picturing things that made my skin feel warm and true. By the time I heard Frank's footsteps hurrying down the hall, somebody else had taken control.

He shut the door and made a show of locking it, then leaned back against it, looking for all the world like some dashing romantic hero. I had to push back a fleeting image of him standing in front of a polished mahogany casket fantasizing about me while he gave a stirring eulogy to a room full of grieving relatives, but once I'd made that leap, I was half way home.

"You look remarkably sure of yourself," I said.

He tilted his head. "I take it that means yes?"

"Maybe."

"Maybe?"

"You haven't actually convinced me yet."

We were both smiling now. He moved gracefully away from the door and came toward me. "Ah, but I have a plan."

When he gathered me into his arms I could immediately see that his plan had its good points, and so, from what I could feel as he held me against him, did his body. I thought fleetingly of calling Rita and telling her I was going home for the day, family emergency. Had already left, really. But it wouldn't do. Rita would have seen him come in. Still ... I cast about for some other option as he spread kisses down my neck.

Just when I was wondering how I'd ever find the will to stop, and what it would actually be like to have sex on my desk just this once, fate stepped in and made another call. Feeling sudden, intense pain in my leg, I pushed Frank away with all the force of my will and began stumbling around the room, feeling for all the world like some uncoordinated flamingo trying out for the ballet. "Leg cramp," I gasped when I could, then started careening around the room again, bumping into walls and chairs until finally the pain began to subside.

It took me some seconds to get up enough courage to actually look at Frank again. He was standing there, smiling broadly. "Wow," he said, "I didn't realize I had such an effect on women."

I sank down in my chair, deflated. Frank continued to grin at me while I rubbed my sore leg and wondered if the universe had been trying to tell me something.

In any case, the spell was definitely broken. I was mortified beyond belief and as it turned out, Frank, as always the victim of his overzealous schedule, was due at one of those infamous church budget meetings. He left me with an intimate goodbye kiss and a "To be continued." It wasn't until after he left that I realized I hadn't even thanked him for the flowers. Or then again, maybe I had.

So there I was, left in a state I've come to call normal—still completely confused about how to handle my relationships with men. I can have the best of plans. I can set things up so rationally in my mind's eye. But once I'm past a certain point (and I was there now) being rational makes about as much sense to me as Greek, and I only studied Italian.

* * *

I came *this* close to wearing the black dress Saturday night.

Jonah was nothing if not punctual. I could tell I'd made the right choice of attire when I opened the door. First of all, he was casually dressed. And second, he looked at me like I was the very best thing he'd seen all day.

We went to a little place about a block from the beach that features seafood, of course, as well as pasta and salads. The place is a few steps down from the Beach Grille and a few steps up in quality. Comfortable and nice. We ate way too much shrimp and shared a bottle of Wild Horse white zin that was so crisp you could almost taste the ocean in it.

After dinner, we went for a walk on the pier. The sky was just going to twilight, the last bright colors from the sun fading over the now steel gray ocean. Gulls were flying low looking for that one last catch of the day and the pier was empty except for one other couple and a family dragging a reluctant four-year-old back to their mini van.

It was one of those typical fall days when the fog, which hangs around all summer (like the tourists) has finally gone away. The air was still nicely warm and there was that quiet little sea breeze I love so much—like a soft, gentle touch on the cheek.

We leaned against the handrails at the very end of the pier, both looking solemnly out to sea. Dinner had been remarkably relaxed, the conversation easy, but now I felt a tension in the air.

Finally, Jonah spoke. "Elizabeth?"

I met his gaze, feeling a little breathless.

"I ... uh ... I think you might want to move."

I glanced down to where he was looking. The sleeve of my new top was inches away from some very fresh looking bird doo.

He grinned and pulled me away. "I'll take care of you," he said, his voice as warm as the evening air. We moved to the other side of the pier, his arm around my shoulder.

I suddenly felt the need to fill the silence. "If we went straight out from here," I said, referring to the open sea in front of us, "where do you think we'd end up?"

He looked amused.

"Don't you ever wonder about that?"

"Guess I haven't thought about stuff like that since I was a kid," he said.

"Well I do. I can't help myself."

Neither one of us was looking at the sea any longer. He reached out and fingered the small ruby pendant at my throat, then moved his hand up to caress my cheek.

"You have a unique way of looking at things, Libby." I started to correct his nickname usage, but couldn't speak. He trapped my lips against his, kissing me slowly. It was right about then that I began to think that having a nickname might not be such a bad thing after all.

I'd like to say we made out all night, one thing leading to another, till we fell into bed and kept each other happily awake till dawn. Then woke up later and made love till noon. I know that's what Lindsay would want to hear, and maybe I can make something up that will please her. But the truth is, we stood on that pier, arm in arm, watching night take over the sky, savoring the sweetness of the evening, remembering the future.

It seems to me that in the movies these days people meet, feel an immediate attraction for each other and the first time they even kiss, the very first time, they fall right into bed. I don't understand that. It doesn't compute. It's like having your entire relationship over and done with right up front. I guess it saves time, but it holds little interest for me. Where's the drama? Where's the romance? I love the build up, the anticipation. Like the holidays, I don't want to see what's in my packages till Christmas morning finally comes.

Are you saying you've never had a one night stand? Lindsay would ask. She knows, of course, that I have. I purposely set out to have one once just to see what it was like, and a second time it just sort of came up. It turned out to be more tense than fun. It's a different animal than falling for each other over time—like Taco Bell compared to Mexican food. I love a good Bell burrito, but it's not what I'd call real Mexican. It's Taco Bell. So that's it, that's my philosophy, I guess. Quickie sex is okay for what it is, the fast food of love. But it's not at all like the real thing.

Standing there on the pier, I felt Jonah's closeness, his breath on my cheek, and sometimes his lips on mine. I won't say his hands didn't roam around a bit, or that mine weren't around his neck from time to time. But we were in sync, somehow, and neither of us seemed eager to speed things up.

I got home about 11:00. While cleaning out the potted palm it hit me like a ton of bricks. I was in a relationship with a priest who wanted to take me on my desk at his earliest opportunity and a cop who was taking it oh-so-slow.

I didn't manage to fall asleep till sometime after two. Needless to say, it was hard getting up the next day. Feeling the need to sort things out I left Frank a message canceling church and suggested we meet somewhere later. When I crawled back into bed, Peeps got under the covers and snuggled against me, afraid, I think, that he might be losing control. I petted him to calm his fears and he finally fell asleep, curled against my hip, all fuzzy-soft and warm.

Later, padding around my house in my nightgown and slippers, I remembered again the warm look in Jonah's eyes when he'd kissed me goodnight. At first I got lost in the feeling, but then I started to doubt it. After some serious kissing earlier in the evening, he had just left me on my porch as if it didn't matter to him the night was at an end. He hadn't really even made one little attempt to push the envelope. What did that mean?

I was still agonizing over this when the phone rang.
"Morning." It was Jonah.
"Hi."
"It's Japan," he said.
"What?"
"If you went straight out from here, I think you'd reach Japan."
"Oh, yeah. Right." He'd made me smile.
"I didn't get a lot of sleep last night, " he said.
"Mmmm ..." Maybe things were going to improve.
"Yeah. I just kept thinking about Janet Packard."
My face fell.
"Kind of like you having all those dreams. Like it wouldn't leave me alone."

I was still stuck on the fact he had left me alone.

"I guess it was already on my mind, you know. Didn't want to talk about it last night, spoil the evening, but ... You remember Jason Jakes, the car guy?"

"Sure," I said half-heartedly."

"The guy has disappeared. Nobody knows where he is. He's missing in action."

I was trying hard to care. I'd been "Janet free" for a couple days, not feeling persecuted by her presence, and I wanted desperately to keep it that way. I cast about for something to say. "Maybe they were lovers. Maybe she wanted to go away with him."

"Well, she and Hernandez didn't have the best relationship." Jonah sounded as if he was considering it. "Neighbors say they fought a lot. But Jakes? No prospects, no money."

"Maybe he was good in bed." It came out of me before I could stop it.

A low laugh on the other end of the line. "Is that how you decide?"

When I didn't answer, he said, "Last night was ... great, Elizabeth. Really great."

"It was nice, wasn't it?"

I was wiggling my toes inside my slipper so Peeps could pounce. He was now crouched and ready, but I couldn't get him to commit.

"He was last seen in Redding," Jonah said.

It took me a moment to figure it out. "Oh, you mean the car guy?" We were now having dueling conversations, I guess.

"About three weeks ago."

"Ouch!" Peeps had finally made his move.

"Elizabeth?"

"It's just my cat. You little dickens!" I pushed Peeps away playfully.

"What?"

"I was talking to ... Never mind. What about the other guy? Her boyfriend?"

"Still in town, still saving the scumbags of the earth. Saw him at the courthouse on Friday, actually. Didn't look too broken up, if you ask me."

"But, what's in it for him, saving scumbags? They don't usually have that much money, do they?"

"Who knows what his game is. Anyway, we've got no proof of anything so far."

"Could I ... meet him?" Where did that come from? It was the last thing I wanted to do, so I was relieved when Jonah said no.

"I'm just sorry I ever asked you," he said. "About the case, I mean, not the date."

"Okay."

"I don't want you thinking any more about it, okay?"

I almost laughed. If only it were that easy.

Frank called a short while later sounding a bit consumed. "The Bishop's here all this week," he said. "Which is a good thing, actually, because I really wanted to talk to him, but on the other hand, it kind of ... cramps my style. Our style."

"Oh, right," I said, feeling embarrassed, even though he couldn't see my face.

"There's a dinner for him later today. Do you think you could make it?" And when I hemmed and hawed about it, "It's my only chance to see you all week."

Well, if you put it that way.

* * *

Serge Witherspoon and his wife, Paulina are the cream of the crop in our little town. They own Witherspoon's Hardware and Gifts and run with the local bigwigs, and Serge, as I had recently found out, also plays an active role at St. Albans as a member of the board.

I had never been to their home before, a sprawling two-story monstrosity among many sprawling two-story monstrosities out in the canyon. I run with a different crowd.

I arrived in my little red Bug, one of Frank's white roses in my car's bud vase, and parked next to two Mercedes, a Lexus, an Escalade, and a Ford Focus. Frank's car. A champagne colored Land Rover was pulling in as I knocked on the front door. Clearly, I—and maybe Frank—was out of my element.

Waiting for the door to open, I debated how to present myself. Friend of Frank? Girlfriend? Parishioner? In the end I didn't have to decide, because the Land Rover people arrived on the doorstep and I was able to sort of rush in with the lot of them.

Frank latched on to me right away, which seemed both a blessing and a curse. I was unsure about how I should relate to him around the others, especially with his bishop standing by. At one point, he excused us, saying we had some business to discuss, and had the nerve to actually lead me to the front porch, and then out by my car.

"You are a sight for sore eyes," he said happily, leaning in to me as I leaned back against Tilly. "I know this isn't fun for you, this dinner. Maybe it was selfish of me to ask you to come, but it was my only chance to see you. After the other day ..." His eyes said the rest. I'm sure his pants did, too, but I tried not to look.

"There's a bishop in there and ten or twelve church people."

He shrugged. "Bishop Dix is very liberal."

"Not that liberal." I dodged his kiss.

"Later, then?"

"What? You mean after the bishop has gone to bed?"

He grinned.

"Frank, you're confusing me. You seem so ... passionate about your sermons. Really so committed. People think you're sincere. I think you're sincere. But ..."

"I'm consumed by my desire for you?"

"Consumed is a strong word."

"No, it's not, Elizabeth."

I started for the house, but he took my arm and gently brought me back around to face him. "The other day," he said, "you seemed like you were so ... into it."

"Frank, I just ... Well, the circumstances ... You live in a rectory, for God's sake, and I only see you at church or those ... frenetic moments in my office."

"Then you did ... feel something?"

I felt like saying, "Duh!" but gave him what I hoped was a provocative little smile instead.

"Then I'll find a way," he said. "Trust me, I will find a way."

At dinner, I was seated between Serge and a local mortician. A delicious arrangement, I'm sure, if I'd wanted to either make plans for my pre-funeral needs or buy a vacuum cleaner. While they discussed church finances in depth and how much it would actually take to build a new social hall, I focused on the winter squash soup (creamy, light, delectable). As they went into their plans for the upcoming Men's Retreat, I zeroed in on the parsley potatoes (pure starch heaven). And by the time they got through an in-depth analysis of their computer access system, it was only the chocolate ganache (sinful and smooth) that kept me from falling over in despair. That, and Frank. He was seated almost directly across from me and although we couldn't really talk, his behavior more than made up for it. He nibbled on his salmon in tiny, intimate bites. And what he did with his tongue and the chocolate ganache was downright dangerous. Was I the only one noticing?

The longer the meal went on, the more I knew I was in trouble. Good trouble, but still trouble. Maybe it was the whole situation—here we were sitting in a crowd of church people thinking about all the things we might like to do to each other. And isn't the forbidden always the most desired?

When I was the first to excuse myself after coffee, Frank volunteered to walk me to my car. We had gone a very short distance when he scooped me up in his arms and swung me around, then carried me off into a clump of oak trees where it was presumably more private. By the time he set me down, I had to grab onto his arms to hold myself up. My legs had gone to mush.

"I see you're still hungry," he said softly. He started kissing me, at the same time moving me slowly backwards until I was wedged between him and the nearest oak tree. Not a bad place to be, except part of me immediately started worrying about ticks falling out of the tree. Would they get in my hair, and if they did, would I find them in time? Fortunately, the other part of me didn't give a rat's ass. I slipped my arms around his neck and kissed him back while his hands began exploring parts of me that I didn't know I still had. *Better than chocolate*, I thought, when he pressed his body hard against mine. "Better than chocolate ganache," I whispered silkily in his ear.

That really did it. All bets were off. He cupped my bottom with his hands and pulled me up against him so tightly that it left no doubt that, yes, he was happy to see me. I wrapped my legs around him and we began to tear at each other—just as the door to the house opened up and several people spilled out on the porch.

We froze, then groaned in unison. One last long, wet kiss, and he was buttoning his shirt, I was straightening my dress. We managed to get to my car just after the first group of folks drove away and just before the next group came out of the house. I'm pretty sure all they saw was me getting into my car, Frank sedately shutting the door for me. In my rear view mirror I saw him go back into the porch light and stand talking to Bishop Dix. I hoped to God that his clothing was back where it belonged.

Frank left me a message the next day that he'd be busy with the bishop all week long. The rest of the message I won't repeat, but it made my face go warm, my body, too. (I played it a lot) And though I hated waiting to see him again, it turned out to be a good thing. As the days passed, the idea of being more rational came back to me and I started talking myself down, back towards common sense. Did I really want to be the one to have a secret affair with a priest? Was it an illicit affair because he was a priest, like being with a married man? Obviously, the church wouldn't approve of him having sex without marriage. My body was all for it, but my mind was trying to slow me down.

I hate it when I get like that, trying to be sensible in the middle of a storm. You can't reason your way out of a storm. Storms blow you around, they get you soaking wet. They aren't about caution, they're about emotional release. Fighting them just makes you tired and cranky.

※ ※ ※

After some serious soul searching, I thought I was doing pretty well. That is, until Wednesday morning and Sandy Roget. Sandy wanted to talk about sex. I had never seen her so down. She didn't even try to smoke. As usual, though, she started right in.

"No sex," she said hopelessly. "I've had no sex for ... Well, it seems like forever." She seemed embarrassed at her admission. I wondered how she'd feel if I told how long it had been for me.

"He just teases me, you know? I get all worked up, we're just ready to do it, and then ... He puts the brakes on the locomotive and we never quite ... make it into the station."

Well, it had finally happened. My life was imitating my art. Lost in my own recollection, I had to force myself back to the situation at hand. "Do you think maybe he's still worried about the biting thing?"

She tapped her teeth half-heartedly.

"I thought we discussed that, Sandy. I thought you were going to change your behavior. But it sounds to me like you're still using it as a threat."

"It's just a joke."

"Maybe, but apparently, he doesn't find it funny."

"So my better half is afraid of me?"

"Well, probably not, but ... It could be that you surprised him so much, he's not sure who you are any more. Have you thought about that?"

She did now.

"He thought he knew you, then you did something completely out of character. He's probably wondering what else he doesn't know about you."

She nodded, beginning to see the light.

"On the other hand, if you'd sit down with him, reassure him how you feel, talk about things you could do that he would like, I'll bet you'll see a change. Offer him something else, but something that he'll like. Sex in a different room, an illicit fantasy ... Maybe even outside?"

She seemed to like the idea. So did I.

"The other thing, is, Sandy, maybe the thing you're doing with your teeth means you really do want to scare him, exert some kind of power in your relationship, have more control."

She looked startled, but pleased.

* * *

I had some free time and there was something I knew I had to do. Two things, actually. I was still working on my rational approach to living, but it was slipping fast. In order to shore it up again, I needed to do some research. I went by the police station to talk to Jonah and find out how it would feel to see him again. Since he wasn't there, I moved on to that other thing I needed to do. I went to see a lawyer.

Brad Hernandez has an office in a very fine old Victorian in the original section of town. Lawyer Row it has become, but the upshot is that the lovely old houses have been restored rather than being torn down.

My plan was a bit sketchy going in. I was going to scope out his office to see if I could get anything noteworthy on the guy just from being there. Turns out I should have been a little more specific in my plans, but the Janet thing was beginning to bug me again and I was really getting sick of it. It's like having a burr under your saddle (if you're a horse, I guess). You'll do just about anything to get rid of it, even if it means putting yourself in a bind. Or, in danger.

The receptionist looked surprised to see me. "But, no appointment?" She scrunched up her little mouth, and I could tell she was considering what to say next. I was hoping for something like, *He's not available*, a logical expectation. But to my dismay she said, "Let me just go check with him and see."

She disappeared through an exquisite beveled glass door while I ran around in my brain trying to figure out what I could say to the guy if I had to actually face him. Quite sure it would never come to that, I sat down, leafing nervously through an *Architectural Digest*, half expecting to see a glossy spread on his office featured there.

It wasn't all that long before she returned. "You're in luck," she said, "Turns out Mr. Hernandez had a cancellation. Which is rare, I assure you."

"Gosh," I said, trying to hide my panic, "I don't really have that much time right now. Maybe I should come back."

"Nonsense." She fussed around getting some papers together, then handed them to me, the standard forms. "If you'll just fill these out I'll have you in there in no time."

She did.

Brad looked taller than he had in his picture. Either that, or he looked more menacing. Maybe it was the fine suit he was wearing in place of the Hawaiian shirt and shorts. Maybe it was his surroundings, plush and lush—tropical plants, leather couches, a desk the size of a Humvee. Maybe it was the undercurrent of ruthlessness looking out at me from civilized brown eyes.

I got through the usual formalities without too much difficulty.

"Elizabeth Brown ..." He looked perplexed. "Have we met somewhere? You look so familiar."

"I don't think so."

"You sure I didn't do some work for you before?"

"No. Never." I'm not that kind of a sleaze ball.

He sat back in his chair, still curiously checking me out.

"I have a generic face," I said.

He sort of smiled, but it wasn't pretty. "So, what can I do for you?"

I had thrown the story together in the way too short minutes I'd had in reception—my Grandma Betty to the rescue. Her health was failing. In fact, it had failed big time ten years ago, bless her, when she died of a heart attack. But I didn't tell him that. I told him how, being her only living relative, she'd asked me to help plan her estate.

He frowned. "I don't usually handle estate planning," he said. "Is it a … large estate?"

Something told me to say yes.

He looked more interested. "Exceptions can be made, of course."

We discussed the particulars, which were few and far between based on the fact I was just now making them up. "I don't have the actual figures with me today," I said. "Grandma's kind of private about things like that. Not very talkative in her old age. But from what I understand, total, it's worth somewhere around ten million."

He seemed to take a lot more interest in Grandma Betty after that. He took down her name and some other basics, then settled back, called his receptionist, and told her to bring us coffee. "You sure I don't know you?" He was looking at me closely again.

"People always think they know me," I said hastily.

"What do you do for a living? Maybe I know you from there."

He was still frowning when I left with a new appointment and a promise to bring my grandma and all the paperwork with me when I came back.

Unsettled, I walked on the beach. He was a strange man, strange energy. Not so easy to judge in person when I was trying to keep my wits about me as when I could just stare at his face in a snapshot. He was intelligent, well read, smooth. And very powerful. That feeling of power was still there, the same as it had been in his photograph, even after I left his office.

I tried not to think about the fact he knew my name, refused to consider that he might remember me from the article in the paper. In a few days, I'd call up and cancel the appointment. Grandma changed her mind. He'd never think about me again, never even remember I'd been going to bring her in. It would be over and done with, there and then. But something in my heart told me it just wasn't so.

I puzzled over whether to tell Jonah, pretty sure he'd be upset at what I'd done. In the end, I stopped by his office again. As before he was out. I took that as a sign to leave the subject alone.

He found me eating lunch at an outside table at a bagel place. "Join you?"

"How do you keep finding me like this?"

He grinned. "Tricks of the trade."

He ordered a sandwich, then came and sat down. "I heard you were looking for me."

I made some excuse about wanting to ask about the case, as if my interest now was only a casual one. Any news of Janet or the car guy?

He shook his head. "You aren't having those dreams again, are you?"

"No." Well, not last night, anyway.

"You aren't … obsessing over it, are you?"

"I haven't thought about it much," I lied.

He seemed pleased as he went to retrieve his order, then sat back down. "I really didn't get it before, how much it would bother you." He took a big, happy bite out of his sandwich and chewed thoughtfully.

He really didn't get it. Once it's turned on, once you know about something like that and the energy has connected with you, it's almost impossible to turn it off and walk away. I thought of Brad Hernandez. He was involved, someway, somehow. I was sure of that now, though I didn't know the particulars. No words had come to me, no visions of what was going on. But after seeing him, I just knew. What I didn't know, was how to share that information with Jonah.

"You ever get anything on that lawyer? Hernandez, wasn't it?"

"The guy's got an airtight alibi. He was at a meeting with three other lawyers the night she disappeared. Of course, that doesn't mean he wasn't involved."

"I suppose he could have arranged for somebody else to do it?"

"That's our best theory right now. But proving it …"

I didn't dare push the subject any further. We talked about the weather, how the Giants had done this past season, our favorite movies—he likes historical and crime, I like historical, comedy, and romance. No surprises there.

"Maybe we could go see a game sometime."

"Sure," I said, "Just don't make me watch it on TV."

There was a historical drama opening on the weekend—action, intrigue, and romance. We set a date.

As I was leaving, though, Jonah seemed a bit concerned. "Okay, Elizabeth, you never told me what you wanted to see me about."

I shrugged. "I'm just glad we ran into each other."

I left him with a puzzled expression on his face. It wasn't going to be so easy, fooling him for long.

* * *

There was another message from Frank that night when I got home. Peeps and I sat down after dinner and considered our options. Peeps decided to curl up on the coffee table and purr while I stretched out on the couch and thought about men. Seeing Jonah had done just what I thought it would, made me think twice about getting in so deep (pardon the expression) with Frank. It was beginning to feel like I was going too far too fast. Still, when I thought of how it had felt being up against that tree ...

Frank was like candy. He gave me a rush and left me craving more. Was it possible I just wanted him for sex? Could I be that callous, that ... male? He hinted at marriage and wanted to have sex with me. I just wanted to have sex.

By Friday, the Frank vs. Jonah debate seemed miniscule because I was pretty sure that at least once that morning and once the night before, somebody had been following me. I even had a couple of hang up calls. When Jonah arrived for our date, I checked carefully before answering the door. It was only a few blocks to the theater, so we walked. I was feeling creepy and he must have noticed I kept looking over my shoulder. For once, I was glad to know he was probably carrying a gun.

I felt safe in the theater, safe to be with him, and everything was going just ducky until we came out into the lobby at the end of the show and ran into my old neighbor, Soni Baker. A mother to one of my friends when I was growing up, she was now well past middle age, but still her spunky self. Her face lit up on seeing me there.

"Lizzy." She grabbed me into her arms, hugging me hard.

When I introduced her to Jonah she at first look confused, then smiled and said, "Oh, of course. I couldn't think where I knew you from. You're that detective who came by the house last spring."

"What?" I was sure she was mistaken.

"I remember, it was a Saturday. I was outside sweeping off the porch, getting ready to put out the lawn chairs for the season."

Jonah looked almost pained

"That's quite a coincidence," I said.

"No, dear, but this certainly is." She smiled broadly. "The fact he came by to ask me about you and now, here you are, the two of you together." She seemed to think it was a grand idea.

I looked to Jonah expecting a denial. *It couldn't have been me*, he would say. *Detectives, we all look alike.* But he was silent, uncomfortable.

I don't remember what I said after that. It was the usual polite conversation with an old friend when you no longer have much of anything in common. When Jonah and I walked out into the now dark night and started down the street, he didn't even try to take my hand.

I walked quickly, trying to process it, trying to find some reason, some excuse. I finally stopped and looked at him. He gave me a half-hearted smile.

"You talked to my old neighbors."

"We did a little ... checking."

I started walking again. "Who else? Who else did you talk to?"

He stopped me. "I didn't think you'd ever need to know."

I was ready to cry. Or yell. I couldn't decide which.

"It was just a standard background check," he said carefully, as if trying to calm an angry child. "The Chief ..."

"The Chief?"

"Look ... After you found Hannah the way you did, the department had to check you out, make sure you didn't have some involvement. I mean, come on, Elizabeth, it's not everyday somebody walks in out of the blue and knows exactly where to find a missing person."

I knew there was some truth to that, but I wasn't ready to see it.

"Like I was a criminal." I was suddenly cold and wooden and I walked on, my feelings tumbling to a new low.

"Not a criminal," he said, sounding irritated.

"A suspect, then."

"Sometimes that's how we catch people. They come in with some vital information like they want to help. Turns out, they have the information because they actually did the crime."

I shook my head and continued on. When we got to my house I ran up the steps, but he caught up with me before I got in the door.

"Libby ... Elizabeth, I didn't know you then."

"And you wouldn't know me now, either, would you, if I hadn't checked out to your satisfaction? If I hadn't ... met with your approval."

I yanked my door open, went in, and slammed it in his face. A few minutes later, I heard him drive away. Fast.

* * *

I called Frank and ask him to meet me somewhere. Anywhere. The bishop was still with him until Monday afternoon, so Sunday after church was out. It would have been awkward, anyway. He had some free time Saturday, he said. He would make it work. We determined to meet at a motel in a favorite little beach town of mine a few miles up the coast.

I was too mad at Jonah to think straight. And being mad always makes me reckless. It was like he had done an inspection; like I was a side of beef and he had to stamp me with the USDA seal of approval before I was safe to eat.

I drove up the coast by myself and checked into a quaint little place where I'd always imagined staying. It was not on the beach, but in town, near interesting shops and cafes. No need for an ocean view; we wouldn't be looking out at it anyway. After an hour or so of puttering around the stores, I went back to the room. I had brought something pretty and lavender that Lindsay would have definitely picked out for me, if she'd only had the chance. Come to think of it, I think she has the same negligee, only in black. I laid it out on the bed and waited for Frank.

Frank hadn't even bothered to change his shirt, which in his case, of course, meant he was still wearing his clerical collar. I prayed (briefly) that no one had seen him come in, and I admit it, pulling it off of him turned me on a little bit. I don't know whether it was my anger at Jonah or my anticipation of some afternoon delight, but the two of us were like caged tigers finally let out to play. It was the most imaginative sex I've ever had, or could ever imagine having, and it was well worth the wait. I let go of everything—all my anger, all my fear, and went happily to a whole other place.

The time went by way too fast and after Frank left, I decided to stay on. After all, the room was paid. Peeps had plenty of food and water, a fresh kitty box, and of course, the potted palm. Happily exhausted and more relaxed than I'd felt in a long, long time, I slept for awhile, then went out for a walk and a light dinner. It felt right and good to be alone.

Jonah Speaks

Jonah was sitting in his living room, his hand gripping the portable phone so hard he wondered briefly if he might crush it. It had been a bad couple of days.

He heard Lee laugh on the other end of the line. "Your friend ran me a pretty race today, Jonah. First we took a little shopping trip downtown …"

"Oh?"

"To Victoria's Secret," Lee said with relish.

"And …?"

"Yeah, I was only sorry I couldn't follow her in."

"You don't have to get that into it," Jonah said with a half laugh.

"Well, I aim to please."

"Right."

"Now we're up in Cambria."

"What's she doing in Cambria?"

A moment of silence, then, "As near as I can tell? Having an affair."

"That doesn't sound like her."

"I didn't think she looked the type, either, but then … Victoria's Secret."

Jonah wished he'd just get to the point.

"So, anyway, she checks into a little out of the way motel up here and a couple hours later, sure enough, this … guy shows up."

"She's single. What makes you say it's an affair?"

"Hardest part of my job, Jonah, telling people what they don't want to hear."

"C'mon, Lee. I can take it."

Lee paused, then said finally, "The guy is a priest."

Jonah swore under his breath. "You've got the wrong woman." He was as sure of it as anything he'd ever known. Sure enough to be mad.

"You've known me, what—ten, twelve years?" Lee was getting huffy now, too. "Worked with me on a hell of a lot of cases. You know I don't get it wrong."

Jonah stared at the floor, unseeing.

"I'm telling you, Jonah, he went into the room, came out about three hours later, his collar off, his hair ...."

"His collar?"

"I told you. He was a priest."

"Then it couldn't have been her room."

Lee sounded reluctant now. "I ... uh, caught a glimpse of her when she opened the door, the way they greeted each other. Trust me, Jonah, it was her, and they weren't there to talk about religion."

Jonah swore. This time loudly.

"You want me to keep an eye on her or not?"

Jonah grunted his yes. He'd been going to talk to her last night when they got back to her house. It seemed someone was following her—or them. Maybe they'd gotten wind of her working on the case, or maybe it was because she was with him. Whatever, he didn't want to take a chance with her. And he'd noticed how nervous she'd been, looking over her shoulder. Before they could talk about it, though, she'd gotten mad and literally slammed the door on any possible conversation. And she hadn't returned his calls. Hard to say what was really going on, but he felt the need to protect her until he found out.

He'd noticed a car lingering when they were walking to the show, and later, after walking her back, he'd noticed what looked like the same car parked down the street a ways. He drove around the block so he could swing back by, but the car had taken off by then and he couldn't locate it.

He'd made a couple more trips by her house during the night, then called up an old friend, a private eye, to keep watch on her for the rest of the weekend, at least, since he knew she wouldn't let him do it himself. If anything was going on, Lee would report back and Jonah would take it from there. But this wasn't what he'd expected at all.

Jonah got up and walked the room, unable to sit still any longer. "Give me the name of the place."

"You know that's not a good idea."

"She's twice as vulnerable up there. You know that."

"Which is why I'm here, right?"

"You've got to sleep sometime."

Lee sighed.

"I can find it anyway. Her car is hard to miss."

"You're gonna hate yourself in the morning," Lee said.

Karma Is As Karma Does

Once back in my room, I had expected to spend the evening feeling cozy and content. Unfortunately, my mood faded right along with the daylight leaving me restless and ill at ease. Sometimes motel rooms will do that to me—maybe it's all the mixed energy left over from people who have been there and gone. When you feel energy physically like I do, it can sometimes be a bothersome thing. I seriously considered driving home, but felt anxious about going out in the darkness and driving home alone.

People think I can simply tune in to my guides when I'm in a tough spot and they'll bail me out, but it doesn't work like that. For one thing, when I feel anxious enough or scared enough, things sort of shut down. Like one of those automatic steel doors you see in the movies, the alarm sounds, the heroine barely makes it through to the other side before her fate is sealed there. Only I'm still here. On the wrong side.

I happen to believe it's because I choose to do my own stunts. As I said before, it's my life and I have to make the choices and suffer the consequences, good or bad. If I let somebody else do it, somebody *up there*, whose life would I be living anyway?

I turned on the TV, propped myself up in bed, and clicked through umpteen channels hoping to find something, anything but a reality show. Think about it. We spend millions sending contestants out in the so-called wilderness with a camera crew, medical team, etc. so they can pretend to forage for their existence while people all over the world really are starving to death every day. It seems to me that we could put those millions to better use.

By ten I had enough of all the back stabbing (must we continually showcase the worst in people rather than the best?) and was thoroughly disgusted. I turned off the light, tiptoed to the window—don't ask me why I felt the need to tiptoe, and peeled back a tiny corner of the curtain to look outside. Nothing moved. The light from the motel shined bright on a quiet parking lot. The place appeared to be almost full.

That felt better. No movement out there and lots of neighbors if I needed to cry out. I went to bed and snuggled up, happily remembering with delighted detail the things Frank and I had done together. Even by myself, my face turned red just thinking about them. But then, things began to go downhill fast. Curled on my side, I started getting little glimmers of what I'd actually done. Little sparks of realization started going off in my head. Never mind the immediate gratification of pure physical pleasure. I had acted on impulse and anger, run off half-cocked, so to speak, which seldom turns out to be a good thing for me. And even though the sex had been remarkable, I could feel the consequences coming already.

At some point I must have drifted off. A soft *tap tap* finally woke me up. I wasn't sleeping soundly anyway. I heard it again. It was at the door. I switched on the light beside the bed, then slid completely under the covers, hiding my face and head and curling up into a tight, frightened ball. Well, that would do me a lot of good.

I moved the blanket off my face so I could listen. I heard more tapping, very soft, and then a low, deep voice. I couldn't really hear what was being said. I screwed up my courage and got out of bed. I could stay there and wait for something to attack, or I could take the initiative. I went to the door and said, as boldly as I could, "Get away from the door. The police are on their way."

The tapping stopped. "Damn it, I'm the police."

I thought I was hearing things. I looked out the window and saw Jonah standing there. He motioned for me to let him in and I was too stunned to think twice about doing so.

I opened the door a crack.

"Let me in, Elizabeth."

I moved back to let him enter, realizing only when I saw the look on his face that I was still wearing my little lavender number.

"Just a minute." I shut the door, raced to the bed, and yanked the bedspread onto the floor. The pillows landed there, too, making the place look for all the world like a wild party had been going on. Well, technically, it had.

I pulled off a sheet and wrapped it around myself, trying to muster some dignity as I went back to let him in.

He surveyed the room, his eyes lingering on the bedding now lying haphazardly on the floor. Then he looked at me. A little too thoroughly.

"What are you doing here, anyway?" I clutched my sheet and tried to look angry.

"I thought you might be in some kind of trouble."

"Trouble?" I was beginning to wake up, and it was a rude awakening. Jonah was standing in my room in the middle of the night, looking at me like I was some kind of freakish creation he'd never seen before. Maybe it was all just some weird coincidence he was here. Except, I really don't believe in coincidence, weird or otherwise. Besides, if he knew I was here, he knew about Frank.

"There's no ... trouble," I said, sharply. "I'm all alone here."

"Good." He sounded as tense as I did.

Good?

"Nobody's been ... bothering you, then?"

I couldn't stop myself. "You know, I guess that depends on your definition of bothering."

I could tell that he was fighting off a harsh retort. He glanced toward the door as if he wanted to escape. "Obviously, I shouldn't have come."

"No shit."

I marched to the door and started to open it, making a big show of my outrage. He followed me, so I reversed direction and headed into the bathroom, slamming the door in his face. Thankfully, I'd discarded most of my clothes there when Frank and I were deliciously meandering our way around the room. I pulled on my jeans and buttoned a cardigan sweater over my teddy, remembering with dismay that my panties had been carelessly discarded out in the room, beside the bed, right next to where Jonah had been standing.

He spoke through the door. "I think you better come out so we can talk."

"Why don't you go fuck yourself?" I said under my breath. Aloud I said, "Since when do I need to report to you?"

I stared at my reflection in the mirror. My hair was tousled—nicely, actually, and my eyes were bright with—what? Afterglow from wild sexual energy, or *Oh, God, Jonah thinks I'm a slut*? Either way, I actually looked remarkably good, satisfied somehow, and certainly as wide awake as I'd ever been. There are worse things then having two men in a motel room on the same day. Things like, *Oh, God, Jonah thinks I'm a slut.*

I had to pull it together.

"Elizabeth?" He sounded tense. "Open the door."

I made a silent face in his direction. God, I can be mature when I want to be.

I heard him try the door handle. When it didn't budge, he said, "Look. I think somebody may be following you."

"Oh, I already know that," I said. "He's talking to me right now."

Jonah hit the door with his hand, and then I thought he moved away. All was quiet on the western front for so long I began to think that he might have actually left. I opened the door cautiously, only to find him waiting there, his hands on the doorframe. He stopped me from closing it with one hand, then wedged his foot in the door.

The only way to deal with this was confidence. Confidence. "Okay, so you were in the neighborhood, and thought you'd stop by?" I tried to move past him, but he didn't budge, looking down at me in an almost threatening manner. I had a flashback to the one romance novel I'd ever been able to force myself to read clear through. The hero was grim looking and always looming at the heroine. Is this what they meant by *looming*? After all these years, had I been officially loomed?

"Is this some kind of attack?" I said. But I wasn't afraid and he knew it.

Still, he relented and moved back a bit.

Feeling his eyes on me, I casually strolled around the bed, and sure enough, there were my pink flowered cotton panties, my standard wear. I'm not usually the Victoria's Secret type, but then today hadn't been one of my usual days. I picked up the scattered pillows and fluffed them, taking way too much time. As I put one of the sheets back on the bed, I managed to drag my panties over to me with my bare toes, pushing them under the bed, hoping he wouldn't notice.

"Looks like you've had a rough night," he said dryly.

I couldn't believe he actually said that. When I finally got the nerve to sneak a peak at him, there was a half smile on his face, which made me angrier than ever. I dragged the heavy bedspread back onto the bed and tried unsuccessfully to restore it to its natural order.

"Need some help?"

"What I need is for you to get out."

"I can't help you, Elizabeth, if you won't let me," he said quietly.

He grabbed the other side of the bedspread and started to help me pull it up on the bed. Child that I was at the moment, I started yanking it the other way.

He stopped and stared at me. "My mistake," he said. "I thought you were somebody I knew."

"Yeah, after that background check, you'd think so, wouldn't you?"

I yanked the bedspread again, hard, just as he let go. I almost toppled over backwards, saving myself just in time. I threw the bedspread over the pillows and stepped back.

"And now you're tailing me. What's next, pictures and prints?"

Our eyes met for just a moment, and then I watched in pain as he went toward the door.

"Jonah. Wait …"

"Lock it," he said tersely. And then he was gone.

Where do you go from there? I locked all the locks, got into bed, still in my layered clothing and cried myself to sleep, feeling too cold to maybe ever get warm again. By morning my anger had morphed into a full blown case of mortification. The one time I'd slept with one man when what I'd really wanted to do was to sleep with another—Jonah. And now Jonah had found me out.

※ ※ ※

Back at home, things had really started to pop. I had a message from Lindsay, of course. I nearly always have one. A message from my mom gushing about her latest trip to Florida with her disgusting new husband, Bernard the Butt (My name for him) and, oh yes, an especially memorable message from someone who declined to leave his name. Too scared to listen to it a second time, I sat down on the couch and stared at the recorder. Peeps, still trying desperately to get my attention after my latest absence, sat and stared at me.

Feeling his round, yellow eyes on me, I picked him up and hugged him. Too hard apparently, because he gave his trademark yowl, then jumped down and headed for the nearest chair. He was just lifting a paw, claws out, just ready to give the thing a nice fat slash when I yelled his name. He looked back, satisfied that I was finally focusing on him, then trotted back over and landed on my lap, all sweetness and light. I petted him absently while my mind went over and over the words I'd just heard.

These are the times when I become another person, really—no longer an intelligent woman with a reasonable amount of common sense, I am suddenly too half-witted to know what I ought to do. Fear really bothers me. I mean, I realize nobody likes it much, except maybe mountain climbers and acrobats, but when I feel a dose of good, strong fear heading my way, I do my best to push it away. Not by taking action, which would be a logical choice, but by taking evasive action. I deny it exists.

So I sat there making up stories for myself, finding reasons and excuses for that message I'd received. I couldn't catch all the words; it was like someone had turned the speed down on a record player, the voice low and garbled and nightmare slow. I decided it couldn't have been meant for me. Obviously it was a wrong number. Boy, I'm glad I don't have friends like that. Or better yet, it was just a sales call that had gone horribly wrong. Those computers that make their own calls could easily make someone's words jumbled and elongated, couldn't they? Still, the word *death* had been used at least once, and I think somebody either said something about pain or about pineapples. My frantic mind opted for the fruit.

I wanted desperately to call somebody, but going down my list, I couldn't come up with any good candidates. Frank was still with the bishop and Jonah was just plain out of the question. I thought of Lindsay, but couldn't bring myself to tell her. You tell somebody one little thing about something like this, you have to tell them everything. I just wasn't ready to do that.

I remembered, too, that day I sat on the beach and had the message about a rough patch that was on it's way. The storm I'd seen then had been followed by a clear blue day, which meant to me that, no matter how scary it might get, it would all come round right in the end. My guides have comforted me more than once by reminding me that we humans sometimes choose a less peaceful path with the (eventual) purpose of finding peace. Doesn't mean it has to be that way, it's just the way we are. Lucky me.

* * *

It's hard to go unnoticed when you drive a bright red VW Bug with a license plate that says, "TILLY." People tend to remember something like that. Still, Frank and I couldn't stay away from each other after our meeting at the motel. I don't know what I was to him, but he had become my drug, the illicit substance that kept me from feeling anything and I needed that right now.

It was a risky business. We were both free, but there was that little matter of his being expected to set a moral example for his parishioners. We met wherever and whenever we could, and the funny thing was, the next Sunday at church, I overheard Paulina Witherspoon telling someone she'd never seen Father Frank preach with as much passion as he was doing now. I think it was the first time I realized she had more than a little crush on him.

After coupling in our cars, the park, and various and sundry other semi-public places, we moved on to even riskier business—I went to his place for the night. Wild sex in a rectory, now there's a good idea. But we were sick and tired of contortionist sex in the back seat of our tiny cars, and my house, with it's unofficial neighborhood watch— okay, the people across the street were just plain nosy, was definitely out of the question.

I tried parking my car a couple blocks away from Frank's and walking in. The trick about that was I had to slip out pre-dawn the following morning and hike in the dark to my car, which scared the living daylights out of me. Having seen what I thought was a car following me during the day, and remembering Jonah's words that night at the motel, it wasn't much of a leap of my imagination to think that someone might be following me when it was dark.

After two early hikes, I couldn't take it anymore. I started parking Tilly at the Denny's a few blocks away from the rectory and Frank would pick me up from there. It's a lot harder to notice a Focus.

We went on like this for several weeks. Then things started to surface. My things. We were lying in bed, talking. Frank was stroking my hair. I was dealing with my demons. "I don't know how you justify this, Frank. You and me, I mean. You know, with your job and everything."

He lay back with a sigh and looked up at the ceiling. "Maybe justify is the wrong word."

"Maybe you should think about another career choice."

When he didn't respond, I glanced over and was surprised to see the hurt look in his eyes. I reached out and touched him gently. "I didn't mean …"

"What?"

"You're a great priest."

He was still frowning.

"I mean it, Frank. Your sermons are amazing. Really amazing."

Our eyes met, and I could see how truly important this was to him.

"I'm not just saying that. They're inspired."

"Thanks."

It was a long moment before he spoke again.

"I'll admit I'm a little conflicted. There's so much about the church that feels so right to me." He was looking at me now. "But try as I might I just can't see how making love to the woman I love could be sinful."

My stomach flipped over. He had slipped the "L" word in nice and neat. Like it belonged. Like tuna in a sandwich. I tried to lighten the subject. "I'm guessing your employer doesn't negotiate these things, does He?" I pointed toward heaven.

He shook his head, smiling.

We lay there quietly for a few minutes.

"So, what did you want to be when you grew up, Frank? You know, when you were a kid?"

"I wanted to pitch for the Dodgers." He folded his arms behind his head and stretched out as if he was looking up at a night sky full of stars and enjoying them all.

I groaned. "I'm sleeping with a Dodger's fan?" A Giants' fan, born and bred, I'd been trained early on that the Dodgers were our sworn enemy. Especially when they beat us, which they usually did.

He grinned. "What about you?"

I thought about it a moment. I knew the answer, but saying it sounded a little silly.

"Elizabeth?"

"I ... uh, wanted to be a waitress."

He practically choked. When he'd recovered, he said, "No, really. What did you want to be?"

"I liked the idea of all the food," I said. "I guess I thought you could eat whatever you wanted. You know, for free."

He was still snickering, so I play punched him in the side. For a man of God, he could certainly get a devilish look in his eye. "By the time I was seventeen," he said, "all I really wanted to do was get in your pants."

"So how come you didn't try harder back then?"

"I thought you were a good girl."

I giggled.

" My mistake," he said. "If only I'd known then what I know now ..."

I leaned closer to kiss him, and not in a good girl way.

"You know what they say." Frank pulled my body against his. "Old friends are the best."

And we were off ...

I had to stop this craziness. Eventually. I'd think about it later. Right now I couldn't quite recall just what it was I'd been so concerned about.

※ ※ ※

Not everyone was thrilled when we went public at the St. Alban's Altar Society annual potluck and white elephant sale. Apparently Father Frank had a host of admirers and many of them thought they had some kind of exclusive rights. Ms. Hooters turned up her pretty little nose at me and Paulina Witherspoon was positively surly, outbidding me on the wrought iron umbrella stand to the tune of nearly twenty bucks. During dinner, a twelve-year-old blonde girl (Her name *had* to be Carrie) gave me the evil eye while her parents weren't looking. And George, the impeccably dressed middle-aged man who always plants himself in the center of the very front pew on Sundays accidentally knocked my plate of second helpings into my lap and looked a little pleased about it.

But most of the people, I'd say ninety-eight-point-eight percent of them, seemed very pleased. They immediately started treating me a lot more formally and with what I can only call respect and reverence. Somehow, it was as if my being close to Frank had changed me into somebody who was just a little bit holy, too. It had happened to me before when I worked with people in a metaphysical way. It's like they want to make you special, make you someone better or wiser than they are so they can elevate what you say to The Truth. I hate it. It's granting me power I never want to have.

Besides, if the parishioners had only known …

The sex thing, of course, we still kept to ourselves. But going public meant I got to share the front pew with George during services (not a perk, I assure you), go out on actual dates with Frank, and get automatically volunteered for nearly every church activity that came down the pike. I decided I liked the secrecy better. The public thing was way too much work.

Besides, I felt like I was now living a double life. Make that triple. First, there was Father Frank and his "girl," as they all persisted in calling me, working side by side at the white elephant sale. Second, there was Frank and Elizabeth, the sex addicts who tried out every position in the book (We didn't have a book, but I'm pretty sure we could have written one). Third, there was poor lost Elizabeth, feeling pursued and afraid.

The odd phone calls were coming regularly now, which was another reason I preferred spending most of my nights at Frank's. I was well aware that the strange happenings had started after my trip to the lawyer's office, and common sense told me that he had somehow figured out who I was and wasn't too happy about it. Still, I couldn't really imagine that Brad Hernandez would do anything so foolish, would risk his livelihood and his reputation that way. He was too intelligent for that, wasn't he? Too smooth? Doing anything that obvious might happen in a movie, but in real life?

I didn't know what to do next, though I'll admit, I felt the need to do something. But the thought of having to talk to Jonah, of having to admit to him that I'd gone to see Brad Hernandez, was more than I could deal with. I told myself it would all stop soon—after all, I hadn't done anything else toward trying to find Janet. And mercifully, I hadn't had any more of those awful dreams. I think maybe Frank—and our nighttime activities, were responsible for that.

As for talking to Frank, two things stopped me. First, we spent most of our time doing other things than talking. And second, I still had never told him anything about my extra-ordinary abilities. Telling him about the calls would lead to telling him about Jonah and the work we'd done in the past. Which would lead right back to telling him about my psychic experiences. Could a priest and a psychic co-exist outside of bed? I wasn't at all sure.

* * *

Frank and I were working together in silence preparing lunch. It was Sunday, of course, our standard after church "date," now made mandatory by our status as a couple.

Was Frank pouting? I'd never seen him do that. I sidled over and kissed him on the cheek.

"Something wrong?"

"Not really."

He continued to slather mayonnaise on the bread long past its need to be there.

"Frank ..." I reached out to stop him, certain the bread could take no more.

"I just don't like being without you," he said. "Last night, I mean." He set the knife down. "I've gotten used to having you in my bed."

"I know, but Peeps gets lonely, too."

"Who?"

I cut a tomato into careful slices, frowning. "My cat."

"Oh."

"Besides, I've told you before, Frank, I can't do the Saturday night thing. I can't just waltz from your bed to church. It feels too weird."

"I know." He stuck the mayonnaise and mustard back in the refrigerator and came over to me, looking so dolefully serious that I wanted to laugh, don't ask me why.

"There is a solution, Elizabeth."

I felt my throat start to tighten. Especially when he took my hand.

"We could always get married. Bishop Dix could come and do the service."

I just stared at him.

"I mean it. No more guilt. No more sneaking around." He squeezed my hand. "It would help me out a lot, in my situation. And, God knows, we're certainly compatible."

Feeling like I could barely breathe, I sat down at the table.

"What do you say, Elizabeth?"

When I hesitated, he looked like he was about to get down on one knee.

"No, Frank. Not ... Not now, okay?"

He straightened up awkwardly.

"There's just a lot of things to think about." And when he looked puzzled, "Do they even allow cats here?"

"Cats?" He sounded incredulous. "I'm trying to ask you to marry me and you keep talking about cats."

I was half tempted to say *Peeps* just to see if he'd once again act clueless, but I kept my mouth shut.

He brought our sandwiches to the table and sat beside me, looking ominously amorous, but then something entirely different came out. "I see how you are with my parishioners. You're a natural, Elizabeth. You'll make a perfect minister's wife."

I smiled weakly.

"At least tell me you'll think about it."

"Okay."

He gave me a long look.

"Okay, I'll think about it."

"Good." He got up and went to the refrigerator. "What do you want to drink?"

"You have any whiskey?"

He laughed and pulled out a pitcher of iced tea. I'm not sure why I make Frank wait on me after church. I just do.

I had known in the back of my mind this day would come soon; known and wanted to avoid thinking about it. *Couldn't we just keep doing what we're doing? I kind of like sneaking around.*

Oops, had I said that out loud?

Apparently. He was looking at me like I was being very, very naughty. Which turned him on, I gather, from the way he abandoned the tea and started kissing my ear.

It was another twenty minutes or so before I got to eat my sandwich.

* * *

Walter was back in town for a few days. Lindsay and I met him for an early dinner at The Pizza Party, one of my favorite places on earth, the first being The Chocolate Chunk Emporium, I think. Just as I was settling into my second piece, I had a blinding thought. This was the place Jonah had picked up a pizza the night he'd come to my house, the night we'd first discussed the missing woman's case, the night he'd handed me that watch. It had been the beginning of a circle and it was now coming around again.

Lindsay was yattering on about somebody she'd run into, telling a story I normally would have laughed at hysterically. She was excited that Walter was there—excited and a bit anxious. I was just anxious. I had that feeling of mixed energy I get sometimes, a feeling I can't ever quite put my finger on. The last time I felt it, someone close to me had almost died, so I've learned through time and experience that the feeling can lead to something really uncomfortable. Still, I can never make it go away.

I was chewing thoughtfully on a strangely crisp piece of pineapple when I realized two things: first, it wasn't pineapple; it was a stray piece of green pepper, and I hate green pepper on a pizza, and second, Walter was looking at me expectantly.

"So, what do you say, E.? We thought maybe we'd head over to The Club. Get a couple drinks."

A door slammed shut in my brain. I set my pizza down and stared at my hands. Why, I don't know. They aren't especially nice looking hands, just average. The fingers are a little stubby, actually. Maybe it gave me time to think. First the pizza place, now the Club Contempo? I hadn't been back there since that night Jonah and I had our unexpected meeting of the minds. More energy circle stuff was happening. It was starting to freak me out.

I hate being the third person, anyway, when you're with a couple. In the past, I could have convinced myself Walter and Lindsay weren't really a couple, but now they were suddenly playing Romeo and Juliet, and doing it very well. When we sat down in the bar, all my sadness came crashing around me, encompassing me in a shell of pain. Never mind my fear and my confusion over what was happening at home, the memory of that magic moment when Jonah and I had danced there was almost too much to bear. I wanted to sob out loud and beg for forgiveness. For what, I'm not sure.

I knew I should be happy for my two friends so I determined to keep my mouth shut and just cry in my beer—except I was drinking a Perrier. Two gulps of the stuff and I blurted it out. "Frank asked me to marry him."

Lindsay looked horrified, while Walter looked kindly, like only he can do. He had no clue who Frank was, anyway.

"Tell me you didn't say yes," Lindsay said.

"I didn't say anything."

"Good. Thank God. Walter, talk some sense into her, will you?"

Walter looked willing, but confused. "About …?"

"Marriage."

"What's wrong with marriage?" He was looking at Lindsay, eyebrows up, expectation at the ready.

She looked flustered, something she rarely does. She put her hand over his and squeezed it. "To the wrong person," she said.

"Oh." But Walter, of course, still didn't know who she was talking about. It was about then that what was left of my mood just snapped. Without a word, I jumped up and headed to the bathroom. Anything was better than staying there and staring at the smug look on Lindsay's face. Since when was she such an expert on relationships? The woman has had more dates than she has sense. Since when did she know what was best regarding men?

I hunkered down in a stall and entertained myself by reading the walls, learning among other things less fit to print that *Amber luvs Ben*, and *Jessica duzit best*. I was most taken with the blood-red lipstick message just above the toilet paper dispenser that said simply, *Roz*! Sometimes, simplicity speaks volumes.

I stayed in there as long as I could stand the ambience, hoping for calm, but I still felt mad. I went back out, sat down with a bang, and interrupted whatever cutesy little conversation they'd been having.

"I'm getting really sick of hearing you put Frank down."

Lindsay looked surprised. She and I don't fight, we don't yell at each other, so this was way too close for her comfort, never mind mine.

"I don't see how you're qualified to give advice, anyway. Your track record sucks," I said, avoiding looking in Walter's direction. Hurting Walter would be like hurting a baby seal.

"I just want what's best for you," Lindsay said.

"Well, you're not my mother, so for God's sakes, quit acting like her."

Lindsay set her pizza down slowly. "Actually, your mom doesn't have such a great track record either, does she?" Lindsay sounded cool to my heat.

Walter cleared his throat. "I think Lindsay was just trying to help." And when Lindsay opened her mouth to speak, he said with surprising forcefulness, "Say something nice, Linnie. I know you can do it."

She closed her mouth, and we stared at each other.

Walter put his hand on her arm, then leaned in to whisper something to her that I couldn't begin to hear. She seemed to swallow something hard, then spoke. "I guess he's okay. For a priest."

Walter and I exchanged an exasperated look.

"I don't get it, Lindsay. You make it sound like a crime, him being a priest,"

She started to answer, but then said nothing.

"Really, I want to know, " I said, knowing I was pushing her, wanting right then to push her. "What's wrong with Frank, anyway?"

"What's wrong with Jonah?"

'This isn't about Jonah."

She played with the ice in her glass, but I was pretty sure she was really toying with me. "Dear girl," she said dramatically, "everything is about Jonah."

* * *

It's a good thing Lindsay and I rarely get mad at each other and almost never hold a grudge, because the very next weekend it was time for one of our trips to Solvang, a very Danish little town just an hour or so down the freeway. We hadn't talked all week, which was unusual, but there was no question in either of our minds that we would still go. We just needed time to clear the air.

And what better way than with some Krispy Cremes? I stopped by on my way to Lindsay's house and bought a dozen to soften us up. Oddly enough, two or three were missing by the time I arrived.

I found Lindsay in the middle of a major dish washing operation, surrounded by stacks of plates and pans. A neat and clean person in other ways, she's the first to admit she lets the dishes pile up until there's nothing left to eat on before she finally gives in and washes them up. Apparently, today was one of those days.

I grabbed a dishtowel and offered to help, but she waved me away. "Let God dry them."

I put the cloth back on its hanger and held out a donut so she could take a bite out of it. Still washing a plate, she closed her eyes and smiled as she chewed. "Heaven," she said happily, so I stayed by her till she finished the donut, which didn't take long. As everybody knows who's ever had one, you eat a regular donut, but you inhale a Krispy Crème.

When she'd finished, I sat at the table and pulled out another one for myself.

"You eat all of them, I'll have to kill you," she said, without looking at me.

I grinned. "Yeah, but it will have been worth it."

Leaving my half-eaten donut on the table I got up and stood next to her. "You know, I really do want to know what you think about Frank."

She gave me a sidelong glance, then rinsed the mug she was washing and set it on the rack. "Maybe I should just learn to keep my mouth shut."

"Well, yeah, but it's a little late for that," I said, smiling.

She didn't answer for a long time. Not until she'd washed the last dinner plate and somehow squeezed it into the overcrowded rack. Then she looked at me with that clear, direct look that only Lindsay can manage and said, carefully, "I guess I just find it hard to respect the guy because he screws around."

"What do you mean, he screws around?"

She motioned for me to sit and we both sat down. "Look," she said, "I saw the guy out in front of the church when I was driving by the other day …"

"You just happened to be driving by?"

"Well …"

"And?"

"Well, he's obviously knock-down-drag-out gorgeous. I'll give you that."

"So what's he doing with me?"

She gave me a measured look. "I could describe it, but we'd both be embarrassed," she said.

We were getting into our patter now, happily.

"So, what's the problem, then?"

"He may not be cheating on you, but you've got to admit, he's still cheating."

"On what? His congregation?"

She nodded. "If he'll break the rules in one place, he'll break them in another, right?" She selected another donut and took what looked like a thoughtful bite.

'So, you're saying if he sneaks around with me he might, what? Steal from the collection plate?"

"I wouldn't go that far, but it's kind of like with a cop. Take Jonah, for example."

"Let's not."

"If he continually parked in a no parking zone, wouldn't you wonder what other laws he's willing to break?"

"No."

She looked a bit irritated. "Okay, then let's say a judge parks in a no parking zone. Wouldn't that make you worry?"

I sat back in my chair and smiled. "You're comparing me to a no parking zone?"

Lindsay's look told me she was in one of her rare, ultra serious moments. She pinned me down with her gaze. "Why, in heaven's name, would you let the best thing that's ever happened to you walk right out the door?"

She glanced at her own door as she said it, and so did I. I could almost see Jonah, a tiny figure receding in the distance. He was walking fast and it looked to me like he was carrying a stick with a red bandana tied to it.

She sat back and I could see where she was going. I just didn't want to get there yet. "You're different with him, you know."

I tried stalling, because, having just lost the best thing that ever happened to me, I wasn't sure I could take anything more. "Different?"

"Yeah. Intense. Lord, the other night, just the mention of his name …"

I was feeling like a deer in the headlights, she had nailed me so completely.

And she didn't even know about our meeting in Cambria.

"I mean it, Elizabeth. Where Jonah's concerned, you're positively volatile. Why is that, do you think?"

I looked around the room, trying to assimilate what I'd just figured out, then said softly, "I don't know, Lindsay, but I kind of like it."

We shared a smile.

* * *

By the time we hit the freeway that afternoon, we were back to our old selves, buddies strong and true. All for one, and all that crap.

Solvang has a truly fine outdoor theater and we go there every summer season at least two or three times. We certainly don't go for the food. Correction: the Danish pastries ain't half bad, but the Danish food? Way too much like German, all sausages and stuff. Lindsay isn't normally fond of plays—she says you can see through them too easily. They aren't real. But give her the package of food plus shopping plus the plays and she manages to get into it somehow. Our favorites (besides the pastries) are the Shakespearean comedies, and this trip we would be seeing *Much Ado About Nothing*, which, as far as I'm concerned, is about as close to heaven as you can get.

It was dark when we got to town and the tiny white lights that decorate nearly every store and tree in the downtown area were already working their magic. It's one of my favorite things about Solvang; they keep them up all year, and it makes for a fairyland appearance. After our standard stop for supplies at Mortenson's Bakery, we parked in the lot that's only half a block from the theater, then opened the trunk and began the ritual of layering ourselves. Even after a hot summer day, the amphitheater can get really chilly, and this near the end of the season you can pretty well count on it. All around the theater, you see people standing by their cars, making themselves fat with clothes.

I dug out my heavy socks and put them on, while Lindsay pulled on a pair of hiking boots. As I was putting on one of my sneakers, I suddenly had the sense that I was being watched. It was like a little tickle against my back, something warning me, something strange. I glanced around, but saw nothing but a few parked cars and a nearly empty lot—most of the playgoers park on the side streets.

I pushed the feeling out of my mind. Too much tension lately, and the whole thing was getting the better of my imagination.

"So, who do you think will play the lead?" Lindsay, who was now fully layered, was leaning back against the car with her arms crossed waiting for me. "I hope it's that guy with the hair."

"You mean the one with the great voice?"

She nodded. We have our favorite actors but we seldom remember their names, just their attributes.

I was just tying my last shoe when the feeling hit me again, even harder. Back of the neck. It was all I could do to not turn around.

"Is there somebody behind me?" I hoped my voice was steadier than I felt.

"Just the parking lot," Lindsay said, squinting into the darkness behind me.

"Don't stare."

"Stare at what? There's nothing there."

I straightened up and used the opportunity to quickly check out the area again. She was right. There was no one there. A couple of empty cars, and that was it.

"I hope to God that actress with the nose doesn't play Beatrice," Lindsay said. "When I'm watching her, it's all I can think about. That, and her little mouse voice."

I made a face. "You mean that woman who played opposite the skinny guy in … Oh, you know, the play about the ship …?"

"The one where they had those fake flowers that looked so real?"

"Yeah, that one."

Like twins, we have our own secret language.

I slammed the trunk shut.

"You want to walk?" Lindsay was motioning towards downtown where the streets were nearly empty and the lighting dim, except for those lovely white lights, of course. In the summer we come early enough to do a little shopping, then take a short walk around the neighborhoods once the stores close up; we had learned the hard way, they close up at five. There are some wonderfully unique houses with semi-secret gardens and a bed and breakfast that always makes me want to stay. It's a good way to kill time waiting for the play to start and an even better way to walk off a few of those Danish treats. This late in the year, when it's already really dark, we usually just stroll down the main street and window shop.

My senses were still reacting to something I couldn't see, but I didn't want to frighten Lindsay. I'd told her nothing about the hang up calls or anything else. Besides, it was probably just a false alarm; my fear getting the better of me. As we set off, I could see a few other people down a block or so—an older couple obviously waiting for the play, and a family of four walking with their chihuahua. We wouldn't be alone.

We set off as usual, checking out the fanciful clothing displayed in the window of a favorite shop, pausing to drool over the fancy cakes sitting in a bakery case window. We took time to giggle over the giant clog that sits on the sidewalk and had our usual discussion over how we both swear it used to be bigger. Then, just for laughs, Lindsay tried to sit on it like she always does. Tradition—you've got to love it.

Looking up, I realized we were now the only two people on the street. Several blocks down, and one street over, the theater grounds would be filling up with people, but here, we were alone. A chill ran down my spine at the same time as a sudden breeze from out of nowhere brushed against my cheek.

"Maybe we ought to go back," I said calmly.

"Nonsense." Lindsay checked her watch. "We've still got plenty of time."

Which meant she wanted to head further on down the street away from the theater to see if the needlework shop around the corner might still be open. We'd found it open once or twice on a summer night, and ever since then she always wanted to check, just in case. But that was another two blocks away.

We kept walking, but by this time, my mind was screaming at me that it wanted to turn around. Once, I even thought I heard steps behind us, but when I glanced back, there was no one there. When Lindsay suddenly grabbed my arm and pulled me to a stop I nearly fainted.

"What is it?"

"Look at that." She was pointing excitedly at a yellow cashmere sweater that was prominently featured in the nearest boutique. "I would kill for something like that."

"It's ... nice." My voice barely squeaked out.

She gave me a funny look. "What? You think the color's wrong?"

I shook my head. At the moment, I had no idea.

We continued on, but at the next window we stopped at, I thought I caught a glimpse of him—or of someone, in the glass. Almost directly across from us, he was standing in the dark of a store entrance on the other side of the street. I could see his legs; the rest of him was lost in shadow. How had I not heard him there before?

"You look like you've just seen a ghost," Lindsay said joking. "Of course, maybe you have, being psychic and all." Seeing the look on my face, her smile faded.

"Elizabeth, what's wrong?"

I couldn't see the man in the doorway now. Maybe he had slipped away into the night or moved back further into the shadows. Maybe he'd never been there at all.

Lindsay gripped my arm so tightly that I was grateful she keeps her fingernails trimmed. "What's wrong?" she said again.

"I just think we need to go back."

"Okay."

"Walk slowly."

"Okay." She was looking around us now, picking up my anxiety.

"Don't look around, Lindsay. Just walk."

"Okay, but you're freaking me out."

Maybe he was like a dog—if he sensed your fear, or if you ran, he'd take out after you. But why would someone follow me here, what was the point? As quickly as I asked that question, the answer popped into my brain. *To scare me.* It was all just to scare me. But how far would he—would they, go? And worst of all, did he really even exist?

I didn't catch sight of the man again, and, mercifully, we fell in with other people as we got closer to the play. Still, Lindsay kept her hand on my arm. "You better tell me what's going on," she said when we stopped just outside the entrance to the theater. "You better damn well tell me what is going on."

I was looking around us, but seeing little.

"Elizabeth?"

"I think maybe somebody was following us."

"Oh, hell," Lindsay said. "Maybe we'd better just get out of here."

We both looked toward the empty, dark parking lot at the same time, and apparently both had the same reaction. "Okay, so we'll see the play first," Lindsay said, trying to sound calm. "We will not let some crazy ruin our evening. Am I right?"

I nodded.

"So, then … Why would somebody follow us?"

"I'm not sure."

"Maybe we should call the cops," she said.

"No."

"But …"

"Think about it, Lindsay. What would we tell them? We're not sure, but we think some guy might have been following us? They'd think we were the crazies."

Since the ticket takers were beginning to look at us funny, we went on in through the gate. She stopped me just inside. "Has this happened before?"

I didn't even have to answer. She read my face. "Have you told Jonah?"

"We aren't talking much these days."

"Well, maybe you should start."

***

The performances were especially fine that evening. The guy with the hair played the lead, the woman with the mouse voice and the nose was, thankfully, nowhere to be seen, and the sets and costumes were just what we would have dreamed them to be. But even though we had an extensive assortment of treats from Mortenson's, and a clear, bright evening to watch the stars, we both found it very hard to appreciate the antics of Beatrice and Benedick as much as we normally might have.

As far as we could tell, no one followed us home. I stayed with Lindsay that night and we had a very long talk. By the end of it I had filled her in on just about everything. What she still didn't know, and what I'll never admit to her or anyone else, is how Jonah tried to come to my rescue in Cambria that night. And why I was there in the first place. That's a story I'll never, ever tell.

In the morning, I stayed in bed till the last possible minute. We hadn't fallen asleep till at least three, so I felt tired and almost hung over, though we hadn't had a thing to drink. I hadn't really believed anyone would go so far as to follow me out of town, and I'd half wanted to think that no one was actually following me anyway, even in town. I was about ready to start believing in coincidence again if it would only make the whole rotten business go away—to pretend the cars I'd seen and that man last night were just a random occurrence.

When I finally got dressed for church and dragged myself out to the kitchen, Lindsay was already gone, leaving a note and a pot of fresh coffee. Her young art major boyfriend had called with an offer she couldn't refuse, the note said. She'd see me later.

Messages in a Bottle

Every small town has at least one bar like it. It's been there as long as anybody can remember, a dark little place where regulars named Lou and Del hang out, old guys who show up about nine or ten in the morning and stay most of the day. Women come there to drink alone or play pool at the one warped table in the back. And even though smoking in public places was banned several years ago, you can still practically inhale a pack a day just by breathing in the fumes that permeate the place.

Jonah had been there before, but it had been awhile. The last time he'd been tracking a suspect. This time it was Lindsay. She gave him a sidelong glance, looking pleased to see him as he settled on the barstool next to her.

He nodded his hello. "Buy you a drink?"

"I asked you here," she said. "I'm buying." She signaled to the bartender and ordered another round for herself. "Peach Schnapps."

"Ouch," Jonah said, grinning. "On a Sunday morning?" He ordered a Miller Light.

Lindsay toyed nervously with her empty glass. "If you tell Elizabeth I talked to you about this ... I'll deny it till my dying day."

"I can live with that."

She looked at him fully and he was reminded of when they had met at the station, when she'd accompanied Elizabeth. He'd liked the way she looked him in the eye when she talked to him, the way she seemed to care for Elizabeth maybe as much as he did. There was something about her demeanor, something seductive in her dark eyes. She'd have no trouble picking up men at a bar, especially this one. More likely, her trouble would come from having to fend them off.

The bartender set their drinks in front of them, then moved away to chat with the graying biker guy at the end of the bar.

Lindsay took a sip of Schnapps and reacted to its strength. "I'd take a bullet for her," she said. She gave him another direct look. "I need to know if you think she's in danger."

"Why? What's happened?"

Lindsay took time to answer. "She's scared. Hell, I'm scared ... Look, I tried to talk some sense into her, but no way is she willing to talk to you about it."

"Then maybe you better fill me in." He was still trying to come to terms with the fact that Elizabeth had chosen somebody else over him and, no matter what, he still felt the need and the desire to protect her.

"It started with some hang up calls."

"A lot of them?"

"Not at first, but now it's night and day. It never quits. But then, maybe it's just some kids, right? Somebody who got her number."

"If that's what you really think, Lindsay, then why are you so scared?"

Lindsay swirled her glass, staring at its contents.

"She asked for a trace?"

Lindsay nodded. "Just Star 69, you know. The message says they can't get the number. Cell phone, maybe, or out of the area."

"There's more that could be done."

"She doesn't want to involve the police."

Of course.

"Then the other night somebody left her a threatening message."

"What kind of message?"

"She says it was garbled, distorted. Something about death. Like in her dream." Lindsay started folding her cocktail napkin into tiny triangles. "I think she told you about her dream?"

He nodded, remembering the night he'd spent on her sofa, the way she'd looked the next morning, fresh and full of light.

"Then, last night ..." She seemed to have trouble continuing.

Jonah waited, trying for patience. He finally said, "Last night?"

"We went to a play." Her words were short. She seemed almost breathless. "You know. PCPA. Solvang."

He nodded, hoping she'd continue.

"We always take a walk, kill time before the play starts, and ... The thing is, she thinks some guy was following us."

"Did either one of you get a look at him?"

She shook her head.

"He was following you on the street?"

She nodded. "I think so."

Jonah felt a jolt of anger. Why would anybody go this far with Elizabeth? What could she have possibly done?

When Lindsay spoke, she answered his question. "She's gonna kill me for telling you this, but ... She went to see that lawyer."

"Hernandez?"

"Yeah, he's the one. She made up some story about how her grandma needed estate planning. Only, she's been dead for years."

Jonah swore under his breath.

She took a long, slow drink, setting the glass down too hard. "It was a fucking stupid thing to do." Lindsay shook her head in frustration. "I try to tell her, but she always says things like, *It was meant to be.*"

"It's my fault," Jonah said. "I'm the one who got her into this. Damn it, I thought she was out of it now. I've told her repeatedly to stay out of it."

"She's stubborn. I think you already know that."

"Yeah. And I'm pretty sure she doesn't want to hear from me."

"I'm asking you. As her friend."

Jonah thought about it, his mind racing ahead to just what he could do. Up the ante on Hernandez for one thing, make sure they had him in their sights at all times. But a guy like that always had other people he could call on. He didn't usually do the dirty work himself. "I don't suppose she'd let me hear that phone message," he said. "But I'll do what I can."

"I'm counting on that, Detective." She opened her purse and pulled out some bills, leaving them on the counter for the bartender, then took a final swig of her drink.

"I've known Elizabeth almost ten years. When that whole psychic thing started, I was kind of worried at first. I thought she was having some kind of weird episode."

"And now?"

"She's one of the most balanced people I know."

She got down from the barstool, looking pretty unbalanced herself.

"Maybe I'd better drive you home."

She shook her head. "Got it covered." She jangled her keys in the direction of a young guy sitting alone at a nearby table. "Designated driver." She started to walk away, then turned back. "Oh, and Detective? She might not be as unhappy to hear from you as you think."

Improbable Realities

I left Frank's early Sunday afternoon. I had so much to deal with, so much to consider. I hadn't told Frank anything yet—no answer to his proposal, nothing about my psychic abilities, nothing about the phone calls or about being followed the night before. Come to think of it, I hadn't let him in on much of anything.

I had a funny feeling while I was unlocking my door, something irritating me around the edges. I thought maybe it was my lunch. Opening the door, the first thing I noticed was that Peeps wasn't there to greet me. And as I walked into the living room, I saw that my things were strewn everywhere—papers, clothing, CD's. In the door of the little hallway leading to the bedrooms, I caught a glimpse of my potted palm. It had been upended; the soil was all over the floor.

I backed out quickly and shut the door. My mind was frantic for Peeps, but common sense told me to leave. I called 911 from my neighbor's house and stayed there until they arrived.

The cops came out after a little while and told me I could go back in, as long as I didn't touch anything. I hoped that didn't apply to Peeps. Looking timid and scared, he squeezed his little body out from under my bed and climbed into my arms as if he would never leave. I hugged him hard as I walked around my house, stunned at the condition of it. Whoever it was, they had certainly been thorough. My furniture was still okay, thank God, but everything I'd had in my closets and drawers now seemed to be dumped on the floor. Strangely enough, only my refrigerator magnets seemed to be untouched. We checked for my few pieces of good jewelry, my one framed original piece of art and they were still there. As near as I could tell, nothing had been taken but my confidence.

"You a Jane Austen fan?" The female cop was writing down my full name—*Elizabeth Bennett Brown*.

I nodded. "And obviously, my mother was."

The cop smiled. "Best book ever written, *Pride and Prejudice*."

I couldn't agree more, and it wasn't only because I was named after the heroine. It was the hero I cared about. He was the perfect man. Spoiled me for anything in the real world, I guess. No wonder I have problems with romance.

"Mr. Darcy," the cop sighed. "Tall, regal, rich. What more could a girl want?"

Noble and true, I thought. He was noble and true. That's what I would want.

"I don't know about you," she said, "but I'm still looking for mine." She offered me a copy of the report. Seeing I was still cradling Peeps, she set it on the coffee table instead.

"I'll just take another look around," she said. "A detective should be here any time."

"Detective?"

As if on cue, there was a rap on the open door and Peeps meowed his hello. I didn't have to turn around to know who it was.

"I didn't know you worked on Sundays."

"I don't." Jonah reached out to pat Peeps on the head. His eyes met mine and I could see the concern there. "I heard about what happened, thought I'd come by." He looked around the room. "Boy, they really did a job."

For the first time, I wanted to cry.

"You might want to have a friend take care of him for a few days. Or board him."

He was talking about Peeps. It scared me more than anything, what he'd just said. Even my cat wasn't safe?

"And you, Elizabeth, can you …?" He seemed to be having trouble saying it. "You have somewhere you could stay temporarily?"

He knew. He knew.

"Here," I said. "I'll stay here. Clean things up."

"Time for that later. Right now it's better if you get away. Let us do what we need to do. And keep safe."

I nodded, my throat tight.

The female cop came back into the living room. "Hey, Detective," she said, looking for all world like she'd just seen her Mr. Darcy. She and Jonah started walking around the place together, talking quietly, examining the exposed evidence of my life, now scattered so unceremoniously around the house.

I found an open spot on the couch and sat down, letting Peeps loose for the first time. He headed straight for the potted palm, and for once, I didn't blame him. I watched as he fussed around the dirt and broken leaves trying to find what he was looking for. He came back a moment later with a lost little "Meow." Thanks to our uninvited guests, there was no more potted palm for him to use.

I felt shaky and disoriented. Things were heating up, as I'd known they had to eventually. But did it have to be now? And did it have to be so frightening? I looked up to heaven in silent entreaty. That rough patch was definitely with me now.

I was talking to Frank on the phone when Jonah and the female cop returned to the room. They spoke briefly at the door, then the cop waved a hand in my direction and went out. Jonah remained, staring out the front door at first, and then, as he heard my conversation, he went to stand outside on the front steps to give me some room.

Frank was of the opinion he should come and get me immediately. I managed to convince him it wasn't a good idea.

I called Lindsay next. Once she got past swearing, she settled down. "Of course you'll stay here. I'll come and get you."

"I can drive," I said weakly.

"I can take you." It was Jonah, who had returned to the room with two new arrivals, both men. I don't watch many cop shows but I'm guessing they were there to collect evidence. Of what I don't know. I hung up the phone. After a quick introduction by Jonah (I immediately forgot both their names), they started nosing around.

Jonah glanced down at Peeps who had plopped near his feet and was now industriously and meticulously washing his private parts. "You have some kind of carrier for Peeps?" Why did he always remember my cat's name? Nobody else did. Even at a time like this it was dangerously endearing.

One of the men asked me some questions (turns out he was actually a detective) and I may have lied when I told him I knew of no one who was out to get me. After that I gathered up a few personal items and we were on our way, Peeps safely ensconced in his carrier in the back seat. As we drove off, Jonah turned left, and I wondered for a moment how he knew where to go. As it turned out, he didn't. A block or two later, I realized he was heading toward Frank's.

My nerves were too raw to let that go easily. I waited a couple more blocks, just for the hell of it, then said, "You know, they frown on cohabitation."

His look was a question.

"At St. Alban's. It's that old living in sin thing." I heard a little warning meow from the back seat, but it didn't even slow me down.

"Turns out they have a big problem with that when it's their priest. Go figure." I stared out the window, suddenly and unaccountably angry. At who, I wasn't at all sure.

"Then I guess I'll need directions," Jonah said. Which left it hanging out there that he not only knew the way to Frank's, he had automatically assumed I'd be going there.

"Anyway, I need to take Peeps to the Pet Palace first." An absolute necessity, as Lindsay pretty much hates cats, a fact Peeps seems to know and thrive on. If she sits in my living room, he's on her like a lap robe. If she sits in the kitchen, he's immediately under the table rubbing against her ankles. One time when she'd biked over, he even tried to follow her back home.

Jonah appeared to be fighting with himself. He pulled over to the curb, put the SUV in gear and turned to look at me. "You know, it's none of my business what you choose to do."

"You've got a really funny way of showing it."

"I was worried about you," he said. "Turns out, I was right."

I looked out the window, anything to get away from him. "That woman has the most beautiful rose bushes," I said, preferring a nearby yard to the truth. "I wonder how she gets them so ... exact."

"A place doesn't get ransacked by some kid making hang up calls."

"And I bet a simple break-in of a tiny little house like mine doesn't usually get all that much attention. What did you do, call in the big guns?"

Stony silence and then, "Esther Hunt. Wasn't that your grandmother's name?"

Damn, he was on to me.

"We called her Betty," I said reluctantly.

"I expect Brad Hernandez was more than a little curious when he found out she's been dead for years. And all he had to do was Google you."

It hit me that Lindsay was the only one who could have told him. But, when? I'd only told her last night. When did she have the time?

I could tell by Jonah's body language he was working up to something. It almost exploded out of him. "Does your ... being psychic, protect you?"

"I had this friend once who thought it did." I said it so low, he couldn't hear me.

"What?"

"I knew somebody once who thought they—my guides ..." I pointed up to heaven. "She thought they did all my work for me. You know, drive my car, make my decisions, stuff like that."

He frowned.

"Like I didn't have a care in the world." Volcano Elizabeth was erupting again and I couldn't stop her. "I don't have any stunt doubles, if that's what you mean."

"Then why risk it?"

I sat back and closed my eyes. Visions of my wrecked living room returned to me, the hang up calls, the deep voice saying something about death and destruction. And then, last night, the man who went so far as to follow us down the street in Solvang. The single-mindedness of it scared me more than anything else.

"Just take me to Lindsay's," I said. "Please."

Silence. I opened my eyes to find him looking at me, obviously irritated.

"You just go down to the next light, make a left, and then it's only about another mile or so."

He nodded, but still sat there.

"I guess I'll deal with her when I get there." My voice was remarkably controlled for somebody who felt so broken.

"You should have told me what was going on."

"I never expected to actually see the man."

"Well you could have damned well gotten yourself killed." He jammed the car into drive and pulled out into the street, his motions jerky with anger. "I want you to promise me you'll stay with Lindsay till I say it's safe to go home. You need something, over there, you call me. If you have to go water a plant, you call me. You understand?"

He didn't have to ask twice. I was too scared to do anything else.

✳ ✳ ✳

Lindsay was like a nursemaid, housemother, and sister all rolled into one. At times like this she could be counted on to break out her seldom used cookie sheets and make homemade snickerdoodles, put her best cartoon sheets on the guest bed, and draw me a great big, sweet-smelling bubble bath. She was a saint, an angel, and I always thought she'd make the perfect mother, if and when she could ever settle down.

The funny thing is, Walter loves her dearly. She's known him since college and he's made it perfectly clear he'll wait for her as long as it takes. But something—fear, lust, or maybe just plain old lack of feeling, keeps her flitting about from one doomed relationship to another instead.

She was talking about Walter now. I was all snuggled up in her best terry cloth robe, fresh from my long bath, and we were sitting in her living room seriously engaged in eating as many cookies as possible while they were still soft and warm. Somehow, my anger at her telling Jonah about what I'd done didn't seem as important right now—maybe it was that wonderful bath I'd just had. Or those big, soft cookies.

"Walter," she said, as if it were a statement. "He's coming back into town this week." She selected the largest remaining cookie and took a big, satisfied bite. "You know, I actually can't wait to see him."

"College boy getting a little old?"

She giggled, and I knew what she was going to say before she said it. "I was just using him for exercise." One of our long running jokes. She looked more serious. "But, you know Walter is just so …"

"Mature? Responsible?"

She made a face like that was a bad thing. "Steady." She spit it out like it was an ugly word.

"He's got a great heart," I said. "And I've always thought he was kind of cute."

She looked more interested.

"You know, in a shaggy dog sort of way."

She threw a pillow at me in mock outrage.

"Seriously, I find that rumpled look kind of … sexy."

She bit her lip. "It just makes me so damned anxious when I think about making any kind of a final decision, you know? Marriage just seems so … absolute." She looked at me and her expression changed. "Ah, jeez. Here I am blabbering on about Walter this, and Walter that, when you've just been through holy hell. You need some wine." She got up to get it.

I did need wine. The cookie buzz was wearing off, and although I felt all comfy and warm, I couldn't banish the memory of my poor little ransacked home. I missed my cat, I missed my house. I missed feeling secure, something I wondered if I would ever feel again.

We were into our second glass of chardonnay, and I was just starting to feel all rosy and good when Jonah arrived at the door. Lindsay spoke with him in a voice too low for me to hear, then brought him further into the room. "Jonah wants to talk to you," she said, looking like she was trying to get some message across to me with her eyes. Whatever it was, I didn't get it. "I'll just be in the other room." With a warm smile for Jonah, she headed into the kitchen.

I was curled on the end of the couch, feet under me, a soft rose pink afghan over my lap. A long moment went by in which I could think of absolutely nothing to say. Neither, apparently, could he because he just stood there looking at me. He finally seemed to rouse himself, then sat down on the couch, at the opposite end from me.

"Cookie?" I motioned toward the half empty plate that was sitting on the coffee table.

He shook his head. "No, thanks."

More silence while we both seriously contemplated the earth and sky.

"Looks like she's taking good care of you," he said. The sound of his voice, what was it? Warm, and deep, like amber colored honey. I love amber colored honey.

"She always does." Had Lindsay known all along he was coming back? It occurred to me that she'd done everything in her power to make me look good, insisting I put on her best robe, and then tucking me in under the pink afghan. I felt like I'd been posed on the couch, at my best advantage. She'd even insisted I let my hair dry naturally, which gives it those soft curls she always raves about.

I stared at the wineglass in my hand. It was almost empty.

"I just thought I should stop by, make sure you were okay." He hesitated. "I was maybe a little rough on you earlier."

It was me who had been rough on him, so his words surprised me. Our eyes met and I remembered right then the electric current I'd felt that first time we touched, eons ago, when he handed me the watch. I felt it now without touching him, which made it very hard to stay away from him. Maybe I'd had too much wine.

"I got a friend of mine to repair your back door."

"My back door?"

He nodded. "Whoever broke in, they messed it up pretty bad. But it's fixed now."

"Thanks."

"We're keeping an eye on the place, running down all the angles. Hopefully, we'll catch up with them."

I nodded anxiously

"The thing is, Elizabeth, they'll need to ask you some questions. About Hernandez."

"I know. I should have told them."

"After what happened at your house ..."

"I understand."

"I got them to agree to wait till tomorrow, but that's it." He handed me a card with a detective's name on it. "He'll treat you okay, but you need to be honest, tell him everything. You can expect a visit, probably in the a.m., okay?" He was looking at me closely, trying to dissect my mood, I suppose. "I gave them some background. About how you and I had been ... looking into the case. How you talked with Hernandez."

I nodded.

"We pretty much think it's him, but we've still got to connect the dots."

"It's just hard to believe somebody would do something so obvious."

"You'd be surprised," Jonah said. "One thing for sure, it tells us you must have been on to something for him to react that way. If you want to go clean up, give it a day or so and then check with me first. And when you do go, take somebody with you."

Lindsay and I had already begun to make our plans. I swung my legs down to touch the floor, sitting upright, and ended up closer to him then I'd intended. "You've been a real help. Thanks." I set my glass on the end table, then reached over to squeeze his hand. He locked his fingers around mine, more electricity.

"Promise me you won't do any more crazy stuff, Libby."

"Crazy stuff? What do you mean, crazy stuff?"

"Snooping around, talking to people." In apparent anticipation of my reaction, he tightened his hold on my hand ever so slightly, upping the wattage. "You put yourself on somebody's radar screen. Not a good idea."

And when I didn't answer, "Elizabeth …?"

"Make up your mind," I said, sharply. "Elizabeth or Libby. Which is it?" I tried to pull my hand away and he finally had to let go of it.

"Sometimes you're one, sometimes the other."

Okay, so the playful tone in his voice made me look at him again.

"Elizabeth wants distance, needs respect. Libby …" He smiled. "Well, Libby is something else entirely."

Our eyes locked.

I heard Lindsay walk into the room behind us. "Oh, shit," she said softly, but it was too late. We moved apart as if we were guilty of something grand.

Jonah stood up. "Well, it's late. You've had a long day. Better try to get some sleep … Elizabeth." Private joke, I could see the humor in his eyes.

"Yeah, well … Goodnight, then." I was trying hard not to care that he was leaving, and certainly not to let either one of them know I cared.

"I'll keep an eye on her," Lindsay said. She handed him a baggie full of cookies. "For the road." She followed him to the door and watched him go down the walk, then came back to sit beside me.

"He sure beats the hell out of that priest of yours."

"How can you say that? You've never even met Frank."

"And now I never need to."

I relaxed against the couch, took a moment to tuck the afghan around me again and then said, casually. "So, interestingly enough, Lindsay, Jonah knows I talked to Brad Hernandez. He even knows what we talked about."

I saw the moment of hesitation before she spoke. "Oh, you know," she said, her eyes carefully dodging mine, "It's kind of like you being a psychic. Cops just seem to know things."

She was up and out of the room before I could say anything more.

* * *

Tuesday morning Lindsay and I went back to my house, first making a quick, though emotional detour to the Pet Palace to visit Peeps. He had called me the day before just to say hi. Well, actually, Hermoine, the lady who runs the place had called me and then put Peeps on the phone so he could hear me talk. It no doubt meant a great deal more to Hermoine and me than it did to Peeps, but that's what I like about the Palace. They pay great attention to every detail.

The police had gathered all the evidence they could, which wasn't much—no fingerprints, so the cops thought it had been a professional job. Which wasn't going to help me sleep any better at night, but at least I was now free to try to make some sense out of my poor, jumbled belongings. As I had suspected from the first, nothing had actually been taken. Would anyone actually go to all that trouble just to scare me? Both Jonah and the helpful detective who came by to see me the day after my house was ransacked seemed to think so.

"You've got to figure he hired somebody to do the job," Jonah said when I talked with him Monday night. He didn't have to mention Brad Hernandez by name for me to know exactly who he meant. We were talking on the phone at Lindsay's. He'd called to give me the all clear to go back to the house. Once he was satisfied that Lindsay would really be going with me, he hung up.

It took me half an hour or so of walking from room to room staring at the mess and crying before I could finally settle down enough to dig in. We were well into the afternoon before we even began to see any results. I was down on all fours peering under the couch, pulling out pieces of broken tape and CD covers—boy, those people had been thorough—when I heard a man say hello at the open front door.

"Look, we're busy." Lindsay was using her no nonsense voice. "And besides, we don't buy anything door to door."

We? I raised up to look over the couch. "Frank?"

He looked relieved to see me, Lindsay surprised. Since Frank was sans clerical collar and she'd only seen him from a distance before, I guess she hadn't figured out who he was yet.

I got up, dusting my hands against each other, seeing the dismay in his eyes as he looked around the room. "Really, I'm not usually this messy." My poor joke failed. He still looked dismayed.

"You should have seen it six hours ago." Lindsay sounded irritated and impatient, but Frank ignored her, reaching out to pull me into a warm embrace.

"I've been so worried about you, Elizabeth." It was the first time we'd seen each other since the break in. It felt good to hang on to him for awhile. Over Frank's shoulder I could see that Lindsay had her hands on her hips, surveying us both. I didn't much like the expression on her face. I pulled away to introduce them, but before I could say anything Frank had already turned to shake her hand.

"Lindsay?"

She nodded, smiling rather tightly. "I guess the word's out about me."

Frank cleared his throat, clearly uncomfortable. "It's good of you to help," he said lamely.

"What are friends for?" she said pointedly. "She needs all the help she can get, you know." She plopped back down in her chair and resumed her work, untangling the one unbroken wind chime someone had so carefully tried to smash on the rug.

Frank watched her for a moment, as if he was trying to think of something else to say, but apparently never came up with it. "Can I talk to you, Elizabeth?" He was looking toward the bedroom; a private talk.

I nodded. I'm not sure, but I think I heard Lindsay say something like, "Any loud noises, I'm coming in," as I followed him into the bedroom. I glanced back at her, but she only gave me an innocent grin.

Frank surveyed the room. "Nice and cozy, just like I imagined," he said, and I realized with a shock he'd never actually been in my house before. Then he noticed the bed, which had been freshly made. "You aren't staying here tonight, are you?" He was frowning.

I shook my head. I'd thought about it, but once we'd arrived this morning, once I'd seen everything, I didn't really know when I'd be able to come back. I was still just too damned scared.

"Why don't you come over to my place tonight?" He put his hands on my shoulders and started rubbing them gently. "Make you forget about all this for awhile, Elizabeth." His voice was so soft, so compelling. I closed my eyes and leaned into the massage, feeling the tension slip away. "You need some tender, loving care," he said. "It will do us both a world of good." He kissed me softly on the forehead.

The drug was being offered, the deal made.

I left Lindsay's just after dark to drive to my usual Denny's. It was odd, really, how frightened I could feel now when all I was doing was something I used to do every day without even thinking about it—go out driving with Tilly. I watched the rear view constantly. Cars came and went, but no one vehicle seemed to stay. Maybe that was all it would be—they'd given me a good scare, and now they would leave me alone. I hadn't even done anything else in regards to Janet's disappearance, so what were they so upset about anyway? The only explanation was that someone—be it Brad or somebody else, wanted to make damn sure I didn't go any further. Which meant they must have known enough about my history of helping the police to be afraid of what I might do.

I pulled into the Denny's parking lot and found an empty spot in the back row, near a light pole where my car would hopefully be safe overnight. It felt spooky, though, and I sat there wishing I'd told Frank to pick me up at Lindsay's. Next time. I turned on the map light so I could examine my face in the aptly named vanity mirror. Satisfied, I snapped it off, checked the parking lot for anyone suspicious, and got out, thinking I'd just go wait by the front door of the restaurant. It was 7:35. The usually punctual Frank was already five minutes overdue, so he ought to be arriving any minute now. I knew I'd feel more secure standing in the light.

As I started to walk, though, I had a sudden sense of danger, that feeling that someone was right behind me. I whirled around just as Jonah stepped out into the light.

He looked all cop.

"Oh God, you frightened me."

"What are you doing out here, Elizabeth?"

"What are you doing out here? I'm beginning to think you really are stalking me."

He ignored my remark. "You shouldn't be out here. Seriously, what the hell are you thinking? You want to let somebody find you out here alone?" He looked away, as if trying to calm down. "For somebody who's supposed to be psychic, you act like you haven't got a clue."

I was just ready to launch into him, but then, he was right. "Look, I probably don't need to tell you this. You already seem to know just about everything I do. I'm meeting someone."

Just then I saw Frank's Focus pull into the parking lot. He swung his car around towards where we were standing, slammed on the brakes and jumped out. "Elizabeth?"

"I'm okay, Frank."

He took my arm protectively, sizing up Jonah as he did so.

"This is Jonah Haley. He's a detective." And to Jonah, "This is my … This is Frank Emerson."

I didn't like the look on either one of their faces. Two lions facing off in a Denny's parking lot. Film at eleven.

They shook hands almost grudgingly.

"I guess I should thank you for … watching out for her," Frank said.

Jonah nodded shortly. "Just doing my job." The look he gave me then made me remember why he'd never believe I really wanted to be with him—he kept catching me with Frank.

"You ought to tell her to stop being so foolish," he said to Frank, as if I couldn't hear him. "Stop putting herself in harm's way. Maybe she'll listen to you."

Frank put his arm around my shoulder. "I'll see what I can do," he said, smiling down at me like I was the little missus. It was that male thing that says, *Back off, sucker, she's mine.* I've noticed that men use it freely, usually when they don't have a clue as to where your loyalties actually lie. *Especially* when they don't have a clue.

Jonah didn't look all that impressed. "I guess I'll take off then," he said directly to me. "Goodnight." With a quick nod to Frank, he walked away.

I wanted desperately to go after him, and when I sat down in Frank's car, I could still see Jonah in the side view mirror. He hadn't gotten into his SUV yet, and, in fact, had opened the back hatch and seemed to be looking for something. That did it for me.

"I'll be right back, Frank." I flew out of the car before he could stop me and walked quickly towards the SUV.

"Jonah?"

He looked up, obviously surprised.

"I don't want to leave it like this."

He smiled ever so slightly, pulled his jacket out, and slammed the hatch shut. Hard.

"I was … Well, you know, I've been pretty … ungrateful about everything."

"I wasn't looking for your gratitude."

"Still …"

He put on his jacket, glancing at my short sleeved top. "You must be getting pretty cold."

I was, but I couldn't seem to care. I shrugged it away.

Jonah crossed his arms and leaned back against his SUV, watching as cars pulled in and out of the parking lot. Then he looked back at me, into my eyes, and somehow, in that brief period of time, the wind had changed. He glanced toward Frank's car. "He doesn't look very patient."

"I know," I said, "I'll go in a minute, but I just wanted to … thank you, Jonah, for all you've done." It sounded so lame.

He nodded.

"I mean, really. I've been …" I couldn't think of the right word.

"You've been scared." He said it so softly, so almost kindly, that it took my breath away.

"But still, that's no excuse for me to …" I tried unsuccessfully to gather my wits, but they seemed to have run off. I couldn't even complete a sentence.

Why, then, was he so together? "When you're ready, Libby, give me a call." He unlocked his door and opened it before looking at me again. "And try to stay safe, will you?"

I think I sort of nodded as I backed away.

Frank was quiet on the way back to the house, and he didn't mention Jonah again. Really, he didn't mention him even once, but somehow Jonah was there anyway, unseen when we made love, when I curled against Frank, tried to sleep and couldn't, and, later, when Frank woke me up in the middle of the night and wanted desperately to talk.

He has an especially fine way of waking me up, bit by bit, kiss by kiss, and touch by touch.

I stretched against him sleepily.

"Elizabeth." He was talking directly into my ear, while kissing it. "How come you don't want to marry me?"

That woke me up. "I never said that."

"You never said yes."

"That's because I'm still thinking."

He sighed. "Bad sign, still thinking."

"Well, if you want an answer tonight, Frank …"

He pulled me into him. "What's there to think about? We fit together like hand and glove." At which point, he moved to illustrate how well we fit together, but it had little to do with either his hand or my glove.

"What's my favorite color, Frank?"

He pulled back to look at me, frowning.

"You don't know, do you?"

"Blue."

I shook my head, smiling.

"Give me another chance."

"Okay. What's my favorite sexual position?"

"This one."

"That was a gimme. We're one dimensional, Frank. Great in bed, but … You don't even know how much I happen to love the color …"

"Purple?"

"No, silly. That was a book."

He grinned. "The rest will come. Eventually. Speaking of which …" He started moving against me, his body teasing mine to come along.

After awhile, it did.

***

Thursday I went back to work feeling like a stranger in a strange land. Rita looked me over suspiciously. "Whoa," she said, examining my face closely, "Your eyes look like two burnt holes in a blanket."

"Thanks a bunch."

She grinned. "Seriously, though, I'm glad to see you're still in one piece. You get your house back in order?"

I nodded, feeling suddenly pained. The truth was, my house might be pretty much back to its normal state, but I was far from being back to mine. I was still staying at Lindsay's and I just couldn't quite bring myself to go home.

On top of everything else, I was having Peeps withdrawals. I had no warm, soft Peeps to cuddle with at night, no daily turf wars with Peeps over the newspaper where he'd stretch out across whatever page I was most wanting to read, no potted palm to worry about. No Peeps, period.

"They find out who did it?"

I shook my head.

"Probably some kids, huh?"

"Yeah, probably." I didn't have the interest or the energy to get into it with her.

With a sigh, I started down the hall to my office. Rita followed me. She smiled at me sympathetically, as if she was about to make a very special pronouncement.

"How are things with the guy?"

"What guy?"

"Oh, you know. Whichever guy …"

"Everything is fine."

She crossed her arms, smiling like she saw right through me. "You know, Elizabeth, too much sex can be every bit as bad as not enough." I opened my mouth to answer her, but closed it again. She seemed to be speaking from direct experience. Besides, it was none of her business. And besides that, I had pretty much decided to stop having sex. I had stayed away from Frank's after the night I ran into Jonah in the Denny's parking lot. Something in me had just snapped then. I couldn't do it anymore.

I felt two-faced, and I couldn't exactly explain why, so I chose to avoid Frank instead.

It was a temporary solution, but it would work for awhile.

"I'll just be in my office," I said, leaving her standing there watching me as I walked away. I fumbled into my door without looking back and slumped sullenly at my desk.

Remembering I'd stuck a small hand mirror in one of the drawers, I pulled it out and stared at myself, horrified. My face was pale, with the undeniable beginning of dark circles under my eyes. I dug my makeup bag out of my purse and did my best to improve the situation. It was no use. Nothing felt the same anymore. Nothing was the same.

Rita had graciously rescheduled my appointments to make up for the days I'd been gone. Most people had been moved ahead to other weeks, but the few who really couldn't stand to miss their fix were squeezed into Thursday and Friday. And wouldn't you know it, one of them was Sandy Roget.

Sandy, it turned out, had decided to bring a guest, the much discussed and apparently easily intimidated James. I wasn't in the mood. James turned out to be a tall, well-dressed, continental looking man even though I would have bet serious money he was a hefty, slow-talking good old boy.

"I'm not going to pull any punches, Ms. Brown," he said, as soon as we were all seated. "I'm not sure I like the way Sandra's been acting since she started coming in here."

Oh, wonderful. He was a "Ms." man. I hate the way guys who have a problem with women make use of that word. It began as a word denoting a woman's right to be identified by something other than her marital status, but to men like James Roget, it's a sword he uses to try to cut you down.

He perused my office as if he was looking for some evidence of my unsuitability.

"Could you be a little more specific?" I said carefully, all the while wishing I had a gun and knew how to use it.

So he launched in. There were issues, he said, issues of role reversal; women trying to be men, and men being expected to take whatever women decided to dish out these days. The feminization of America. "It's cruel and misleading, Ms. Brown."

"What's that?" I had zoned out minutes earlier and had to get back on track.

"To get a woman like Sandra all stirred up, reading junk food books about sex and whatnot."

Whatnot?

I waited for Sandy to speak up, to mention the fact that the little junk food book on sex, as he called it, was her idea, but she just sat there like a prim little schoolmarm, a small, tense smile on her face. I wasn't about to out her, which left me to defend myself.

"I ... uh, imagine she was only trying to please you, Mr. Roget."

"If she wants to please me, I'd be glad to tell her how." He smiled at Sandy as if he'd just said something incredibly wise, then leaned forward earnestly. "In future, I'd prefer it if you'd stick to other subjects rather than sex." He patted Sandy's hand. "God knows you've got issues with your mother, sweetheart. You can talk about that till the cows come home."

Sandy gave him a sickly little smirk of a smile, and I thought for a moment she was going to snap her teeth. I was rooting for it, anyway.

"As a therapist, I'm afraid I can't promise what we'll talk about," I said. "Nor can I tell you what we do talk about. It would be counterproductive to the entire process."

He actually snorted. "Is that what you call it, a process? Teaching her to take charge? If God wanted women to be in charge, he would have made them the strong ones."

I'd heard this argument before, from my ex-husband, so I was ready for him.

"So then you're saying those who are physically stronger naturally make better leaders?"

He nodded, apparently pleased I was seeing the light.

"But, doesn't that mean we'd end up with somebody like Mike Tyson for president?"

He stared at me, unable to think of anything to say.

"You know, " I said, quite aware I was losing my grip on professional, but trying to at least hold on to sane, "it's actually not such a bad idea. It could save us a lot of money and time. Instead of elections, we could hold prize fights. It'd cost a lot less. In fact, they could actually make money on the fights, what with pay per view and all that. And it would probably be a hell of a lot more interesting."

You can't change a person's point of view, their beliefs. They only change them for themselves, when they're damn good and ready, and after hearing Jimmy's spiel for an hour, I don't think he's liable to change much of anything anytime this century. Me, either. We made a deal, though. He agreed that Sandy had a right to "talk through her little issues," as he put it. She could continue to come to the appointments if she wanted to, and the only limitation he put on that was that he be allowed to come to appointments with her any time he chose.

I know his type, though. He'll most likely never show up again.

Not all that interested, really. Just needed to come in, blow off some steam, and make a few meaningless proclamations. Which told me just how strongly Sandy's unexpected change in behavior had thrown him. He was out of his comfort zone and looking for a fight.

When I shook his hand to say goodbye, I couldn't help picturing it—Sandy's big white pearly teeth clamping down hard. And if I had anything at all to do with it, it would not be on his shoulder.

* * *

The dream wasn't the same now, but it was still frightening. I woke up in a panic, turned on the light, and realized I wasn't at home. The dream had taken place in my kitchen this time, but I woke up in Lindsay's guest bedroom, the one with the forest green curtains and gold shag rug. The bedspread covering me was a bold gold and black plaid design that clashed mightily with the Sponge Bob sheets. Enough to give anybody a nightmare.

I took some deep breaths and tried to calm down. No luck. The dream was still so clear, so vivid; it wouldn't let go of me. With the light still on, I curled up on my side.

I was *this close* to sucking my thumb; it was that bad, and from what my mom has told me, I never sucked my thumb as a child.

Every time I tried closing my eyes, the dream was right there, playing itself out across a movie screen I couldn't turn off. I sat up, hugging myself, though it didn't help. I got up and circled the room several times, but it still wouldn't go away. There I was, standing in my own kitchen, dressed in my lavender nightie, endlessly separating eggs into bowls. The yoke would break every time, and I'd know I had to do another one, and another one. I must have gone through dozens of eggs. Then, suddenly I felt someone standing right behind me. I turned, panicked, only to find Jonah there. His eyes were so intense. Though he only looked at me, I knew he was about to reach out for me.

I don't know what would have happened after that. I only know I didn't want to find out, which is strange, really. It could have been a really romantic dream, depending on what happened next, of course. But it only made me feel afraid.

Lindsay rapped on my closed door and then came in without waiting for me to respond. "I thought I heard you up," she said. She took a good look at me. "What the hell is wrong? You want to talk about it?" She sat down beside me, concerned.

The "no" was out of my mouth before she'd even finished speaking. Fortunately she was already on to something else. "I'm sleeping with Walter," she said, a moony look on her face. Walter had arrived late this afternoon and was staying a few days.

"Not exactly a news flash."

She sighed happily and flopped back on my bed. "He's just so … good," she said.

Okay, I'd play the game. "Good in what way?" I was lying on my side next to her, one arm propping up my head, trying for pajama party when what I really felt was *Children of the Corn.*

"Oh, you know …" She was so gone I don't think she even knew she'd stopped in mid-sentence. Then she rolled on her side to face me, a somewhat serious look in her eyes. "But, the thing is, E., I just don't want to move too fast, you know."

"You've known him almost 15 years. I don't think anybody would say that was too fast."

"Still …"

I shrugged. "One thing for sure, the guy worships you."

"Yeah, but that's the problem, isn't it? What happens when he finally sees the real me, warts and all?" She answered her own question. "Knowing Walter, he'd give them all names." She grinned. "He's snoring. Can you hear him?"

"It that what that is? I thought maybe it was garbage day."

She giggled.

"You know, something like that can get old really fast," I said. But he could have been banging on steel metal with a turkey drumstick for all she cared.

She got up and drifted towards the door.

"Lindsay?"

She turned.

"You ever have trouble … separating eggs in a bowl?"

She looked only momentarily confused. "That's why I always scramble them," she said, then floated right on out, closing the door softly behind her.

I looked to the ceiling. "You ever realize you could love somebody, but you've screwed things up so bad, it's never going to happen?"

There was no response from the room.

Channeling Jonah

He couldn't stop following her. Not all the time, but at least once or twice a day he would get the uncontrollable urge to check on her, make sure she was safe. At night, it wasn't so bad as long as he knew she was staying with Lindsay. But during the day, anytime he knew she might be running around—lunch, getting to work and back, that kind of thing—he needed to know she was okay.

The hardest part was wondering if she'd go to the rectory, but strangely enough, she hadn't gone there even once these last few days. He wondered why. He didn't know what he'd do now that the weekend was here. Or once she went back home and was alone again.

Part of it was foolishness, he knew. You don't get involved with somebody you're working with; it clouds your judgement. In a dangerous situation, it could mean life or death. But he wasn't really working with her, was he? He'd taken her off the case, so to speak, if she'd only stay there. Still, he felt responsible for her predicament, for all the things that had happened, even the ones she'd brought on herself. If he'd never asked her for help, she wouldn't be in any danger now.

It was frustrating, this case. Not only because every lead seemed to lead nowhere in regards to the missing woman, but also because they couldn't even seem to solve the simple things, like finding out who had trashed Libby's house. Everywhere, they ran into walls. He knew damn good and well that Hernandez was behind it, which made him more certain than ever that he was also behind the missing person's case. Even so, the man was apparently really expert at covering his tracks.

Jonah rested his head against the headrest and closed his eyes. She'd be coming out of work any time now, heading home to Lindsay's. He thought again of the last time they had talked, in the Denny's parking lot; how it had felt to have to watch her driving away to another man's bed. He could have sworn she was interested in him. She'd certainly seemed to be those times they'd gone out, and even other times, when their eyes had met unexpectedly. Either that or he was losing his touch, his ability to know things like that where a woman was involved. It frustrated him that he still couldn't figure this one out. Especially since he was beginning to realize just how strong his feelings were for her.

He saw Libby come out of her office, checking around her as she walked. Good, she was being at least a little cautious. He watched her as she went to her car, watched the sweet sway of her hips, the movement of the dark skirt she was wearing. He could almost see himself walking up behind her, pulling her back playfully into his arms. She would laugh and turn her face so he could kiss her—or run away screaming. He grinned, remembering what she'd said about him stalking her. It was now close to being true.

As she pulled her car out into the road, he waited, giving her space, then followed at a distance, noticing right away that she wasn't going to Lindsay's. At first puzzled, his smile grew as he realized that she was turning into the Pet Palace. Apparently Peeps was calling her name.

He parked down the street in the parking lot of a mini-mart and waited. Exactly twenty minutes later, she emerged, got in her car, and drove away. She was such an unexpected mix—cooking him a dynamite breakfast, gently making over her cat, boldly seeking out the likes of Brad Hernandez, meeting some guy in a motel for what had to have been some wild sex … He had to admit it intrigued him, especially the part about the wild sex.

He almost missed his turn thinking about it, then turned off a few blocks from Lindsay's, circled back around and drove past the end of the street just to be sure the little red car had safely arrived, that Libby was safely there.

Destiny: Can't Live With it, Can't Live Without it

I went back home on Saturday. I needed to give Walter and Lindsay some breathing room anyway, and trying to sleep in a house where Walter was snoring was damn near impossible. Besides, watching them melt over each other, sweet though it might be, was more than I could stomach right now. I was liable to get diabetes.

I won't say I wasn't nervous to be back in my house, but I convinced myself that the squad cars that occasionally cruised by would somehow keep me safe. I also had the sneaking suspicion that someone else might be watching out for me now and then. I was pretty sure it was Jonah. Not that I'd seen him, but, especially since the night he'd been at Denny's, there were moments when I just *knew* he was around. Though I would have felt angry about it in the past, my feelings were different now, and I was beginning to think of him as my earthly guardian angel. It made me feel all soft and warm.

The hang up calls appeared to have stopped and things seemed to be settling down. I told myself it would just take some time to get my life back. Happy to be reunited with Peeps, he was equally happy to be with me. I had bought him a new, very large potted palm, so big it would be hard for anybody to overturn it, a catnip-scented kitty scratching pad, and a jumbo box of his favorite treats. Between my lap and his new treasures, he was in hog heaven, kitty style.

I didn't sleep well the first night, but then, neither did Peeps. Still, the weekend was wonderful. Just being home, in my own place, my own bed. I didn't go anywhere. Except for returning the frequent check-in calls from Lindsay and Walter, I didn't do much of anything except play with Peeps and eat whatever I wanted. Oh, and I watched *While You Were Sleeping* twice. Somehow, it always makes me believe in love again, and I needed that right about now. Frank called a couple times, but I let the recorder pick up.

He showed up at work first thing Monday morning. I found Rita fawning over him when I came in the door. He followed me into my office. I hung up my jacket, then turned to face him and we ended up in an awkward hug.

"I almost came by last night, I was so worried. Are you okay?"

"Yeah, just really tired."

"No wonder, after all you've been through. I wish you'd let me help you more," he said, letting go of me at last.

"I appreciate that, Frank, but there's really nothing anybody can do."

"So, you feel pretty safe at your place now?"

"I'm not sure I'll ever feel safe again. Anywhere." I sat down and so did he.

"I suppose they're keeping an eye on you."

Okay, so he really wanted to ask about Jonah. I gave him a questioning look.

"The cops," he said. He sat there looking at me. "I've really missed you."

"I know." I felt sad that he looked so ... sad.

He leaned forward anxiously. "You want to tell me what's going on?"

"Nothing. Nothing is going on."

"I remember the last time I was in here." He raised his eyebrows, remembering. "So, what happened, Elizabeth? Was it my proposal?"

I squirmed in my chair. "I guess I just really need some time right now."

"Seems like you keep saying that."

"Well, maybe you should listen."

He nodded, but went on ahead. "Look, we can cool it on the whole marriage idea for right now but why don't we do something fun? Fly down to Cabo, maybe?"

He hadn't heard me at all. "Maybe some other time."

He looked pained.

"I feel like I sort of need to reevaluate, Frank."

"Reevaluate ...?"

"My whole life. And, you, Frank. I need to ... think things through."

He obviously didn't like the sound of that. My guilt made me reach out to him. I got up and went around the desk and he stood, too, taking me gently into his arms and just holding me there. So nice. Almost home. Which was exactly why I needed some time by myself. I felt like I was being blown back and forth by the wind. A nice, handsome wind, but still ...

When we broke apart, I said, "Actually, I might be going away myself."

"Oh?"

"Just for a few days." I walked over to look out the window as it came to me. "Up north, maybe. Tule Lake, or Klamath Falls." I watched a screaming yellow Humvee try to park between two monster SUVs. What is it with those giant cars, anyway? Is it one of those *size matters* things for guys—I'm bigger than you? And if so, why do so many women drive them?

"What for?"

I turned to look at Frank. "I don't know. See the sights?"

"In Klamath Falls?"

"I hear there are some very nice bird sanctuaries up there."

"I didn't realize you were into birds," he said halfheartedly.

I didn't either. "I'm just feeling sort of ... pulled there." Something hit me in the stomach as I said that, a powerful feeling, unexplained.

He didn't know what to say to that. Neither did I. Until this moment, I'd had no plans to travel, and if I did it certainly wouldn't have been going to Klamath Falls. It had just popped right out of me from God knows where.

"Doesn't sound like your kind of thing, Elizabeth."

"I know." The bird thing was freaking me out. What was going on?

Frank sighed heavily, the weight of the world. "They miss you at church. And I miss you terribly. Paulina Witherspoon has been dropping by my office a lot lately." He was trying to joke, but neither of us even cracked a smile.

"Oh, Frank," I said, then looked down at the floor, having nothing more to say.

"Maybe I pushed you," he said. "Maybe things just happened too fast." He came over to me and leaned down to gently kiss my cheek. He seemed for a moment interested in trying for my lips, but then backed off. He was hurt. I could see it in his incredibly blue eyes.

"I just need a little more time."

"Keep me posted," Frank said, tightly, then turned on his heels and left.

✷ ✷ ✷

It was one of those dreaded Tuesday nights. Lindsay was depressed because Walter had to go back home and attend to his business. There were rumors (most all of them mine) that he was thinking of relocating to our little town, but it wasn't at all definite yet. Trapped in a state of emotional disrepair, she insisted I go out with her even though I was feeling bone tired and lost. Her boss had given her two tickets for a fundraiser—free spaghetti, all you can eat.

My first mistake was in not asking her a little more about it. Turns out it was the annual "Cops for a Cure" dinner, something I might rather have avoided, had I only known. Not two minutes after we arrived, I heard Ruby buzz out of the kitchen and head past me into the busy room. If Ruby was present, could Jonah be far behind? He was, after all, a cop, and though part of me wanted desperately to see him again, the other part wanted nothing more than to run the other way.

"God, Lindsay, we've got to get out of here. Now." I grabbed her arm to distract her from watching the buffed up guys wearing aprons and serving food. "I mean it, Lindsay. I've got to go. That woman over there, in the red dress ..."

"You mean that tall, striking one that's headed right to us?"

Ruby arrived with a broad smile. Hands on hips, she surveyed me like I was a prize and she was the winner.

"How you been, Miss Elizabeth?"

I choked out a weak, "Pretty good."

"I keep telling Jonah he ought to bring you by," she said, "But you know how he is."

I nodded, trying to smile. I introduced Lindsay, hoping it would spur Ruby to leave. Didn't the woman have enough to do without loitering around our table all night?

Right about then, I saw Jonah emerge from the kitchen, looking particularly frilly in a ruffled red and white checkered apron. He was carrying a tray with two baskets of bread in one hand and a carafe of salad dressing in the other.

"Look who's here, Jonah, " Ruby called to him sweetly.

He checked his movement, only for a moment, nodding in our general direction. I'd never seen Jonah look embarrassed before, but he was doing so now. Then he headed on to the table he was serving across the room. Ruby kept an eagle eye on him, though, and as soon as he'd deposited his bread and turned away from the table, she motioned him over.

Reluctantly, he headed our way. "Hi," he said, to both of us at the same time.

"I think you know Lindsay." It was all I could think to say.

He nodded. "How you been?" He was asking her, not me, and I was close to being jealous, especially when Lindsay rewarded him with one of her trademark smiles. He set his tray on the table and glanced around to make sure he wasn't needed, then turned back. "Actually, Lindsay, I'm glad I ran into you. There's a guy down at the station who keeps bugging me to introduce the two of you."

"How does he know about me?" She quickly answered her own question. "Oh, God, the interrogation room?"

Jonah smiled. "The story's pretty much out." He pointed out a forty-something guy, stocky build, short cop hair. "Ted Byron," he said.

Lindsay hesitated, which surprised me. But then she said, rather halfheartedly, "Sure, why not?" I think I heard Walter groan from somewhere far, far away.

"Listen," Ruby said to me, obviously trying to bring the conversation back to her little world, "I'm having a little soiree next weekend. Nothing special, just a few couples, some good wine. Why don't you and Jonah come by?"

Dead silence. Lindsay chose that moment to slurp her iced tea, bless her, but it didn't help much.

I couldn't think of a thing to say.

Jonah turned to his sister and said quietly, "We aren't dating, Ruby."

"You ... What?"

"We were working on something, that's all."

She read the look in his eyes.

"It's ... finished now."

"Oh. Well ..." It seemed to roll off her back. I imagine everything does. "Some other time then," she said crisply.

"Nice seeing you." Jonah was speaking to Lindsay and me collectively, never just to me. "I'd better get going." He motioned toward his table, which was now filling up. But just before he left, he looked directly at me, into my eyes, and I remembered why I had longed to see him so.

Ruby patted my shoulder. "Told you he was slippery," she said.

Fortunately, just about that time one of her equally social butterfly friends got her attention, muttering urgently about there being a definite shortage of sourdough. They'd had a bigger turnout than expected, and what were they going to do if this many people kept eating bread? She excused herself and ran to the rescue while Lindsay and I both quickly filled up on sourdough.

"I really don't get it," Lindsay said, as she munched on the last piece of bread. "What's the problem, anyway?" She was watching Jonah from afar, as he played waiter to a table full of preteen girls and their mothers. The girls were giggling up at him happily; the mothers looking at him a little more seriously. "He seems like a great guy."

I had to quickly come up with something, so I chose the obvious. "He's a cop."

"So?"

"Macho. You know."

"Doesn't seem macho."

"Well, no, not in that apron."

She crossed her arms and sat back, tracking Ted Byron as he worked the opposite side of the room. "Sometimes they have to be macho."

"Well, then, I guess it's just not meant to be."

"Oh?" She looked completely unconvinced. "You obviously like him."

"I like lots of things that aren't good for me. Together, we're like ... " I was going to say *oil and water*, but what popped into my head was, strangely enough, exactly what Lindsay verbalized.

"Abbot and Costello?"

We both started to laugh. It was like that, only not as funny.

"It's just not ... right, I don't know. Every time we've tried being together, we get into some kind of a mess." But I didn't mention anything about the guardian angel part.

"I suppose it's that whole volatility thing?"

"Yeah."

"Seems like that would just make it more exciting."

Damn her for knowing too much, but I wasn't going to admit it. I just shrugged.

"I think that psychic wand of yours needs some serious adjustments," she said.

She picked up the empty breadbasket and examined it carefully, as if that would suddenly produce more sourdough. "Where did our waiter go, anyway? I hope the spaghetti isn't running out, too."

Our cop, Rusty something-or-other, had left us with bread and beverages and we hadn't caught sight of him since. Eating was going to take twice as long as it should have, when I wanted nothing more than to get out of there fast. It was just too awkward seeing Jonah again. I felt pulled and repelled at the same time. He didn't want me there, that was obvious, and I can't stand to be where I don't belong. It was like I was in hell and it was happening in slow motion. Come to think of it, maybe that's what hell is, anyway.

"Will you look who just walked in?" Lindsay said.

Does everybody in this frigging town have to come out on the same night to eat spaghetti? Are they all that cheap, that low on imagination? Isn't there anything else going on around here worth doing? I slunk lower it my chair as Jerry, my latest ex-boyfriend, and his date walked into the room and settled grandly at the next table, not five feet from where we sat. Never mind that it was me who broke up with him, or that it was a brief relationship, seeing him again wasn't high up on my list of hopes and dreams.

It was only a moment before his eyes fastened on me. I couldn't read his look, never could. Then he smiled. "What's happening, Elizabeth?"

I could have listed a few choice things, but I only smiled back.

After that, it went from bad to ... very bad. I could have slid under the table and stayed there. I don't know how I even got out of there alive. It was like all the cosmic forces in the universe came together then and there to embarrass and humiliate me and every person I didn't want to see, with the possible exception of my Uncle Rick, who always wants to play touchy-feely, showed up. It didn't help that Jerry was dating a woman named Muffie or that she kept playing with her hair, twisting the long strands around her finger, then letting it slowly unravel again while you watched in horror wondering if and when it would fall into her marinara sauce. And, if so, would she try to eat it? To make matters worse, Ruby kept giving me pity looks every time she passed by. And, of course, we had to stay and finish our food.

"It'd look a lot worse if we high tailed it out of here now," Lindsay said, as she tucked into her second plate of food. At least Rusty had finally delivered on the goods.

To top everything off, near the end of the evening's ordeal, out of the blue, I had the sudden urgent need to talk to Jonah, the kind of need I knew I wouldn't be able to ignore for long. It wasn't a physical need, but a psychic one. I sat there trying to fight it, wanting to just get up and leave, but the feeling was too intense, too strong. These are the times that try a psychic's soul.

I noticed that Jonah glanced my way now and then, but he had plenty to do taking care of the tables he'd been assigned. He had made good on his promise to introduce Lindsay to Officer Byron and she was now somewhere across the room getting to know the guy while I tried to avoid watching Jerry eye Muffie's cleavage and paw her pouty little butt. Unlike me, there was someone in the room that Lindsay actually wanted to see.

Jonah's table was finally thinning out so as he made his way back toward the kitchen, I waved half-heartedly, trying to get his attention. He came by, looking really rather cute in his little red apron. I did my best to hide that fact, making some inane comment about how busy he'd been and trying for nonchalant.

He nodded towards Lindsay and her cop. "Looks like they're hitting it off."

Why did he have to look at me like that? Okay, so he was actually just looking at me like he'd look at anybody else, but I was still suddenly hopelessly and deliciously tongue-tied.

"You wanted something, Elizabeth? More bread?" Oh, God, he had noticed how much sourdough Lindsay and I had sucked down. But he was joking, and I liked that. Like we were old friends. Which made it hard to bring up the subject I had in mind, so I just blurted it out.

"I've been, uh ... Do you remember those birds I told you about?"

His expression changed, like his good mood had just crashed into a telephone pole.

"I've started seeing them again."

I swear he looked almost mad.

I stumbled on. "Well, the thing is ... I think I've figured out where they might be."

He shifted his stance.

"Klamath Falls."

"Oregon? Elizabeth ... I'm in the middle of serving people here."

"I know, but Jonah ... It's where she is. Where Janet is. I think."

It seemed like he was having trouble keeping a civil expression.

"I ... uh ... Actually, I'm thinking about going up there. Maybe ... you know, take Lindsay with me, make it kind of like a vacation. Nose around." My voice trailed off at his expression.

"Nose around?"

"You know, see what it feels like."

"Isn't that what you were trying to do with Brad Hernandez?"

He had me there.

"It's a really bad idea," he said.

"But it's really starting to bother me, Jonah. There are just certain things I can't ignore."

He shook his head and went on toward the kitchen. I sat there waiting, knowing he'd be back. He served another round, joked with the people a few minutes, then came back my way.

"How many times do I have to tell you I don't want you involved anymore? Use your head, Elizabeth. It's too damn dangerous."

I nodded my head, a compliant child.

"What about what happened to your house? What do you think will happen the next time?"

"I know. You're absolutely right."

"Good."

"But it's just not that simple."

"Why did I know you were going to say that?"

"I'm sorry, Jonah, but it's like having a ... burr under the saddle."

"A what?"

"You know, a horse has a burr under his saddle, he has to do something to get rid of it."

"You've lost me, Elizabeth."

"When I get a strong feeling like this, I have to do whatever it takes."

"And going up there would do that."

"Hopefully."

"What makes you so sure that's where she is?"

"I'm not a hundred percent sure. It's just that, well ... It was me on the train—in the dream where everything was going fast. I knew it seemed familiar and I finally remembered. I really did go through there once on the train, and that's what I saw. I was sitting in the observation car, the birds were flying, the train was going fast."

"Still ..."

"Everything was going really fast, exactly like in my dream."

He was obviously fighting for patience.

"And that dream is always connected to the other one. The one in the kitchen." I felt a shiver snake it's way through my body, remembering the one where he'd been standing just behind me. "Anyway, I won't know for sure unless I actually go up there. And it's going to keep pushing at me until I do, so ..."

"But you'll really take Lindsay with you?"

A nod wasn't a lie, was it? I hadn't spoken any actual words.

He seemed to be considering it. Then someone called him from across the room. "Don't leave until we talk again, okay?" he said, and went back to his work.

Lindsay returned a few minutes later, finally ready to go. I had the idea we could just slip out without seeing Jonah again, but as we were going out the door, he caught up with us, following us outside.

"Leaving so soon?"

Although I pretended I hadn't heard him, Lindsay stopped and turned around, forcing me to follow suit.

"I hear you two are planning a little getaway," he said to her while I tried to make meaningful signs to her so she wouldn't say the wrong thing.

"Uh ..." And then, quickly, because she finally got my drift. "Oh, yeah. Sure. Absolutely."

"So, you like bird watching, then?"

She glanced frantically at me, and I nodded. He turned towards me, almost catching my response. Seeing the look on Jonah's face, Lindsay said, "I think I better just wait for you in the car, E," and went on ahead.

Standing there in his frilly apron, Jonah might have looked silly except for the serious expression on his face. "We were lucky last time, Elizabeth. Things worked out okay, but this ... If there is anything to it, and I'm not saying there is, you could get yourself into all kinds of trouble."

"I know it could be ... difficult," I said. "But I'll be careful."

"I know about your being careful." He almost smiled and I caught a glimpse of the guardian angel in him. He glanced back through the door. "They need me in there," he said, obviously irritated by that idea. "I'm going to have to go. Look, Elizabeth, why don't you try to ... get more info on it, however you do that, and then we'll contact the authorities up there, see what they can do."

"You know it doesn't work like that," I almost whispered.

He grabbed the door, ready to go back in. "Why are you doing this to me?"

Something made me reach out and touch his arm. "Because I can't make it stop, Jonah. I can't stop it."

Our eyes met and held. "Well, I sure as hell can't let you go up there alone," he said, but he said it mildly.

At that point I think we both knew we were practically on our way.

* * *

I went to see Frank at his office the next day. It was time to come clean. About what, I'm not sure. Being psychic? Not wanting to be a church wife? Taking a trip with another man? I decided I'd try to let him down easy, which, in my experience, almost always turns out to be the hardest way.

He was writing his sermon long hand. Frank hates computers and pretty much lets everyone know it. When I walked in, he was frowning at what he'd just written.

"Hey," he said, "Sit down." He wasn't mad at me, just in the middle of a thought.

He erased furiously while I practiced what I should say.

The thing is, there's something about Jonah. When I look in his eyes, I always feel like I could swim down deep and come up with something bright and shiny. No, that probably wouldn't do.

He was looking at me now.

"You know that trip I mentioned?"

He nodded.

"I'm leaving tomorrow. I'll be gone for several days."

"I hope you can get some rest."

"Thanks." Maybe I was going to get off easy after all.

"Going alone?"

With that one little question, those two little words, I suddenly realized I was going to have to tell him everything.

"Not exactly."

"Lindsay?"

Shit.

"No. Uh ... Actually, it's ended up being sort of a work thing," I said. "We're trying to locate somebody."

"We?"

"You remember that detective I introduced you to? Jonah Haley?"

Storms whirled in his eyes. "Since when are you working for the police department?"

"I'm not, but ..."

I told him everything. I told him about being psychic; the whole story. After I labored through it all, and what had happened when we found the little girl in that campground by the lake, he said calmly, "I know, Elizabeth. A couple of the ladies from the church filled me in, showed me the articles they'd cut out and saved. They had some concerns you might not be appropriate for a vicar's wife, as they put it."

"Oh."

"Didn't you notice when Alice Cartwright started wearing that huge gold cross? How she sort of fingered it whenever you were around? I think she was trying to ward off the evil psychic." He was obviously amused. "I wish you'd told me sooner, but I'm okay with it. I don't care."

"You don't?"

"As long as you don't do anything weird with it."

How to answer that?

Just as I was about to try, he said, "But, why do you need to go away with that cop? Let me go with you, or at least take Lindsay."

"Well we're not really *going away*," I said, using my fingers to put the words into quotes. "We're just trying to find that missing woman. And being a cop, he's got the necessary connections, you know, so it makes sense he'd go along."

"He has no right to ask that of you, Elizabeth. Put you in danger like that."

"Actually, I asked him."

Frank looked pale. "I see."

I started to try to tell him about getting that burr out from under my saddle, but decided to take another tack. "I have these strong urges, Frank, and I have to do whatever I can to get rid of them." Oh dear, that sounded wrong.

"I can understand that," Frank said dryly. "Since we've stopped having sex, I feel pretty much the same way."

"I meant, as a psychic I sometimes get these feelings that can't be ignored."

Frank looked pissed, something I'd never seen him do before. "Look, Elizabeth, all I know is that I haven't seen you for days, we've stopped having sex, and now you're going off to satisfy ... strong urges with some cop."

How had I gotten myself into such a corner? I spent the next ten minutes trying to make myself clear, but it didn't seem to help very much. I know what it's like when somebody's trying to give you the brush-off, not being honest with you, playing you along. It hurts like hell, and, no matter what, you always know when it's happening to you. Eventually, there was nothing more I could say.

Frank clasped his hands, as if he was praying, probably for patience.

"We'll talk when you get back, then, I guess," he said. "If you come back."

I assured him I would, all the time feeling just a little bit angry with him for putting pressure on me. Still, I understood his feelings. I could pretend all I wanted, but I was going away with another guy. I wouldn't want somebody doing that to me. I gave him a hug before I left and I could feel his eyes on me, watching from the window, until Tilly and I drove away.

* * *

Poor Peeps. He was just home from a way too long stay at the Palace and now he was going back there again. He knew it right away, even before I started packing. I think he reads minds, actually. I can make a vet appointment for him while I'm at work (so he never even hears the conversation), and about ten minutes before I go to scoop him into his kitty carrier, he somehow knows to run and hide himself under the very middle of the bed.

He was pacing nervously around my bedroom and soon after I had spread the suitcase open on the bed and begun to pack, he jumped up and threw his little body into it, stretching out across the flowered undies I'd put in the bottom, staging a kitty sit-in to protest my trip. He was purring, but with a hint of a threat. Making a statement. Giving me a very furry ultimatum.

I sat down on the bed to pet him, which caused the lid of the suitcase to slam shut on him. He gave an angry yowl, but seemed quite content to stay where he was once I had opened the lid up again. "No fleas, I hope," I said. I swear he looked at me the same way Frank had just before I left the rectory. The males in my life all seemed to want something from me I just couldn't give right now.

I scratched Peep's chin, wondering what it was Jonah wanted I couldn't give.

Why was my dream about him a nightmare? Was he the man who had threatened me before in that other dream? It was a totally crazy idea, but it was starting to make sense—not that Jonah was that other man, but that I did feel threatened by him. I felt threatened by his heart.

* * *

It's a long trip up the length of California, even when you're starting in the middle. I always forget just how long until I'm actually on my way, and then I begin to wish I lived in Rhode Island or Vermont. Interstate 5 is an endless highway that never even makes the effort to curve until you're almost to Stockton, and then it only manages a token jog. Riding high along the edge of the San Joaquin Valley, you look out over it and most days see very little—rain or fog, if it's winter, smog most of the rest of the time. The best days are in the very early spring when the almond orchards lining the freeway are ripe with blooms. You don't need to see far then, just deep into the endless acres of flowering trees.

Taking a long car trip with someone you don't know very well is maybe even worse than eating pizza on a first date. You've got hours to fill but you just don't know what to do with them. If I'd been driving, I could have at least had something to keep me occupied but as a passenger, I was left with nothing to do. So, I fell asleep, letting myself weave in and out of those strange little dreams that come when you're just barely out of it in the car: thoughts, memories and moments blended together with the sounds of the trip itself. I was on some distant planet trying to levitate. I was floating in the sea, happy as a clam. I was teaching a sex education class to people with giant heads. Where did that come from?

I woke with a start, my heart pounding wildly, thinking Jonah had driven off the road. He had, actually—he was just pulling into a rest area. He shut off the engine, an odd expression on his face as he looked at me.

When we got out, I caught sight of a woman's reflection in the car window, her hair lopsided and piled high on one side of her head. Reminiscent of my grandma's old Cupie doll. Now I knew why Jonah had looked at me that way. I've known women who can sleep eight hours on a plane and come out with a perfect do. I'm not one of them.

I made a beeline to the restroom. When I came out, at least somewhat repaired, Jonah was surveying a map posted on the bulletin board. He turned as I approached, and I liked the look in his eyes. Must have been my hair.

"This is feeling a little ... strange," he said, stretching to relieve his stiffness. He took a moment to massage his neck.

"Coke?" I was looking at the drink machine.

He nodded, so I got him one and then another for myself. We stood there drinking them, watching people.

"You mean going somewhere, the two of us?"

He frowned at his soda for a moment and then said, "Yeah, partly." He took a last long swallow, then threw the can behind his back, perfectly lobbing it into a nearby trash container, basketball style. "C'mon," he said, motioning toward his SUV. "Maybe it's time you and I had a little talk."

"Okay." But did we have to do it now?

Once we were back on the freeway he let a few miles slip by before he actually spoke. "If we're going to spend the next few days together, I, for one, need to figure out what we're doing."

"Oh, well ... Looking for Janet, I guess?"

"Right."

"Well, we are, aren't we?"

He gave me a look that said he thought I was being a little too coy. "We've done some things, had things happen between us ..."

I nodded, feeling a strange sense of excitement starting to build. He had just verbalized exactly what I'd been thinking ever since we started this trip.

"It's been pretty much like a roller coaster."

I smiled.

He glanced at me. "I think maybe I need some ground rules."

"Ground rules? Like what?"

"Like you let me call the shots when it comes to your safety. No running off on your own somewhere."

"I can live with that."

"I'm serious. You stick to what you know best, I'll do what I know best."

"Okay."

We drove on a little further. "And I don't know if calling this a business trip is working for me," he said. But he didn't look at me when he said it. He kept his eyes on the road. After that, thick silence filled the car and I started remembering, in great and intimate detail, how it had felt to kiss him in this very same car, in the rain. I would have bet Grandma Betty's diamond hatpin he was remembering that, too.

Since I felt like it was my turn to speak, I finally did. "I kind of thought we could try doing the friends thing."

"The friends thing?"

"Being friends," I said, "Traveling like ... two friends."

His eyes met mine briefly and I knew what he was asking.

"So, you're one of those people who think a man and a woman can't be just friends." I tried to say it lightly, but my heart was beating fast.

"I didn't say that. I just think once they get past a certain point, it's hard to go back."

Of course, he was right, and we'd certainly gotten past that point.

"But we can always try," he said. "If that's what you want."

I nodded, though my heart wanted to scream *No!* "I just need to ... I don't know, keep it simple," I said. "My life is way too complicated these days, you know?"

"Is it?"

It would be if he didn't stop looking at me like that. I looked out the window for awhile, watching the fields whip by, empty now of their summer harvest, some already tilled into perfect, dark rows, others still a tangle of dried plants and roots, long dead.

It was Jonah who finally broke the silence. "Big valley," he said.

"Yeah. I remember when you could see the Sierras on the other side. Now it's too smoggy most of the time."

"Nothing stays the same. Not places, not relationships ..." He drummed his fingers lightly on the steering wheel, then said, casually, "So, how are things with the priest, anyway?"

He had caught me by surprise. I just looked at him.

"You being my friend and all," he said, emphasizing the word *friend* ever so slightly. "Are congratulations in order?"

"Oh, I don't know ..." I had fallen into his trap. "Wait a minute, how did you even know he'd asked me?"

His look told me he didn't.

"Just because I spent some time with him, don't assume ..."

"I never assume," he said. "But based on observable facts ..."

"Gathered by somewhat questionable methods."

"Trust me, Elizabeth, there were times even a blind man could have seen."

I sat there trying to build up a head of steam, but it just wasn't there. Strangely, I was enjoying myself.

"Elizabeth ...?"

I turned to look at him.

"I thought friends were supposed to be able to talk about things like this."

I cleared my throat and said carefully, "Frank and I haven't made any definite plans."

He said something under his breath that sounded like, *Hallelujah!*

"What did you say?"

He didn't answer for some time and when he did, it was hardly an answer. "Whatever happens, you deserve to be happy."

That threw me. Right into a very nice place.

Jonah sped up to whip past a very large RV that seemed to be swaying dangerously with the breeze, then pulled back into the slow lane. "Guy ought to be off the road," he said, glancing back in his rear view mirror, adjusting it as he did so. "So, anyway, Elizabeth, we still haven't answered the important question. Are we going to be friends or sparring partners?"

Sparring partners sounded like much more fun. "How many times to I need to tell you," I said. "My name is Libby."

The look he gave me nearly knocked my socks off, and I wasn't wearing any. Suddenly, Libby didn't feel a bit sleepy anymore. Or a bit like a friend. I had to find some diversion. Fast. "Let's count Volkswagens," I said quickly. "Five points apiece. Ten for red."

"You mean like Tilly?"

Good Lord. Now he even knew my car's name. But, oh yeah, it was on my license plates and he had been following me, after all.

"Tilly's a great car," I said, trying for huffy.

He smiled. "So, what do I get if I win?"

I thought about it awhile. "I'll pay for your dinner."

Then he thought about it awhile. "What if it's not dinner I want?" he said.

And then, just as I was smiling, just as he was grinning ear to ear, I swear I saw him literally shake himself, like how they describe it in a book or a movie, and after that, his mood changed. He got much more into his driving and we didn't look at each other again for a long time.

By the time we actually stopped for a meal, we were way past Sacramento and almost to Redding. We hadn't counted a single VW bug, though we'd certainly seen a few. I'd gotten fifty points on red ones, alone, but only in my head.

Why he chose a truck stop I'll never know, but when we split up to hit the bathrooms, I was reminded of why I personally never stop at a truck stop when two guys the size of Ohio ogled me in the hall. As I passed by I heard one of them say, "Hey, sweetheart, you all alone?" I heard the other guy snort in response.

I didn't look around and walked on, congratulating myself for taking the high road and ignoring their behavior, but then, I heard it—

that smacking noise I first heard years ago in junior high. I didn't think men used it anymore, but there it was. It's not a growl or a whistle; at least I could live with that. It's loud and it's rude and it's more of a smirk with tongue than anything else. Totally disgusting.

I whirled around. "Why don't you shut your fucking mouth?" I said, just as Jonah swooped down on me from behind and took my arm. I tried to push him away. "I can take care of myself," I hissed at him, surprised and just a little irritated to see the humor dancing in his eyes.

"I'll just bet you can," he said, but he pulled me away with him anyway.

I was still smoldering when we sat down to eat and it took me awhile to settle down. While Jonah read his menu, I stared at mine, thinking instead of the two men, savoring the idea of them standing there flummoxed (Sandy's word comes in handy again) that such foul language could come out of such a sweet looking gal. I'm quite sure they would have called me a gal first. And much worse after the way I talked to them. I once went through a period where I could have signed onto a ship and fit right in with the crew—my mouth was worse than a sailor's. I got a charge out of shocking men, a real kick out of being able to swear with the best of them. I had some foolish notion it had something to do with equality. I thought I was over that. Till now.

I took a drink of water, then ruthlessly crunched a piece of ice until it was gone. "That sound they make, do they do it to impress each other? Because I'm absolutely certain it never got any guy into any woman's pants."

Jonah lifted his eyes from the menu just long enough to look into mine. "You're probably right," he said. "It sure never worked for me."

It was only the pure delight in his eyes that kept me from sticking out my tongue at him.

By the time we got back on the road, it was totally dark. This time I curled up against the seat facing him so that every so often I could watch him through the dark and see that profile, such a nice one. He might not be classically gorgeous like Frank, but there was something about him all the same. I didn't even mind when he found a jazz station. At least he kept it low. And when I finally did fall asleep, I dreamed the nicest dream. It involved Jonah, of course, and strawberry ice cream, lots of it. And licking it off his fingers, one at a time.

Thank God the motel was a decent one. My face was already too red after that dream to have to handle any further embarrassment. Of course I'd gotten us separate rooms. Turned out they had a connecting door, like in the movies. Don't two people traveling alone but together always have a connecting door? In the movies, I mean.

That way, they can have their romance.

But this wasn't the movies. Jonah knocked on my inner door and I opened it carefully. I noticed him glance around my room. It was just like his, only opposite, so I don't think he was looking at the design and décor. Maybe he was hoping to catch a glimpse of that knockout lavender nightie. I was beginning to regret leaving it at home.

"What time you want to leave in the morning?"

I had such a sensation that wasn't what he really had to say.

"I was thinking we ought to leave early," he said. "You okay with that? That way we can get up there before noon." We only had a few more hours to go. If we'd left earlier today, we could have been there by now, but Jonah had to put in a few hours at work before he could take off.

Why don't we just cut the crap and sleep together? The voice in my head was talking so loud I wondered for a moment if I'd actually said it. But no, he wasn't responding that way. He had gone back into his room and was fiddling with the alarm on his clock radio, trying to make it work. But he hadn't closed his door.

I went into him.

"We'll have to try your radio," he said, giving up on his.

Then the two of us traipsed back into my room where I sat on the bed like a helpless female while he set up the clock. Note to self: *Helpless females have their place, but seldom get what they really want. Maybe you should just tell him?*

He set the radio down and looked at me. I could almost see the struggle in his eyes. He was trying for businesslike again, and me, I wasn't sure what I was hoping to do. Ever since our conversation in the car, we'd moved back to square one, away from getting personal and back toward the black hole we'd fallen into shortly after we met six months ago.

He checked my front door locks, then headed toward his room, stopping at the connecting door. "Sleep well," he said.

He shut the door, but didn't lock it so I spent the next forty-five minutes or so lying there in the dark imagining what would happen if I just got up and waltzed through it and landed in his bed. I knew he wouldn't turn me away, but, still, I just couldn't do it. Turns out I'm not all that brave.

I spent a good part of the hour after that imagining him opening the door and slipping into my room, taking me into his arms, etc., etc. It would so take the pressure off me if he made the first move. Turns out he wasn't that brave either—or maybe that foolish. I woke up the next morning alone.

The Handwriting on Jonah's Wall

At first he had thought it would be easy, never seeing her again. After that night in Cambria when she had gone off on him and seemed so crazy and it had shaken him to his core that she was seeing another man, he'd decided to simply put her in the past and walk away. He'd certainly done it before with other women, but he couldn't seem to do it now. Fate and circumstance and, ultimately, his desires, had brought them back together again and again.

He rolled on his side and stared, unseeing, at the shadows on the wall. He hadn't had to deal with such powerful emotion for a long time, not since he and Ginny had married right out of junior college. Since then it had been the Helens of the world he'd chosen to hook up with; nice women, pretty women but women he felt safe with because they kept their distance and let him keep his own as well. But with Libby there was no distance no matter how he tried, no matter how far away she might be. And right now, she was way too close, a few steps away through an unlocked door. So close he had heard her alarm go off a minute earlier.

Not that he'd been asleep. Sleep had pretty much eluded him since somewhere around three a.m. when he woke up, dreaming she was with him, in his bed.

Hearing a light tap on his door, he raised his head slightly.

"Time to wake up, Jonah," she called.

"Okay."

He waited. It was one of those motels where you could hear just about everything and, sure enough, a couple minutes later, he heard her shower come on. He practically groaned. It was too much to ask, really, for her to be so close, so accessible, and yet so very far away. His imagination took him through the connecting door and almost into the shower with her before he could force himself to stop. It would do no good, and it would only make him miserable. But still, he could almost see her, how surprised she'd be to see him there. A little shy, but he liked that about her. In his fantasy she'd open up her arms and pull him into the shower with her.

But that was definitely a fantasy. He jumped out of bed and started moving around. It would always be the same with her. He'd just begin to get close and then all hell would break loose again. Maybe she'd enchanted him, ensnared him somehow. But he knew better. Despite her more unusual aspects, she was as normal as anybody else most of the time. He smiled, knowing that would please her, because it was obvious that normal was something she wanted very much to be.

How had he learned to know her so well when they saw so little of each other? It scared and pleased him at the same time.

He forced himself to think of Frank Emerson, the man with whom she had spent many a night. The guy obviously had a claim on her. They were old friends and it was quite apparent they must be good together in bed. God knows, she might even marry the man. He'd asked her after all. And she'd certainly chosen the priest over him on more than one occasion. Chosen him of her very own, very free will. It should have helped to remind himself of that but it didn't seem to help at all.

This trip would tell the tale, he knew it would. He was still just a little anxious to see how the story would end. Libby had feelings for him—there were times when it had been more than obvious, even yesterday in the car. He had no idea, however, if they were anything near as intense as his feelings were for her. When they'd talked the other night at the spaghetti dinner, he'd at first wanted to do everything he could to stay away from her but once she started talking about this trip, he was lost. Damn if he didn't need to keep an eye on her anyway. And besides that, a chance to be with her twenty-four-seven was a chance he couldn't pass up.

He hopped into the shower, unable to ignore the fact that she was still taking her own shower just on the other side of the wall. Probably only about a foot or so away. It was enough to drive him mad, but it was, unfortunately, as close as he was going to get to her for now and maybe forever.

The Road to Enlightenment is Paved with Good Intentions

As we neared Klamath Falls, the marshland along the road started to suck me in—I mean the feeling of it started to suck me in. It triggered something in my gut; some memory, or some event to come. Which told me we were in the right place, or at least going in the right direction.

"Could you turn there?" I pointed towards a narrow road that headed off into the country.

Jonah had to slam on the brakes, as the road was coming up fast. He made the turn, then looked at me. "You have some kind of plan?"

I made a face.

"I figured as much," he said.

"I can't ... plan. It just sort of takes me there. At least, I hope it will." And to his unhappy look, "Remember when we went up to the lake? It wasn't a straight shot."

He nodded, a slight smile on his face as if it was a pleasant memory. He wasn't smiling quite so much after we'd driven nearly ten miles and I had to ask him to turn around.

"It's not an exact science," I said sheepishly.

After lunch at a small downtown café, Jonah went off to check with the local PD. He'd phoned them before we left and he wanted to see if anything new had come in. I don't imagine he told them I was there. And he wasn't on work time, anyway. He'd taken vacation time for our trip.

He hadn't been telling me anything about the case for some time. He'd stopped doing that when he'd realized how much it affected me. Things could have happened, evidence could have been found and people questioned, but he didn't tell me about it one way or the other.

Still, since he'd agreed to come with me to Klamath Falls, I had to think that meant he had some idea that our trip was worthwhile, that Janet might really be around.

While he was at the station, I took a walk through town. There wasn't a lot to see; it wasn't exactly a bustling metropolis. But I like small places, old places. Places that haven't been shined up and polished. Places that scar and stay that way. It reminded me of some of the mill towns I'd seen back east.

There was a tiny shoeshine stand in front of Nick's Barber 'N Shine. A scrawny little man was propped up on it reading the sports page and absentmindedly scratching his nearly hairless scalp. Probably had been there thirty years or more, both he and the shop.

Seeing me, he lowered his paper. "You looking for somebody?"

I shrugged. "Just looking, I guess."

"Not much to see." He rubbed his chin thoughtfully, then seemed to come to some important conclusion. "By my mind, you'd have more luck over by Tule Lake."

"Excuse me?" He was looking at me and talking to me, but it felt like the message was coming from somewhere else.

"More likely you'll find what you're after," he said, and I saw it again, in his eyes. He might be doing the talking, but the words weren't coming from him. It's happened to me before, several times, but it's always a shocker.

"Tule Lake?" I managed to stammer.

He nodded. "Not the town, so much. Over near the bird sanctuary. It's maybe, oh ... five miles out of town."

Of course. The birds.

"Best place to find what you're looking for," he said. He winked at me and I saw that he was returning to himself. I thanked him and went on my way, grateful for the guidance. I don't know how it works when it happens like that but I do know that it's always helpful.

* * *

"I should thank you," Jonah said. "The scenery here is something else. I probably never would have come up this way if it wasn't for you."

We were standing beside the SUV looking at the landscape, the foothills silhouetted behind it, a deep blue sky puffy with clouds above it all. The air was pure and crisp, with that feeling of fall that comes in late October. It was one of those days when you can no longer deny that another seemingly endless summer has slipped away. In fact, it was feeling a little too crisp. We got back in the car.

As we drove along the edge of the wildlife refuge, two hunters were just returning to their truck, unloading their catch. Seeing us coming, one guy proudly held up one of his poor duck victims, dangling it by the neck. I rolled down my window. "Nice day for killing," I yelled angrily, catching their startled expression as we flew by. When the second guy gave me a bird of a different kind, I pulled my head in and rolled up the window.

"It is hunting season," Jonah said dryly.

"I like a fair fight. Hunting is not a fair fight."

"You one of those people who thinks we should arm the wildlife?"

I smiled, picturing mallards armed with smart bombs and big bucks sporting camouflage caps and carrying Uzi's. Suddenly I had an upsetting thought. "You don't hunt, do you?"

"No, but it's necessary, Libby. It keeps down the populations."

"Never mind global warming. The real problem is too many ducks."

We shared a grin.

It was already getting dark by the time we found a place to stay, an old west style hotel in a small town not far from the refuge. The lobby was downstairs, situated next to a rather rowdy sounding bar. Add a swinging door and a tinkling piano, and you'd have the classic gold rush saloon. We got separate rooms again, of course, on the second floor. And this time there was no connecting door. In fact, there were two rooms between our rooms.

We had eaten lunch so late I wasn't even hungry. Jonah went downstairs to get a sandwich and I bought a bag of cheese crackers and a soda out of the vending machine down the hall and retired to my room, intent on calling Frank. Having spent the day with Jonah, I owed it to Frank to at least call. Besides, it was starting to feel very necessary to distance myself from Jonah. It was too damn hard to think of anything but him when he was nearby.

I dialed Frank's number several times before I realized it wasn't going through. The phone was dead. I jammed the little buttons up and down and even got down under the desk to wiggle the cord and check its' connection. Nothing. It's a testament to how distracted I was that I then decided I'd better call the front desk to report the problem. I looked carefully at the list of numbers posted by the phone and was already dialing before I stopped to realize that wasn't going to work either.

I don't do cell phones—can't stand the beasts, so I started down the hall to ask Jonah if I could use his phone, then thought better of it. I needed to stay away from him for the evening. I'd use the phone in the bar and report my problem phone to the front desk at the same time. Brilliant. But when I made my grand entrance, Jonah was the first person I saw. He was sitting at the bar and talking intently with one of the cowboys there. They were laughing and carrying on like old friends, crunching spanish peanuts and drinking Coors.

Better he didn't see me anyway. I slipped over to the pay phone hanging on the wall near the back of the bar and did my best to stay in the shadows. Frank answered on the second ring and sounded relieved to hear my voice. He related his day for me. Mrs. Cary had lost her bid to unseat Emily Potter, long time head of the Altar Society, and there were rumors of voting irregularities. (All from Mrs. Cary) The bishop had given him the green light for a new series of classes for teens and he was jazzed about that. And, of course, he missed me something fierce.

I told him what I had for lunch and how cold it was.

"So, have you been thinking things over, Elizabeth?"

"Well, I haven't had much time so far. A lot's been going on."

"Has it?"

"I know we need to talk, Frank, but it's really hard long distance."

"Exactly my point."

"I do think it's a good idea about us taking some time …" I couldn't say the rest, though Lord knows, I wanted to. Surprisingly, Frank didn't press the point.

"Well …" he said, sounding more uncertain than pleased, "So I guess I'll see you … when?"

I told him it was very hard to say. At which point Frank pulled out the big guns and proceeded to tell me how he could make me feel better, if only we were together. In bed, of course. When confronted with uncertainty, he always seems to go straight for his sure thing—sex. It did sound nice, especially the part about being in bed. Asleep. I was really feeling very, very tired.

I closed my eyes and listened. Frank is nothing if not imaginative and it wasn't long before he made me smile. "If the church people only knew what a devil you really are, Frank, they would …"

I looked up to find Jonah waiting patiently beside me. "They would … Uh …"

We stood there looking at each other while I turned several shades of red. Then Jonah gave me an odd little smile and turned away. But he didn't move away.

I put my hand over the receiver. "Do you mind?" I said to his back.

He glanced back at me with a look that said things I didn't have the heart to hear, then moved away. I almost thought he was angry.

I tried to focus back on my phone call. "Anyway, Frank …"

"Who was that?"

"Just somebody in the bar," I lied. "The phone in my room isn't working."

"*Your* room?" He was making a point of it.

"Yes, Frank. My room."

I could see that Jonah was still within hearing distance, damn him.

"I wish I was there with you."

"I wish you were here, too," I said, well aware that the lie was more for Jonah's benefit than for Frank.

"Promise me you'll be careful." And when I didn't respond, "Elizabeth?"

I was watching Jonah's back. "I'll be careful." Was Jonah purposely staying close by just to embarrass me? I wanted desperately to embarrass him. "Besides Frank, I know how to take care of myself. A well placed knee ..."

Frank laughed and then there was silence on the other end of the line while everything that couldn't be said was said. "Come home soon, Elizabeth," he said finally, and even though I didn't acknowledge it to myself at the time, I could hear the defeat in his voice.

"I will," I said. "Bye." I hung up quickly before I had to say anything remotely like, *I love you.*

"You want a get a drink or something?" Jonah was back, standing right behind me.

I turned to look at him, trying to read his expression, but coming up blank. Like his expression. "No, I don't think so," I said as crisply as I could. "I think I'm getting a really bad headache." I took off upstairs before he could say anything more.

* * *

It got a little weird in the car the next morning. We were once again sharing that small space without the appropriate words to fill it up, and now we had the awkwardness of the previous evening wedged in between us. Between our verbal sparring/flirting rituals in the SUV the first day and my overheard phone conversation with Frank the night before, who knew where we stood? In no time at all that morning we managed to go from a cheery, though impersonal conversation at the breakfast table about the relative merits of oatmeal as opposed to eggs, to a stilted discussion of the weather: *Gee, isn't that wind cold today?* And from there? Well, it got very quiet in the car.

The map was my salvation. I poured over it, looking for something that grabbed my attention. I gave Jonah directions, and sat back to stare silently at the country passing by. It was beautiful in a sparse, rugged way and there were, of course, more and more of those damned flying birds.

I asked Jonah to pull over so I could get out of the car and get the lay of the land. I was feeling so tense, like something was coming over me. Once out of the car, I closed my eyes and took some deep breaths. When I opened them again, I caught Jonah looking at me curiously.

"There's a big house," I said. "Some kind of old fashioned structure. I can't quite tell, but I think I'd know it if I saw it." I felt a wash of feeling come over me, some of it frightening. "I don't want to, though."

"What is it?" Jonah came closer.

"There's ... a lot of fear."

"Does that mean we're close?"

"Maybe. I don't know." And then I just sat down, unexpectedly, on the side of the road. My legs wouldn't carry me. "Wow," I said.

Jonah squatted down beside me. "What's going on? Are you okay?" And when I didn't answer because I couldn't seem to speak right then, "Are you sick?"

I shook my head. "The fact that I'm feeling this way must mean we're on the right track."

I saw the worry in his eyes. "I'm not sure it's worth it, Libby, if this is what it does to you." Our eyes met and I felt drawn in by his gentleness. He took hold of me and helped me up. "Maybe I should take you back to the hotel."

I shook my head and he let go of me carefully, as if he was afraid I'd break. He was being so delightfully soothing, but he really didn't understand. And if I told him, it would probably freak him out, because I was pretty sure that at least some of the feelings I was feeling weren't actually mine. They belonged to somebody else.

I had to get a grip. If there's one thing I learned early—and learned the hard way, it's that you need to keep your own psychic space, your own energy, clear. I had let somebody else's energy in, something I didn't do very often any more. And once you let it in, it can be difficult to get it out again, because any energy that's pushy enough to force it's way in is probably going to want to hang around awhile.

I leaned against the car, warning Jonah off with a wave of my hand. "Give me some time." I closed my eyes to center myself and started working to consciously clear my energy. I pictured white light all around me, expanding out in every direction. Feeling the power of that, I let my hands move freely in their familiar and comforting dance of energy. I must have looked like I was directing jet parking at the airport, but I had learned the graceful movements long ago. It had just been a long time since I'd needed to do them as much as I did now.

Jonah wasn't near me when I opened my eyes, but he was watching me all the same. I got in the car without a word and waited until he got in. "That way, I think." I pointed east. I could see the big old house in my head and I could also feel the fear, both there and in my heart. While he drove I convinced him to tell me what he knew about the case. It was a matter of safety really, a matter of our lives.

"If we should find the place, (I could tell he thought it was a big *if*) I'll contact the sheriff," Jonah said. "It's out of my jurisdiction. Besides, I'm not taking you into something like that."

We drove in silence while I processed what he'd told me. No one had seen Jason Jakes, the former used car dealer, for a couple months, but that wasn't all that unusual. The man had a way of insinuating himself into situations, and then disappearing when things got too rough. There were a couple reports, however, that someone fitting his description had been spotted in the last month or so in places like Redding and Shasta, which weren't far away from where we were right now. Unconfirmed sightings, but the police had no reason to doubt they were true. They had also discovered that he'd rented a panel van around the time of Janet's disappearance, and while a search of the van had revealed nothing, they thought it might be significant. He had chalked up a lot of miles in only a few days.

Brad Hernandez was dating again, one girl in particular, and the affair appeared to be hot and heavy and moving fast. He was as busy as ever representing scumbags, and he was apparently wasting little time grieving over the loss of his former live-in love.

We were driving along, both quiet, when Jonah broke my reverie. "You still never really told me. What did you think you'd accomplish by talking to him, anyway?"

Rats. He was talking about Hernandez. I tried to look clueless.

"You know who I'm talking about, Libby."

I sighed. "I told you. I was just trying to see what the energy was like. I thought maybe being in his office might tell me something."

"I can't believe you actually went in there."

"Well, I didn't expect to actually see him. I didn't know ..."

"He'd be so deadly?"

I swallowed hard. "I just wish Lindsay would stop shooting off her mouth."

"Yeah, it's a real problem, her wanting to protect you."

I did it again. I smiled.

I directed him to take a dirt road that felt right to me and we bumped down that for awhile until it dead-ended into the Tom-Tom Turkey Ranch. After a quick chat with the eager, and apparently lonely, manager of the place, during which we were treated to way more facts about turkey production than anyone should ever have to know, we declined his offer of a guided tour and headed back.

I could see Jonah was dying to make a comment, but he held it in until we were almost back to the main road. "It's not an exact science," he said, grinning.

After lunch, we headed out again, and ended up driving at least four or five miles on a dirt road past several private ranches until the road dead-ended at a locked gate. There was a rusty *No Trespassing* sign and a faded wood painted sign that may have said something like *Rancho Park*.

We got out of the car and stared at the road, as if that would somehow tell us what to do next. I certainly wasn't getting any signals. The road continued to curl off into the distance, winding through low hills. It was impossible to see its' eventual destination

Jonah played with the lock, but it wouldn't budge. "You think we ought to pursue this?"

"I don't know," I said miserably. My confidence had been shaken by the false starts, especially the turkey ranch incident.

We continued to stare at the road a while longer.

"It'll be dark in a couple hours," Jonah said. "If you think it's important, maybe we should come back tomorrow, get an earlier start."

"But what if it's just around the corner?"

"You willing to climb the fence?"

"I'll just squeeze under." I'd done it before, as a child. I tried pulling up the lower wire, but it barely moved.

"I can boost you," he said.

We looked for the lowest spot we could find and he lifted me over as effortlessly as if he was Baryshnikov and I was his partner. Not being built like a ballerina, however, I said a quick prayer for the protection of his back. He seemed unaffected, vaulting over the fence rather gracefully, and making a perfect two point landing by my side.

"I sure hope there aren't any bulls in here."

"Bulls are probably the least of our problems," he said.

We stayed close to the hills rather than following the road. The pasture was deeply wet; our feet sunk down in it in some places. There were clusters of wild mushrooms, small dark ones, and I wondered what kind they were, remembering a time in my past, my now distant past, when wild mushrooms of a certain kind held some fascination and delight. Eating them was ugly—they tasted horrible, but afterwards, they sent you off into a different and sometimes pretty magical place.

"What kind of mushrooms, do you think?"

Jonah's look made me send my silly fantasy back to the past. You don't do magic mushrooms with a cop. Besides, with my luck, they were probably the poisonous kind. They'd send you off somewhere, but you'd probably never make it back.

We trudged on a mile or so, winding around hills, always expecting to see something that would show us where we were going, but the farm house, if there was one, was elusive.

We had stopped to consider turning around when we heard the low rumble of a plane. We had just enough time to duck under one of the rare trees around the place before it flew over. A Cessna four-seater, I think. It was coming so low that we knew it must have just taken off.

The plane made us both just curious enough to continue. Plus, I wasn't ready to give up on my vision of an old farmhouse tucked at one end of a very private valley. It sounded so scenic and romantic, never mind what I'd originally hoped to find there.

It was right about then that I stepped into a hole and twisted my ankle.

"Probably a sprain." Jonah rubbed my ankle gently, feeling for breaks, but finding none. "Anyway, looks like we'd better get you back."

But how? I couldn't put any pressure on my foot. "I'll just sit here awhile," I said, trying for heroic. "We've come this far. You go ahead, see what's up there."

He thought about that, then agreed. He'd be back in twenty minutes, he said, and left me sitting on a rock beneath a tree. At first I enjoyed the solitude but as it was getting towards dark I began to entertain unpleasant thoughts of coyotes and mountain lions, and even started wondering about bobcats. Were they big enough to do any damage if they happened to be really, really hungry? It was with great relief that I saw Jonah approaching. There was a long-haired man with him, young and rather heavy—your standard couch potato. Before they even got close enough to carry on a conversation with me, I had decided to name him Spuds.

"How's your leg, sweetheart?" Jonah was playing the boyfriend card. He came up to me and squatted down to take another look at it. I groaned a little when he actually touched it. If anything, it was getting worse.

"It's posted no trespassing," Spuds said gruffly from behind him.

I looked up at him with what I hoped was an innocent air. "It's my fault. My aunt had a ranch around here. I used to come up here as a kid and when I saw your road, I was so sure this was the place."

Jonah looked appreciative of my creative touch. "You know how women are," he said. "I tried to tell her, but ..."

I gave him a withering look, just for effect.

"I still think it might be her old place," I said. "Is there a barn, a two-story house with a wrap around porch on three sides?"

But Spuds was having none of it, a man of few words.

"Appreciate it if you could give us a ride back to our car," Jonah said.

The guy considered. "I guess," he said, finally. He trudged off down the road. He wasn't in a hurry, but then, couch potatoes seldom are.

"What did you see?" I asked as soon as Spuds was out of earshot.

"Old air strip near the house, grown up a little, but still useable. Didn't get up to the house, he caught up with me before that. Looks like a big spread, something out of the early west—a large barn, outbuildings, a corral."

"And the house?"

He looked a little grim. "Two story with a wrap around porch on three sides."

"Oh," I said, feeling both pleased and scared at the same time.

Jonah was looking at me as if he was waiting for something. When I didn't speak, he said, "It's starting to feel a little too close for comfort, Libby."

"Well, I ..."

Seeing I was shivering, he took off his jacket and put it around my shoulders. Chivalrous. I wasn't sure I could handle that right now. "It's not far back up there," Jonah said. "He'll be back in a few and we'll be out of here before long."

Comforting, except it was almost dark already. "Were there any cattle?"

"None. Makes you wonder what they're ranching."

Jonah offered assistance, putting his arm around my shoulder to help me up, then supporting me as I took hesitant steps toward the road. "I have to admit, it's got me curious," he said, "but I've got no excuse to go up there again. Tomorrow I'll go talk to the sheriff, see what they know."

A pickup came around the corner, its' lights silhouetting us in the gathering gloom. The cab smelled of hay and tobacco when we climbed in. Wedged in the middle, I leaned toward Jonah as far as I could and he held my hand as the truck bumped off down the road. The girlfriend thing was feeling pretty nice and the zing I was getting from sitting so close to him, felt even better.

By the time we got back to town my ankle seemed to be loosening up, so when Jonah suggested we try to find a doctor, I refused. Besides, I was pretty sure there wasn't much you could do for a sprain anyway, but just lay off of it. With a little extra help from Jonah, I made it rather easily to the top of the stairs. Call me crazy, but my resistance to seeing a doctor might have had more to do with the desire to keep Jonah helping me than it did with anything else.

While Jonah went back to his room to take a shower, I tried to nap. But once I was lying down, I knew it was hopeless. I was sore, stiff, and too wound up to sleep. I changed clothes and freshened up a bit, then waited what I thought was the appropriate time before limping down the hall to Jonah's door. Since I had promised to keep in touch with Lindsay, I knew I'd better call her before it got too late. Since my own phone still wasn't working, I had to go to him.

I sat on the bed by the phone while Jonah sat in the one chair in the room, his long legs stretched out in front of him. His hair was still damp from the shower, his feet were bare, and he hadn't buttoned his shirt all the way up yet—I could see his undershirt underneath it. For some reason, I felt almost giddy by the time Lindsay picked up the phone.

"Lindsay?"

"Oh, Elizabeth, thank God." It sounded like she was eating a sandwich. "Hold on," she said, "I was just eating a sandwich." She was back a moment later. "How's it going up there?"

"Well ... Okay, I guess."

"Find anything?"

"Lots of birds."

"Birds?"

"It's a long story."

"Well, so how are you guys getting along?"

It was anybody's guess, so I changed the subject. "We took a long hike today. Really pretty up here. Cold, though. I stepped in a hole and I twisted my ankle."

"Oh, dear," she said, and then, without missing a beat, "But, you're getting along?"

"Yeah, things are ... fine. I'm actually calling from Jonah's room." This elicited a knowing *Ooh* from her, which I chose to ignore. "We're just gonna go get something to eat. It's been a long, hard day."

"You need to relax," she said. "Have a drink, then maybe have a ... long, hard night." She giggled, the rat.

I groaned.

"So, what's he doing, anyway?"

"Who?"

"Jonah."

Other than looking edible? "Do you want to talk to him or do you want to talk to me?"

She wanted to talk to him. As soon as I handed him the phone, I figured I'd made a big mistake. I started limp-walking around the small room, nibbling on my nails, hoping Lindsay would have some sense and keep her mouth shut.

"Hi, Lindsay." He listened, then said, "No, not so far. There's a lot of open country around here, a lot of places to look. I think we may have found a drug operation, though."

I looked at him, startled, and our eyes met. It hadn't occurred to me until he said it out loud, but of course, it made sense—the remote ranch, the plane, no livestock.

"Never mind finding people," I said, " I could always get work as a drug-sniffing psychic."

He gave me a blinding smile, then listened again, still watching me make my tour of the room. "Don't know yet, " he said, "but if nothing comes up in the next day or so, we'll probably head on home."

I felt a sudden sense of letdown. Head home? Back to reality, decisions, and consequences? I suddenly felt like my ankle would just give out, there and then.

"So, how's Byron treating you?" Lindsay and Officer Byron had been trying hard to be an item. It just hadn't turned out to be a very interesting one. He grinned at whatever she said. "Tell him he'll have to answer to me."

Should I be jealous? He was having a longer conversation with her than I had.

He listened a few moments longer. "Yeah, okay. I'll tell her," he said, and then hung up.

When I could wait no more, I said, "Tell me what?"

He hesitated. "Not to be a hero."

From the look on his face I could tell that wasn't what she'd said at all. I was sure of it. "C'mon. What did she really say?"

Another hesitation, and then, "She said we should make hay while the sun shines, Libby." His look was a little too direct.

"Uh ... Oh. Okay." I cast about for some escape and took the only one available—the bathroom. "I'll just be a minute," I said. Once inside, I stared at myself in the mirror and spent a few unsuccessful moments trying to recall what Frank looked like, then felt forced to flush the toilet as my excuse for being in there. It was so loud that I came out more embarrassed than I went in.

Jonah gave me an amused look, then followed me out and helped me down the stairs without even being asked. We ate in the bar where we had huge, juicy burgers and steak fries. Turns out the food wasn't half bad. For some reason, when Jonah ordered beer, so did I. It just seemed to fit the night and the place. I don't think I could have uttered the word, *wine spritzer* if my life depended on it.

We sat in a back booth in comfortable red plastic seats. The tables, dark gray formica with silver metal edges, were marred by years of neglect. In front of me RJ & CK were obviously in love forever, as one of them had so artistically carved, and in the very middle of the table it said, "Question author ..." as in *Question authority*, I suppose. Apparently, the artist was discovered and kicked out by the *authorities* before he could finish the job. There were dusty plastic plants on shelves above us and beer signs on every wall. Groups of locals and hunters filled the other booths and tables and all, it seemed, were drinking beer. After all these years, for an hour or so at least, I felt like I finally fit in.

Jonah was looking at me funny. I could have sworn I felt his leg brush against mine under the table, but just as quickly it was gone. We were just starting on our second pitcher of Coors, I think. I'd lost track somewhere during my second mug full. In any case, the beer taste had gotten easier to swallow and Jonah was looking dangerously close to being irresistible. And don't guys always know when you're feeling like that?

"You know, we really shouldn't spend so much time just sitting around," I said, suddenly anxious. "We're wasting time when we could be out doing what we came for."

He seemed to find that funny. "What do you mean, doing what we came for?"

Why did that sound so suggestive? "I meant looking for Janet, of course."

"What, in the dark?" When I didn't say anything, he said, "It's damn near bedtime, Libby."

That set off bells that usually wouldn't have rung.

"After the day we've had, we should both be in bed." He looked at me, a steady look.

The whole church bell choir was ringing now. I didn't realize they could make that much noise. I put all my attention to finishing my beer, then put my hand over the top of my mug when he offered to pour me some more. "*No mas*," I said, feeling smugly bilingual, even though it was about the only Spanish phrase I know other than *No hablo espanol aqui,*(or something like that) and *Yo quiero Taco Bell.*

I watched as he poured himself another glass, then sat back and crossed his arms.

"I was just thinking about that night I brought the pizza over to your place. Remember?"

I nodded. A little unsteadily, but I nodded.

"It was the first time we ever really got a chance to talk."

I nodded again. "Peeps liked you right away." Oh, God, was that too revealing?

He grinned. "So then, I passed the test?" He took a drink of his beer, then looked at me intently. "Seems like you were kind of nervous that night, too."

Okay, nothing makes me more nervous than to have someone point it out to me. It's like when somebody says to you, *Don't be so shy. I won't bite*. It shuts you up faster than anything. I picked up my fork to play with it, but it slipped from my hand, landing with a lot of commotion on my plate.

Jonah once again seemed amused. "Libby," he said softly, " I won't bite."

That did it. I got up, rather roughly as it turned out because my leg had stiffened up big time while we were sitting in that booth. Fortunately, he's quick—he jumped up to steady me just as I started to topple over.

"Thanks," I said curtly. Managing to regain control, I moved away from him and started for the door. It was agony. I could hear him right behind me, but I wasn't about to let him know how much I needed a hand. Getting to the doorway, I stopped to catch my breath and my momentum.

"Just give me a minute," I said, not looking at him, though he was now standing very close.

"Last thing I wanted to do was make you mad," he said, his mouth close to my ear. "Last thing I wanted to do."

"I'm not actually ... mad." Seeing the warmth—and the humor in his eyes, I grabbed onto the doorframe for support.

He looked from me to the steep, narrow staircase ahead of us. "You do realize there's no way you're gonna make it up those stairs by yourself, darlin'."

Darlin'? How'd he know that was my endearment of choice? A stranger called me that once in a Circle K store and I just about melted into his arms and promised to bear his children. I let go of the doorway and practically fell into his arms.

"That's better," he said.

Still, it was a struggle to get up those ancient stairs. By the time we reached the landing, I absolutely had to rest. I leaned my back against the wall for support and closed my eyes, trying to drum up the gumption to go on, wondering if I should have accepted Jonah's earlier suggestion that we find a doctor.

"We could probably still find a doctor to take a look at that ankle," he said.

I opened my eyes. "I'll be fine."

I was grateful to have his arm around me now, around my waist. He practically carried me up the rest of the way. By the time we got to his door I was thinking less and less about the pain in my ankle and more and more about the feelings I was having just about everywhere else.

I'm not sure exactly what happened after that, but I'm pretty damn sure I had a lot to do with it. The next thing I knew I was leaning back against his door and he was leaning over me, his hands propped on either side of me, giving me the exact same look Harrison Ford gave that Amish woman in *Witness*. You know the one—in the barn, over the top of the car.

The old light fixtures gave off a dim, rather pink light, making it feel intimate even standing in the open hall. Neither of us spoke, we just locked gazes, I guess you'd say. And then he smiled, not with his mouth so much as with his eyes, and I was mush.

He leaned in to kiss me, softly at first, then more determined, then pulled back reluctantly as another hotel guest walked by. I put my arms around his neck and pulled his mouth back down to mine. I never knew beer could taste so much like honey. I never knew the touch of his hands could feel so electric, and, at the same time, so true. Like he knew me. Well. Like we were quite happily the only two people in the world. Like it could have been at any time or any place in history and it would still have been the same.

Energy alike, energy aligned.

"I've been wanting to kiss you all day," he whispered, nuzzling my neck. I tried to summon the will to speak, but it came out as a little moan. Still, he must have felt some hesitation on my part. He pulled back just enough to look down at me. "You want to go in where it's more private?"

"It's not that."

"Good," he said. He started kissing me again, long and lingering; the kind of kissing I dream about. The man was definitely not playing fair. Which made it twice as hard to ask him to stop. So I didn't. For awhile. But when it really started to get serious, when his hands were sliding up under my sweater right there in the hall, I snapped back to reality, this reality, and made a half hearted attempt to pull away.

"Jonah. We have to stop."

He was looking at me like I was crazy, like maybe it was a joke.

"I know it seems like I want to ... I do want to ..."

I had to look away from him. I couldn't keep looking at him and not keep touching him. Or letting him touch me. I tried to go to my quiet place, a perfect little mountain stream that babbles its way through a flower-strewn meadow on a bright spring day. It was now a torrent, raging and full of energy, ready to overrun its' banks.

"Libby?"

"Oh, God, you probably think I'm playing hard to get."

"No, I don't."

I struggled to think of something coherent to say. "It's just … Well … You know how you said we needed to have some … rules?"

"That was a really stupid idea." His voice was thick with wanting.

Okay, so there was only one way out. I had to speak the words. I owed it to my old friend, didn't I? "I promised Frank I was gonna think things through. And this is hardly … thinking things through."

I caught a flash of humor in his dark eyes. "Nothing like a good physical workout to clear your head," he said.

I had to smile. And think about it.

He was waiting, watching me closely. He was still holding me and he still looked like he just might devour me, a delicious thought.

"I'm having a major attack of the guilts," I said reluctantly.

He dropped his hands from me and I felt immediately adrift. I stared off down the hall, as if some answer would come to me, some solution.

"You think maybe you could have thought of this a little sooner?" he said.

"I'm so sorry, Jonah."

I could tell he was trying to pull himself back, hold himself in check. His eyes fastened on mine. "You're sure about this?"

I did sort of a shrug-nod.

"Okay, then. Fine."

We stared at each other a moment longer, as if each was waiting for the other to change their mind, then he followed me as I limped to my door.

"Frank knows," he said, tensely. "For God's sakes, Libby, Frank's a smart man. He already knows." And then he walked away. I stared at him as he went back to his own door, unlocked it, and went in.

I felt like I had just tumbled down into a very deep, very dark hole. Getting into my nightshirt, I felt a little numb. I climbed into bed, feeling numb. Could I still feel my legs, my feet? I wiggled my toes to be sure, groaning when I had to move the sore ankle. I stared at the ceiling, feeling numb. Maybe I was having some kind of weird attack, or a stroke or an aneurysm. Don't they say heart attacks are the real killer of women? Maybe I was in danger right now. I tossed and turned in my lumpy bed for what seemed like hours, though the clock showed it to be more like twenty minutes or so. Whatever was going on, there was only one antidote I knew about, and fortunately, it was located just down the hall.

I leaped out of bed, forgetting about my painful ankle until I hit the floor, then dragged myself over to the door and listened. From the sound of things, there was nothing going on in the hallway, no one around. I opened the door just far enough to peek my head out. The hall was empty, except for the echoes and whispers of Frank. I slipped out, still in my silky blue nightshirt, just as a man and woman I hadn't heard coming made it to the top of the stairs.

"Forgot my toothbrush," I said lamely, and they grinned and went on down the hall, disappearing around the corner. I stood for what seemed like forever outside of Jonah's door, then swung back around and limped back to my door. But I didn't go in. Instead, I paced the hall. I was an idiot. I was complicating things. I was doing the inevitable. When I heard two men laughing drunkenly as they started up the stairs, I panicked, flew back to Jonah's room (as fast as a wounded bird can fly) and knocked feverishly.

Jonah opened the door just in time. The look in his eyes made any last bit of hesitation I had just drain right out of me. He reached out for me just as the two drunks went by. "I'd like to get me some of that," one of them said, but Jonah put a finger to my lips to hush me, pulled me in, and shut the door.

His smile was so warm I could almost taste it. He gently caressed my cheek, then ran his fingers softly over my lips. I couldn't stop myself from kissing them. His gaze was so intense that I felt like he was kissing me already.

"Jonah ..." He leaned down to kiss me and I no longer knew—or cared about whatever it was I had been about to say.

"Come to bed," he said. And they were quite possibly the best three words that anyone has ever said to me. He took me by the hand and led me over to the bed, then pulled me down beside him and wrapped me up into the blankets with him. "I've been lying here thinking about you," he said, between slow, soft kisses. "About all the things I want to do to you. I think it's going to take awhile."

We looked into each other's eyes for one long heart-stopping moment and then we plunged in. And I do mean plunged.

Remember the cute little waitress who had sex with the angel in the movie, *Michael*? She came dancing out of the motel room the next morning, practically floating on air. She had no guilt, no second thoughts. Just absolute joy. I believe that's how sex was meant to be for all of us. We've just gotten lost in the shuffle.

It felt like that with Jonah. Like absolute joy.

Unfortunately, my life isn't that simple—and I'm no angel. I woke up some time later with Frank weighing heavily on my mind. There in the dark, I had to come face to face with my truth. Even if Frank knew about my feelings, I still should have cut it off with him first. I was doing to Frank what countless men do to countless women every day—I was the one having sex, but he was the one getting screwed.

Fortunately, when I turned over to try to go back to sleep, it woke Jonah up. I know this because he moved closer and pulled me against him, my back to his front. "Round two, Libby," he said softly, his mouth against my ear. (Actually, it was more like round three.) I love how it feels when you wake up like that knowing you've spent the night together in a warm and intimate conversation. Even when you were asleep, your bodies were talking. And seeing each other again, warm from the shared bed, you make love slowly, deeply. And never ever want it to end.

In the morning I slipped out of bed quietly so as not to wake Jonah, stifled a moan when my sore ankle hit the cold floor, and headed into the bathroom to try to make myself more presentable. My essence of Cupie doll was definitely back and my mascara, what was left of it, was giving me a sort of haunted effect. For that matter, maybe I was feeling a bit haunted. I scrubbed myself clean, used Jonah's comb to rearrange my do, washed various important parts, and used Jonah's toothpaste on my fingers to try to freshen my teeth.

When I went back into the room Jonah had just gotten up. He was sitting on the edge of the bed in his underwear, running one hand through his hair. In what universe was it fair that he looked so together when I was so apart?

"Morning." He smiled lazily. He strolled past me to the bathroom, reaching out to touch my cheek as he went by.

I got back into bed, shivering. I'm not entirely sure it was from being cold or ... hot. When Jonah came back and slipped under the covers with me, I couldn't wait to touch him again. He wrapped his arms around me, kissed me soundly, and then buried his face in my hair. "Too bad it's pouring outside," he said. "We may have to stay in bed all day."

I was aware of the rain on the roof and the feeling of Jonah surrounding me with some kind of special comfort. I felt safe, private, and completely secure. I snuggled into him and promptly fell asleep.

It was still pouring at a quarter past ten when I woke up again. Seeing that Jonah was still sound asleep, I staggered out of bed and got into the shower. I was just noticing how small and cramped it was in there when Jonah appeared and climbed in with me. It didn't take me long to discover that sometimes being cramped can be a very good thing.

Later, Jonah brought me my things from the other room, then went downstairs to, as he put it, "Rustle up some grub." Obviously he'd been spending way too much time with those cowboys. I fished through my clothes, but couldn't find anything that looked as inviting as his flannel shirts. On impulse, I put one on. Happily, it was long enough to cover my necessary parts and ample enough to button easily. It was soft and comforting and it felt incredibly good to be surrounded by his energy in that way. I sat down to wait for him, feeling very open and alive.

Jonah tapped on the door and I let him in. I noticed that he almost did a double take when he saw what I was wearing, but I said nothing and neither did he. He handed me my bowl of oatmeal and a plate with buttered toast, then took the rest of the food—an omelet with the works, over to the chair and sat down.

"Thanks," I said happily. I sat on the bed, curled my bare legs under me for warmth and tucked happily into my oatmeal.

Dead silence. I looked over to find Jonah looking at me. A slow smile spread across his face. "If you insist on wearing my shirt like that with nothing underneath, don't hold me responsible for the consequences," he said.

"Hmm ..." I ate a few more bites, pretending to be thinking it over, then took my spoon and began very carefully licking every last little piece of oatmeal off of it. Slowly. And trying (none too successfully) not to giggle. Poor Jonah—he didn't get a chance to finish his breakfast until it was really pretty cold. But then again, he didn't seem to mind a heck of a lot.

It went on like that all day. It felt like fate had given us a time out. It poured so hard that there was no way we even began to feel guilty about having put our quest for Janet on hold. And I'm not sure we could have left the room anyway. Being there together like that felt too much like a gift from God.

Besides, I needed to keep my ankle up, didn't I? Fortunately, I was pretty much off my feet for most of the day.

※ ※ ※

The next morning, after another hot and steamy shower, Jonah went downstairs while I finished getting ready. It was still raining, but only a light shower here and there now, so we figured we'd better get back out there and see what we could find. It didn't come back to me until I was alone in the room and the dewy feelings of our night together had started to move back to accommodate the light of day that I realized I'd had that dream again, the one in my kitchen. I covered my face with my hands, remembering—and not wanting to remember. The dark figure of the man was there again and he was reaching out for me. And it certainly wasn't Jonah.

When Jonah returned, he pulled me playfully into his arms and kissed me. But when I saw his eyes, they looked surprisingly serious. "Somebody broke into the car, Libby." He said it so gently, it took me awhile to realize what he had actually said.

"What?"

"Somebody broke in. The stuff you left on the front seat—they took it."

Was this becoming a theme in my life?

"My tote bag." Damn, they'd gotten my Josh Groban tote bag, my AAA Club Tour Book and map and my appointment book, something I always carry, don't ask me why. It had names, dates, and, most importantly, my name, address, and phone number. I pulled away, wanting to cry. The energy had just taken a turn for the worst. I could feel it in my bones. It made me scared, but most of all, it made me mad.

By the time we got out of the room, breakfast was definitely lunch. While Jonah went into the sheriff's to report our break-in and talk to them about the ranch, I dashed into the Olde Thyme Antiques Shoppe next door. Hungry as I was, I needed something to occupy my mind until we could get some food.

It was bothering me that I was suddenly so off balance, so off base. After all the time I'd spent on this, all the distance we'd come, why didn't I have more of a clue about what was going on? The dream of the night before had warned me that something was still out there, but I couldn't seem to make any kind of sense out of it right now. It was like everything had suddenly cut off—the energies that had led me to Tule Lake were no longer evident. Was this trip only about being with Jonah? Some kind of cosmic dating service meant to bring us together? I mean, I appreciate that, but come on!

I noted that the rickety little lady in the antique shop was following me around. For a fleeting second I wondered if she thought I was going to shoplift, but then she said, "Do I know you?" She seemed so excited by the prospect that I checked the shop to see if she might be talking to somebody else, but I was the only person there.

"You're somebody famous, aren't you?"

I tried to smile graciously and briefly thought of making something up so as not to disappoint her, but no, it just wouldn't do.

"Now don't tell me ..." Her soft gray eyes were alive with delight, probably the most excitement she'd had in forever. "Weren't you in that western with that fella ...? Oh, you know the one ... Big guy. Tall. He had the nicest eyes. He was trying to find that killer? You got kidnapped from the stagecoach and for the longest time, he thought they'd killed you."

She was describing just about every western ever made.

"He ended up saving you, of course. It was so romantic."

"Oh, yeah," I said. "That movie. No, wasn't me."

She went to her jewelry counter and pulled out a drawer, carefully selecting an item and bringing it over to me. "I want you to have this." She placed a small object into my hand and closed my fingers over it. It felt good to me, calming, and when I opened my fingers to look at it, I found a lovely old brooch—antique silver work framing a perfect piece of deep green malachite.

I tried to give it back, but she wouldn't let me.

"It reminds me of that lady you played," she said. "You know, the early west and all. It's one of my favorite movies. And to think you came in here today."

I left the shop feeling uncertain about what had happened. Was someone trying to tell me something? My brain was so unclear, my senses cloudy. Maybe there *was* such a thing as too much sex. I tried hard to conjure up the movie she'd been talking about, thinking maybe there were some clues there, but it could have been any one of many.

Back in the car, I closed my eyes, put my head back, and tried to relax. It was still sprinkling, the car was cozy, and I must have drifted off somewhere because I woke with a start when Jonah opened the door. Seeing his smile, it suddenly hit me—Jonah would have been a sheriff if this were the early west.

I'm happy to report that the sheriff was a good kisser. He kissed me twice. The little lady was watching and waving eagerly at us as he started the car.

"What's that about?" Jonah asked.

"Just one of my adoring fans," I said, opening my hand to show him the brooch I was still holding there. The energy of a rock can feel so good, and this one, this kind piece of malachite, was no exception.

I handed it to him and he reacted strongly when he took it. "Jeez ... What'd you do to it? It feels ... burning hot." He examined it in his open palm, frowning.

I grinned at his puzzled expression. "Some rocks sort of ... interact with me."

"Oh, it's the *energy*, right?" I almost expected him to pat me on the head like a child—a foolish child, as he handed it back to me. But he had felt it all the same.

He changed the subject, telling me that the sheriff's office hadn't been all that surprised about what we'd seen. They were aware that a single man (Spuds, no doubt) had been living there for several months, apparently alone, and this made them question what was going on out there. The ranch was leased, with little obvious ranch activity and Spuds made himself very scarce in town. It didn't add up, and the plane we saw was just another piece of evidence leading them to believe there might be more going on. But they had no evidence and absolutely no reason to believe that Janet, or anyone connected with her might be there. At this point, neither did I.

Jonah had spent too much time at the sheriff's office, we'd had no breakfast, and lunch was by this time way overdue. Hunger makes me mad or mean (sometimes both) and I was beginning to get just a little cranky. I was also feeling more and more mixed up about a multitude of things, not the least of which was how the energy had changed so dramatically that morning, how I hadn't found Janet, and how I had lied to my good friend, Frank. Any other insecurities would just have to get in line.

At the top of my list, I had a gnawing feeling that my romantic interlude with Jonah might be about to change. Reality was rearing its ugly head, and when it pops up one place, it usually pops up another. When I wanted to remain in the simplicity of my romantic fantasy, we instead had sheriff's department meetings and thieves breaking into our car. I remember once coming back from a vacation with my husband. We'd had a really special time, one of the few good times that kept us together against the odds, but when we drove into town, the first thing I noticed was the row of garbage cans out by the curb. It was garbage day and it hit me in the face. We were back to our harsh reality. Forget the fun we'd had, forget the escape we'd shared, we were back to the daily grind.

I noticed that Jonah was trying to be sensitive to my needs, and that, for some reason, only made me more anxious. What if he was trying to back out? Now that he'd bedded me, had he lost interest? Men still do that, you know. And after all, Jonah was, most definitely, a man. That thought got me so off track that my anxieties had to take a back seat while my memories of Jonah's ... attributes and abilities took over. And then, of course, those memories eventually brought me back around to my doubts about whether such delights would or should continue.

It's an exhausting, circular process.

We ate lunch at the hotel bar, no beer this time, sharing more questioning looks than actual conversation. I didn't want to risk saying anything that sounded the least bit needy, so I said very little. And I think Jonah, being a guy, probably thought he'd done something to piss me off and was tiptoeing around just about any subject that might come up. He got up to pay the bill, which actually did kind of piss me off. Did he think he ought to pay for everything?

I went around the back of the building to find the john. The last thing I saw of Jonah he was standing at the bar waiting for his change and making what appeared to be easy conversation with some guy sitting there. He can strike up a conversation with just about anyone, anytime. Must be nice, being so fucking well adjusted all the time.

I sat in the restroom stall awhile contemplating my next move. It was starting to dawn on me that my irritation with Jonah was really just a coping device. I had made myself vulnerable to him, and now I was afraid of the consequences. What do you do when you meet a man who makes you feel like you've finally found home? Losing something like that, now how would you live with it? My inner neurotic was working overtime and it had unleashed it's own little herd of fuzzy, raging insecurities that were now scurrying around my feet. I had no idea how to gain control of them. I, who had the gall to counsel other people on how to relate, was right now doing everything exactly wrong.

I spent a couple happier minutes thinking how I could write a book about that. It would probably be a best seller, make a truckload. A counselor who gives you detailed advice on how to do everything in the worst possible way, now there's a fresh concept. It would be a road map leading directly to relationship disaster. And I certainly had the experience and the credentials to back it up. Isn't that the real reason people like me become therapists, anyway? We're so in need of figuring ourselves out, we have to do it on a full time basis.

At least we're smart enough to find a way to get paid for it.

Still, one should never underestimate the power of the human spirit, especially when it's *in love*. By the time I flushed that toilet and headed out the door, I was coming out of my funk. I had kicked all those silly little insecurities to the curb and even stepped on a few of them when I got the chance. Now all I wanted to do was see Jonah again, get back to what was real and true and dear to me. We were not ending, for heaven's sake; we had just barely begun. I could feel him singing in my blood, my heart, and my soul. I couldn't wait to feel him in my arms.

Looking back I realize I should have seen it coming. I was getting that mixed up energy feeling again. It makes me anxious and unable to settle; I can't pick a mood. That's the only way to describe it. In fact, it can't really even be described. I was feeling it that afternoon but the circumstances had made me interpret it as a bad mood instead. Maybe if I'd seen it for what it was—a warning, I could have saved us both. I guess it wasn't meant to be.

When I finally went back into the bar, Jonah was nowhere in sight. I peeked outside, but didn't see him there, either. The man he'd been talking with at the bar had disappeared and the bartender was in the back doing whatever it is that bartenders do back there. When I finally managed to get his attention, he didn't have a clue. The front desk clerk was a little more helpful—he thought he might have seen him standing out by his car a few minutes earlier. He just wasn't sure.

Jonah's car was still outside with my purse and everything else a woman might need inside of it, but I had no key. The rain had backed off and a stiff wind had come up, half clearing the clouds from the sky. I fussed around another ten minutes or so, told the bartender to keep Jonah there if he should return, and started walking.

Jonah Does Some Energy Work

By the time the sheriff gave Jonah a ride back to the bar, it had been a couple hours since he'd left. He had expected to find an angry, or at least impatient Libby waiting for him by the car, but she was nowhere in sight. He pushed back the anxiety that was beginning to trouble him around the edges and went into the bar to find her. There was no one there.

"Haven't seen her for some time," the bartender said, frowning as he tried to wipe a speck from the glass he was drying. "Said to tell you to wait, though."

Thinking that maybe she'd gone back to the room, he was halfway up the stairs before remembering that he had their only key. Still, she could have had the maid or the desk clerk let her in. He went on up to the room, happily imagining he'd find her there. Instead, he found the room disturbingly empty, the bed still unmade. For a moment he let himself remember the night they'd shared, then went back downstairs to talk to the front desk clerk. No one remembered having seen her there.

He went around back to check the bathrooms. No luck. He could feel the tension starting to build now, the sense that something was out of sync. It was one thing for Elizabeth to act a little remote but quite another for her to disappear entirely.

Not knowing what else to do, he went back to his car, unlocked it and slipped into the driver's seat, realizing for the first time that she'd had no way to get in once he left. Her purse—some kind of large black leather thing, sat quite neatly on the passenger seat.

It had been a crazy day so far and he had the feeling it was about to get even crazier. Earlier, after lunch, he'd sat at the bar waiting for her to come back from the bathroom, thinking about how she was doing it again, moving back from him. How the last couple nights had been one for the record books, as far as he was concerned. And it wasn't just the sex; now there was a surprise. He'd been interested in her since that first day they'd met, when she'd plopped down at his desk, dripping wet, and told him she knew where to find the little girl. He had immediately judged her a kook and a nut case but even then, even in the middle of that thunderstorm, some part of him had known he'd need to see her again and again. They'd certainly had their ups and downs since then. And now, here she was withdrawing from him again, even though nothing but incredible things had been happening between them as far as he could tell. Had he done something? Said something?

When she hadn't returned to the bar right away, he had said goodbye to the interesting guy he'd been talking to, and headed outside to look for her. He knew the bathrooms were around the back, but he didn't want to push her or embarrass her by looking there, so he leaned against his SUV and waited.

A rattletrap car went by and he glanced up at the strange noise it made. He did a double take—the woman driving it looked directly at him for an instant, then looked away. He would have bet his favorite shirt that she was Janet Packard. She was driving slowly, as if looking for something. She turned down the nearest side street, a narrow residential street lined with aging houses. He made a quick decision and took off on foot, thinking he could catch up with her faster by cutting across some yards than by taking the time to start his SUV. There was no time to find Libby or tell her where he'd gone.

He had made it across a couple streets and several lawns—if you could call the browning mixture of weeds and bare dirt lawns, before coming face to face with a hunting rifle. And a very large man in blue and yellow striped pajamas aiming it at him.

"Hold it," the guy growled. "What the hell you runnin' from?" He puffed up his chest, a bear confronting his prey.

Jonah watched helplessly as the Bronco disappeared around the corner and sped out of sight. He still didn't know for sure exactly who he'd been following and now he wasn't going to get the chance to find out. He focused on his immediate problem. "I'm a cop," he said, knowing full well that the man would never believe him. And realizing at the same time that his I.D. was in the SUV.

"Bullshit, you're a cop."

It had gone downhill from there, and it was a good long time before he could convince the guy to call the sheriff so that someone from the department could come out and spring him. Meanwhile, so many neighbors had gathered to watch that he felt like the main attraction at a circus sideshow.

Jonah had to smile, remembering the commotion he'd caused. He and local law enforcement were practically buddies by now, what with everything that had been happening. Well, that was a good thing. He might be needing them.

He drummed his fingers on the steering wheel, still hoping and expecting that Libby would walk up to the car at any minute. He felt such longing, such an urgent need to see her and make sure that she was okay that he could barely sit still. He got out of the car and paced in the parking lot, trying to will her back to him. He could almost see her coming towards him. Somehow he knew she would no longer be distant. Everything would be right again. He'd take her in his arms and hold her till he was sure that she was really with him. Then they'd go back up to their room, something he'd been longing to do ever since they'd left it this morning. Back to bed and stay there.

But Libby still didn't come. He leaned against the car, almost mad now. Mad with worry. Mad at her if she'd gone off and done something stupid again, put herself in jeopardy. He wouldn't put it past her, despite her promises to behave herself. If she'd done something like that, he was going to really have to lay into her, put her in her place. Once she was back again. Once he knew she was safe.

Maybe she'd just gotten bored waiting for him and gone for a walk. He waited another fifteen minutes or so and then he called the sheriff.

The Truth Shall Set You Free

Sometimes I feel so pulled by energy that I can physically feel it in my body. If I don't follow the feeling, a sort of tension builds up inside of me. If I do follow it then the tension recedes and I feel more peaceful again. This was one of those times. The energy pull was really very strong. I walked in the direction that felt right, hoping it would lead me to Jonah. But I guess it wasn't Jonah who was calling me.

I hadn't walked very far before a battered beige Bronco, set high on giant tires, pulled up beside me, and the woman who was driving it reached over and threw open the passenger door. "I hear you want to talk to me," she said.

I frowned up at her, trying to make her out against the light. When I finally got a good look, I realized it was Janet Packard. Small and intense looking, she was wearing worn down jeans, an oversized sweater, and a knit cap pulled low over her eyes. A long, thick braid of dark brown hair hung down her back. She could have been a Midwest farm wife who'd just been out milking cows, but she was Janet Packard all the same.

"Janet?"

"Maybe you better get in." She sounded urgent, glancing in her rear view as if expecting to see something she didn't particularly like. Without thinking, I jumped in, and she roared off before I had even shut the door properly.

"My God, everybody thought you were dead."

"I know."

"Not me, though. I always knew you were alive."

"Yeah," she said bitterly. "That's the problem."

She turned down a side street and drove more slowly. "I'm just looking for a place we can park," she said. She pulled into an abandoned house with a weed-infested driveway and shut off the engine, then gave me her full attention. "Look, I know you've been snooping around. I know you've been to the sheriff."

"You're the one who broke into the car?"

She shook her head. "Word gets around." She fidgeted in her seat and hesitated before speaking again. "Look, I'm asking you woman to woman to just ... go away."

"But, I came here to help you."

"You really want to help me, then go away."

I started to open my mouth to tell her about all the dreams and feelings I'd had about her, everything I'd gone through to find her, but at this point it seemed a waste of time. So instead, I said, "Are you in any danger?"

"I'm okay."

"Then why don't you let people know where you are?"

"It's nobody's business."

"But, people are looking for you. You're a missing person's case. A homicide."

"And I want it to stay that way."

We sat in mute silence for awhile. Then, I had to say it. "Does it have anything to do with ... Brad Hernandez?"

She looked like I'd slapped her in the face.

"Then it's even more important we take this to the authorities."

"No."

"So, you're saying I should just go away and not tell anybody?"

"How many times do you need to hear it?"

I didn't care for her tone. I was there to save her, for God's sakes. I'd spent sleepless nights trying to help her, risked my life. How dare she not want to be saved?

"What about my friend?" I said. "We came here together looking for you. I can't just disappear, then show up again and pretend nothing happened."

"Why not? Tell him you went shopping. Guys always believe that."

"He's not an idiot," I said. "Besides, it's a criminal investigation. Whether you like it or not, Janet, you're front page news."

She slammed her hand against the steering wheel, then started rubbing her wrist like she'd hurt it. "You're messing everything up."

"Why? Has Brad tried to kill you?"

No answer.

"You've got to go to the police. They can help."

"You just don't get it, do you?" she said. "I was fine till you showed up." She revved up the old Bronco and shot us out of the driveway faster than I would have guessed it could go. "Hang on," she said angrily. She didn't even slow down enough going around the corner for me to seriously consider jumping out of the car.

"What the hell are you doing?" I had to yell to be heard over the aging engine.

"I'm just trying to get you to listen, damn it," she yelled back, as she ground the old car into the next gear.

We were out in the country now, fields on either side of us, and I was beginning to feel just a little scary. "Janet. You need to take me back. Now." I tried to sound commanding.

She slowed down a little and I thought she looked ready to cry. "I can't," she said, looking straight ahead as she drove. "I sure as hell can't. Oh, God. What am I going to do now?"

A rhetorical question. I answered it anyway. "We can talk. You can pull over and we can talk. Work something out. "

She kept driving, but looked conflicted.

"Pull over," I said. "You're just going to make things worse."

She slowed dramatically, but kept on going. "What good will that do? You'll just go back and tell everybody. And then ... Oh, God, what am I going to do now?"

She was speeding up again, driving erratically.

"Look, Janet, there's something you need to know. My friend—Jonah? He's a cop."

"Oh, shit," she said, but I realized she wasn't commenting about that. She was looking in the rear view mirror. I turned to find that the pickup Jonah and I had ridden in out at the ranch was following close behind us, flashing it's headlights.

She pulled over without a fight, then sat there pouting like a little child. I grabbed for the door handle, but her words stopped me in my tracks. "I wouldn't do that," she said. "He's got a gun."

Jason Jakes, former used car dealer, currently hopping mad, appeared at her window, his face red with anger. She rolled it down.

"I already know what you're going to say," she said.

He gave me a quick glance, then fastened in on her. "Do you? Do you, Janet?"

She stared straight ahead. It didn't deter him. "When Roger told me you took off for town, I thought he must have gone and lost his senses. No, I said, my little Janet wouldn't go and do something as stupid as that."

Janet crossed her arms angrily.

"Not my little Janet," he said again.

"Stop patronizing me."

"Stop acting like a moron."

A moment of silence. Stony silence.

"Janet?"

"Right now, I can't even think what I ever saw in you," she said.

"Yeah, well, remind me to show you later tonight."

I did a double take. He now had an evil little grin on his face and she was fighting off a smile. None too successfully.

"I just thought maybe I could talk some sense into her, warn her off," she said finally. "You know—woman to woman."

For the first time he gave me a long look and I felt chilled to the bone. Then he looked back at her. "You messed things up pretty good, Janet. What are you gonna do now?"

"Oh, I don't know, Jakes," she drawled. "Go to Disneyland?"

"I swear to God," he said, but he was grinning again.

Janet glanced at me, looking uncomfortable. "Damn it, you never should have got in the car," she said. She looked at Jason. "Couldn't we just let her go?"

Jason snorted.

"I mean it, haven't we got enough on our plate?"

Jason gave me another measured look, then reached out to touch Janet's cheek, suddenly softer. "You're willing to just throw away all our plans? Leave it all behind and take off right now?"

She sighed.

"Because trust me, we leave her here, in twenty minutes time she's gonna be back in town telling her boyfriend all about us." He straightened up, his mood suddenly more somber. "You better drive on up to that road up ahead," he said. "There's a pullout about a quarter mile down. Park there, they'll just think somebody's out on a hunt. We can take the pickup home and I'll bring Roger back later for this."

When Janet hesitated, he said, "Come on, girl, start your engines." He moved away as she did, then went back to his truck while I searched my mind for something I could do.

It was a quick trip to the turnout. Jason Jakes was at Janet's door almost immediately after we pulled in. He opened her door. "Come on out," he said. Janet glanced at me, then got out, and I had a half-second of hope they were going to leave me there. Another half-second of fear he was going to strangle me first.

"You, too," he said to me. "Get out."

I saw a car coming toward us, but it was still way down the road.

We'd look like stick figures to them at the very best. Still, I had to try. I threw open the door and darted away from him and made it, oh, ten feet down the road, and that's stretching it. Then he got hold of me, covered my mouth with a large, disgustingly hairy hand, and dragged me back to the truck. By the time the car I'd seen went by, I was nowhere in sight, tucked neatly behind the seat.

The truck smelled as strongly of hay as it had the day before, and now I could see why—there were bits of hay and what looked like some kind of horse or dog hair on the floor of the truck. Right where I was lying. So much for my Herbal Essence shampoo.

Several minutes after we started moving, I managed to pull myself up enough to see over the seat. Unfortunately, it was to look right into Jason's darkly dangerous eyes.

"Get your head down," he said. And when I didn't budge, "Janet, take the gun and point it at her if you have to, but get her back down out of sight."

Janet looked pained as she turned to look at me. "You never should have gotten in the Bronco," she said. The woman was a font of gratitude.

Jason reached over her to the glove compartment and pulled out a gun. I don't know, it was probably some kind of pistol. And even though I was pretty damn sure Janet had never tried to shoot anything in her life, I ducked my head back down.

More silence, and then I heard Janet say, "I hope somebody remembered to pick up the milk."

Jason swore.

"Damn it, Jakes, I really wanted milk with the chocolate chip cookies. Otherwise, it's just not the same. Maybe Roger could …"

"Not tonight," Jason said shortly.

More silence, then someone switched on the radio and Janet started singing along. It was "Born In The USA" by Springsteen, but she gave it sort of a plaintive blue grass spin. And, she was way off key. We stopped at what must have been the gate. Janet got out to open it and then got back in after we drove through. "I don't want any part of … doing anything," she said.

"You should of thought of that before you went off half cocked and drove into town, Janet. She wouldn't be here if it wasn't for you."

"And I wouldn't be here if it wasn't for you, Jakes."

The truck took a sharp turn, tossing me around like a lumpy bag of groceries. I was miserably twisted up behind the seat, my head now throbbing, my stomach feeling sick. I had found Janet all right, my psychic ability was still intact, but there was small comfort in that right about now. I had spent a lot of time and energy trying to save a woman who didn't want to be saved and now, was I going to die for it?

We bumped on down the road for another mile or so and then the vehicle screeched to a stop. Jason dragged me out of the truck and when he let go, I fell to the ground, my legs too shaky to hold me up. The earth smelled damp and moist from the recent rains, and by the time I righted myself, I felt like a mud wrestler who'd just lost a fight.

Janet helped me up and I caught the dismay in her brown eyes. She took a tissue out of her jeans' pocket and started trying to scrub something off my cheek. From behind me I heard Jason say, "If she's so psychic, why didn't she know better than to snoop around?" I'd heard that one before, in various incarnations. *If you're so psychic how come you don't know the lottery numbers? If you're so psychic, how come you need to ask for directions?* I had to bite my tongue.

"She was just trying to help me, Jakes," Janet said huffily. She handed me the tissue and marched over to confront him. "Don't take it out on her. I'm the one you're mad at." He grabbed her into a bear hug and she giggled, then pushed him away playfully. My God, these people were all over the map. The miracle was, they somehow kept ending up at the same location. They were either mad for each other or just plain mad. And either way, my life was now in their hands.

I took the moment to try to look around. There was a rambling 1940's style farmhouse with a wonderful wrap-around porch that would be perfect for summer afternoons and lemonade, a large reddish barn in surprisingly good shape, several pieces of rusted out farm equipment, and two overgrown corrals. We were back at Rancho Park, all right. But that was the good news, wasn't it? It would probably be the first place the police—and Jonah, would look.

Turns out it wasn't going to be all that easy. Jason took me into the barn where he moved aside what looked to be a heavy, stationary workbench, revealing a very well hidden trap door, then forced me to climb down a long ladder. Beneath the barn floor was an expansive, well-lighted underground room that must have stretched nearly the length of the barn above it. No one would ever know it was there. The dirt floor was smooth and even and there were plants everywhere, lots of them, growing lush and green under banks of artificial light. It was obviously a big time operation—marijuana, and it was almost ready to harvest. I'd seen it before. Back in my wild mushroom days.

He left me alone, slamming shut the trap door. I listened hopelessly as the bench above me was shoved back into place. Grateful they at least hadn't left me in the dark, I prowled the room, hoping for some alternate exit. There was a card table with a stack of outdated Sports

Illustrated magazines, a couple plastic patio chairs, a tiny enclosed toilet and basin combo with a sliding door, and a locked metal cabinet with double doors. Probably where they kept all their guns. Or their dead bodies.

I sat down miserably in one of the chairs, put my head on the table and tried not to panic. Times like this ... Well, I'd never had times like this before hooking up with Jonah. I was on uncharted ground. I thought of him, of the wild course our relationship had taken so far, and of his tenderness and passion the last couple nights when what I'd always waited for finally seemed to be coming true. It felt so far away now that it almost seemed like a dream. And then, of course, I thought of Peeps, who was probably right now dozing peacefully in his own cozy kitty condo. That really did me in.

Maybe an hour later, Janet and Jason reappeared. Janet bounced off the ladder as if she was happy to see me, while Jason, after coming part way down reached up to take a cardboard box from Spuds, who handed it to him from the top of the ladder.

Spuds' face turned pale when he caught sight of me through the open trap door. He threw three army issue sleeping bags and some pillows down from the opening, then climbed down the ladder. "How you doin'?" he said to me, obviously uncomfortable. He followed Jason over to the table and said something low and urgent to him.

Jason glanced in my direction. "Don't look at me," he said shortly. "It was Janet's idea to bring her back from town. Some women go shopping. Not Janet."

Janet, who was pulling things out of the box, used the opportunity to punch him lightly in the arm. "Shut up, Jakes," she said.

Jason grabbed her by the hand and pulled her into him. "You shut up," he said, kissing her to make his point. Janet pretended to pull away, so he kissed her again.

Spuds sighed, as if he'd seen it enough times to be out of patience with them. He walked away looking stormy then turned back to confront the situation. "I don't give a damn how it happened," he said to Jason, "She shouldn't be here."

"You think?" Jason didn't try to hide his sarcasm. He let go of Janet reluctantly and she went back to unloading the box, pulling out sandwiches, potato chips, and bottled water.

"I didn't sign up for ... something like this," Spuds said.

"I told you, I'll handle it."

Spuds nodded, looking thoroughly unhappy.

"Have some food, Roger." Janet was offering him a thick sandwich, but he shook his head and headed for the ladder. Climbing out of the room, he poked his head back in one more time to take another look at me as if to be sure I was really there.

"Call me," Jason said, holding an imaginary phone to his ear, and Spuds nodded. No one spoke as we watched him disappear at the top, then close the trap door. The bench above us slid back into place and for just a second or two you could hear his footsteps as they faded away across the barn floor above. I wondered if anyone else felt trapped like I did. It was like being in a grave. You couldn't get out.

Janet spread a blue cloth on the table then set out flowered blue and white paper plates. Humming, she pulled the sandwiches out of their plastic wrap and arranged them artfully on one of the plates, layering them to make three tiers. "Jakes thinks we're likely to get visitors tonight," she said pleasantly, "so we decided to bunk down here with you, just in case." She put a stack of giant homemade cookies on another plate, then set it exactly in the center of the table, an edible centerpiece. There was, of course, no milk.

"I usually cook more gourmet," she said apologetically. "Julia Child's still my favorite. I don't care what kind of fancy-smancy stuff those new guys try to pull off, you just can't beat Julia for taste and presentation. It broke my heart when she died."

Jason seated himself at the table, picked up one of the sandwiches and examined it carefully, then made a face and put it back down. "God, Janet, was this the best you could do?"

She marched over to him, grabbed the plate out from under his nose and brought it to me, offering me a sandwich; hand cut slices of homemade whole wheat bread, thick layers of ham, and some kind of white cheese. "Provolone," she said happily. "Imported, of course."

I took a sandwich, which seemed to make her day.

She spoke conspiratorially. "Last night it was steak tartare. The night before that we had wild duck with plum sauce. Doesn't matter. He still does nothing but complain."

"What's that?" Jason's ears had perked up.

Janet walked back to the table and plopped the half-empty plate in front of him. "If you don't like it, don't eat it." She sat opposite him, leaned back in her chair, crossed her arms, and stared at him; a challenge.

As much couple counseling as I've lived through over the years, I'm still always interested in seeing how power plays work out and this time at least, she appeared to have won. He picked up a sandwich and slowly started to munch.

Janet got a satisfied little smile on her face. "Jakes and I have some ... trust issues," she said. Since she was still locking eyes with Jason, it took me a moment to realize she was talking to me. She swung around to look in my direction. "Wait a minute. You're a counselor, aren't you?"

No use denying it. They'd seen my appointment book, after all.

"Jakes needs some serious work," she said. "Do you do tune ups?"

Jason peeled off the crust on his half eaten sandwich and threw it with disgust on his plate. "I don't go in for that touchy-feely crap," he said.

"Maybe you should. Maybe instead of growing pot and kidnapping people ..."

"Shut up, Janet." His tone of voice would have frightened me, but Janet seemed immune.

She got up and started wandering around the room, her irritation making her move. "And getting paid to ... Well ..."

"Janet."

This time it stopped her. She circled back around and ended up near me. "You see what I'm dealing with," she said. She squatted down next to where I was sitting on the floor. "So ... Give me some suggestions. What can we do?"

"Yeah," Jason said, "how can we fix Janet?"

She threw him a dirty look, then looked earnestly at me, obviously expecting a serious response.

"This is hardly the time or the place." I felt I was stating the obvious.

Jason got up to throw his plate away, then came towards us. "I thought you were all hot to help her." He was ruthlessly jabbing at his teeth with a toothpick. He was also jumping back over to her side. It was like watching a tennis match where you could never quite tell who was ahead. Just when you thought one side was winning they would purposely miss the ball. Twice.

"Therapy isn't something you can turn on and off. I'd need to spend some time with you. Explore things in depth."

"So?" Jason was now standing over me.

"I'd need to feel safe."

Surprisingly, he backed off.

Janet settled down beside me, resting her back against the wall like I was doing.

"It might soften him up," she said to me in a low voice. "You know. Use your counselor stuff. It might help."

I doubted that, but I wasn't going anywhere. Besides, it just might be the biggest therapy challenge I'd ever face. "Okay," I said, "Why not? Why don't you start by telling me how you feel, Janet?"

"Oh, here we go," Jason said. He walked back over to his chair and sat down heavily. He had once again jumped back over the net.

Janet, however, was showing some interest.

"Why don't you begin at the beginning, tell me how you met?" I was pretty sure I already knew.

"Oh, that." At first I didn't think she'd say anything more, but then, "Well, it was when Brad ..."

"Damn it, Janet, don't go telling her that stuff."

"Well, it's how we met."

"We saw each other at the house a few times before that."

"Yeah," she said firmly, "but we only really ... got to know each other after Brad ..." Her voice trailed off at Jason's expression.

He jumped up and came over, joining us full force. "All you need to know is I treat her like a queen." He was pointing an angry finger at me. "And I didn't do anything to her, did I? She's still alive, isn't she? You see any marks on that girl?" He looked down at her affectionately. "You're still here, aren't you, baby doll?"

What, did he think that should earn him points for being a sweet, romantic guy? Apparently Janet thought so. "He always had a sort of ... thing for me," she said softly.

I was at a loss as to where to go from there. I was in a maze with no way out. I don't think any of my textbooks or journals had ever addressed a situation quite like this, or even any of my professors. The class would have had to be called something like "Hostage Therapy," only I was the hostage. And besides, what Janet needed I couldn't possibly give her. What Janet needed was a lawyer. That, and a healthy dose of common sense.

I tried to start again. "It's ... uh ... unusual to have a relationship based on ... what yours is based on, Janet. But ... Well, let's face it, being with someone ... Being put into a situation like you're in would quite naturally cause you to feel a lack of trust."

Surprisingly, she smiled. "Oh, no," she said, "It's not me with the problem. It's Jakes. Jakes doesn't trust me."

And it went on from there. Actually, though, it helped to have something to think about besides my predicament. But once we unrolled the sleeping bags and tried to sleep, I had nothing left to block my fear. Every scary movie and every true crime program I'd ever seen came rushing back to taunt me. For all I could tell, I was very close to being dead.

When I finally did drift off, it didn't last long. I woke up to the sound of the two of them talking. They were lying side by side, far across the room from me, and I couldn't begin to hear what they were saying. When Jason got up and went into the bathroom, it made me antsy. Would he try to kill me in my sleep? And would Janet do anything at all to try to stop him? I wished I could have counted on her to be on my side, since I'd done so much to try to help her, but after the tennis match I'd been witnessing I had no idea where anybody stood. Especially me.

Jason was making rather unattractive noises in the bathroom. I glanced over at Janet only to find her looking back at me. Seeing I was awake, she came over.

"Lactose intolerant," she said, grinning. "He never should have had all that cheese." Just then there was a loud explosion from behind the bathroom door, followed by two smaller bursts. "Oh, God," she said. "Oh, God!" She sank down beside me, hopelessly trying to control her giggles.

I sat up, feeling rocky. "Is it morning yet?"

She shook her head. "More like 2 a.m. I can't sleep either." She crossed her legs, dropped a small brush on the floor near where she sat, and then began loosening her tangled hair from its' untidy braid.

About then, we heard the toilet flush. Jason came out of the bathroom, turned back to close the door behind him (Thank God) and then frowned at Janet when he saw she was sitting with me. He mumbled something that sounded like "Don't say a wait oolong" which, I think, must have meant, *Don't stay away too long*, because Janet nodded her head and said, "I won't, Sugar Bear." He shuffled off to his sleeping bag and settled down on it heavily. I swear he was snoring as soon as he lay down.

"Sleeps like a tank." She was watching him affectionately. She grabbed her brush and started trying to run it through her hair, then stopped, looking thoughtful. "I'm gonna talk to him," she said. "It's only another week or two before the crop's ready. Maybe once we move on, we could just ... I don't know, drop you somewhere?" She reached over to pat my hand. "I'm sure we can work something out." She smiled as if she'd settled everything. It didn't matter if the idea made little sense. She was happy about it all the same.

If I was going to have any chance at all, I knew I'd better start. A glance in Jason's direction and another loud snorting snore and I was quite convinced he wouldn't wake up any time soon. "Don't you ever worry he might ... turn on you?"

It took her awhile to answer. "I've thought about it some." She set herself to her work, concentrating on her brush strokes, not looking at me. "It's not to his advantage though, is it? This way, he's got me and the money. Everything he wants. You know, it's one of those win-win situations." But the look she gave me told me it wasn't only Jason who had trust issues.

She gestured toward the plants. "We've got it all worked out. We'll have all the profit from this, plus we've got the ten thousand Brad already paid him."

"To kill you."

She looked pained, but ignored my remark. "Lord knows how much that pot is worth." She spent a few moments in happy anticipation.

"And then what, Janet? Even if Brad never figures out you're still around, he's not likely to miss the fact that Jason ran off with the profits."

"By then we'll be long gone."

"What about your two little girls?"

Sorrow flitted across her face. "But I can't go back now. Brad knows I know too much. I could put him away for a long, long time." She leaned forward anxiously. "Have you heard anything about them?" The need in her eyes made me want to say yes.

"Just that they're with your sister. And, I saw their pictures. Very pretty."

She nodded proudly, for a moment a mom rather than a fugitive. "Another month or so ..." Her eyes were teary and she sounded like she was trying to convince herself more than me. "It's been hard, but ... Jason's already got a place lined up, a safe place. For all of us."

"You really want to expose your children to a killer?"

"He's not a killer. He hasn't killed anybody."

"Yet." *What about me?*

She was now braiding her hair back into one large, magnificent braid. From the deftness of her fingers, I could tell she'd done this many times.

"Besides," I said, unable to stop myself any longer, "killer or not, he's a slime bag, Janet."

She gasped.

"Before this, he sold stolen cars. Has he ever done an honest day's work in his entire life?"

She stared at me. "I didn't think counselors were supposed to talk like that."

"I'm not your counselor. I'm your hostage."

We locked eyes and I had her. She wasn't stupid, just naïve.

I pressed my point. "Brad, Jason ... What do you see in guys like that?"

She looked almost embarrassed and then I remembered the way she and Jason had played their game back and forth, back and forth. It didn't matter what Jason was, she was smitten with him. Reason didn't enter into it, something even I could attest to and understand.

"I guess I haven't had much luck in men," she said. "My ex was kind of okay. He was just ... Well, I guess he was just too laid back. He didn't have any ..." She searched for the word, then came up with it smiling, "pizzazz."

I sat there remembering the old leather watch and what it had told me. "He ever commit any crimes?"

"Just a speeding ticket or two."

"Then maybe laid back would have been okay."

Looking crestfallen, Janet began examining her toenails. Apparently they were fascinating, because she didn't speak for several minutes.

I closed my eyes, trying to connect to my inner knowing, trying to feel just a smidgen of my inner peace. It was there, of course, but I had been shutting it out. Fear and imminent danger will do that. It's hard to fight. But there was something there, something quite palpable. I was in that rough patch now, but for all their current power over me, I suddenly understood without a doubt that of everyone at Rancho Park, I was the one with the strength. I just couldn't quite get to it right now, it wasn't yet time.

As if on cue, Janet said casually, "So, what's it like, being psychic?"

I opened my eyes.

She was fiddling with her feet again, not looking at me. "What? Did some voice tell you I was here?" She looked up at me almost timidly.

"How did you know about me being psychic?"

She shrugged. "Brad told Jakes to watch out. Said that you might be snooping around. He said you had some kind of weird ability to find people. 'Course he thought I was already long gone and Jakes figured it was no big deal, us being all the way up here and everything, but then when you showed up in town ... I suppose you saw it in the cards or something?" She was trying to joke.

"I don't use cards."

"Oh."

"I don't use anything. It was more like a feeling. And dreams." I sighed heavily, remembering. "Lots and lots of dreams. Actually, Janet, the voice I heard in my dreams—sometimes it was you."

"Oh." She sounded more than a little spooked.

"I thought it meant you wanted help."

Neither of us spoke for awhile, except Jason who let out a series of low, grinding snores, strangely musical in nature. Seriously, the man should record a CD.

Janet glanced over at him, then continued. "At first, I was afraid he was going to kill me. But that was only the first day or so. Then I realized he didn't really want that. He didn't have the heart. And, besides, I knew what he really wanted." She smiled, but not happily. "Well, at first, it was really weird, you know, and I thought I'd just try to save my life." She was back to her toes again. "Then I realized I somehow wanted to be with him, too. There was this magnetic pull, you know?" She was embarrassed now.

"It's okay," I said, "I've been there."

"Kidnapped?"

"In love when I didn't understand why." My throat tightened. "Sometimes things are just meant to be." I was immediately off somewhere else. Had I met Jonah only to fall in love with him and then lose him? I had to struggle to force myself back to the moment at hand. "Sometimes there was another voice in my dreams," I said, reluctantly. "It was a man's voice."

"Oh, God. Not Brad? You don't mean Brad?" Our eyes met and we both had the same thought at the same time.

She started looking around, as if he'd suddenly pop out of some corner. "If he finds us, it's not death we have to worry about," she said raggedly. "It's what he'll do to us in between."

Her words made me suddenly nauseous. Did she really have to say it just like that? Word for word? The dream—the nightmare—was coming true and I had no idea how to stop it. I got up and started moving around the room, trying to walk off my sick feelings, and wondering if I was actually going to throw up.

She followed me, caught up with me. "So, what happens next?" Her voice was tight, intent.

"Maybe I did something lousy last time out and my karma's coming back to bite me."

She looked pained. "But, what happens next? In the dream, I mean." Her voice was higher now, the panic was palpable, and I couldn't afford to catch it.

"Nothing," I said. "I don't know because I always woke up." I started moving again. I was talking to heaven now, walking in a circle while Janet stared at me like I'd gone off freaking mad. "I never wanted this," I said. "Finding people? Did I ever even once say I wanted to try something like that? I don't think so." I had to stop myself from shaking a fist at the unseen energies above me. After all, they were still my friends.

Just then, Jason sat up. "Why the hell hasn't Roger called? I told him to call and let me know what happened. Why the hell hasn't he called?" He got up, still half asleep, and stared at us, as if we'd know, then climbed the ladder while Janet and I stood frozen where we were. The trap door wouldn't budge, of course, but he beat on it all the same.

Eventually he came back down and started fishing through his supplies, finally pulling out a cell phone. Dialing, he seemed to wait a very long time before someone picked up. "Where the blazes have you been?" He stopped to listen, glancing at me. "No, Roger, she's still here. What did you expect?" He turned away from us, as if it would give him some privacy. "When did they show up?" And then, "How many?"

"How many what, Jason?" Janet sounded urgent and innocent at the same time.

He motioned impatiently for her to be quiet. "A helicopter?" He scratched his scalp in agitation. "Uh huh ... Uh huh ... So, did they come into the barn?"

"Jakes ..."

"Janet, I can't talk to both of you at the same damn time."

Janet relented, backing off a bit.

He went back to his call. "Yeah ... Well, I guess we got no choice but to wait it out, then. Like a bunch of fuckin' rats in the cellar." He sighed, then listened to whatever Spuds said. "You're gonna have to stay cool, Roger, that's the only way it's gonna work out. You got that?" He hung up and turned abruptly to glare at Janet. "Cops were out, just like we thought," he said. "Now are you pleased with your handiwork?"

"Who?" I said. "Who came out?"

He ignored me, but spoke to Janet. "Two sheriffs, Janet. In a helicopter so they didn't have to get through the gate. It's just a good thing they got no cause for a search warrant or we'd be big time screwed." He glanced sharply at me. "Two sheriffs and one .... boyfriend. Damn it, Janet, of all the women you could have kidnapped, you had to pick one whose boyfriend is a cop?"

For a moment it felt like a gift from the gods, comforting somehow. Just to know Jonah had been close, maybe even overhead, gave me some kind of hope, and I wanted to believe it was some kind of sign that help was on the way. After that, though, reality set in and it made me even lonelier, and more afraid. Jonah had come, but he had also gone away. Would he ever come back? And if so, how could it possibly be in time?

Sleep was even more elusive after that. When I woke up for the umpteenth time and got up to stretch my anxious legs, I found Janet sitting at the table looking positively fried. "At least it's finally morning," she said, munching halfheartedly on a leftover cookie. "God, I'd kill for a glass of milk."

I could hear Jason in the bathroom again. Sounded like he was directing a Souza march.

It was right about then that we heard sounds above us, the workbench being moved, the trap door suddenly thrown open. For a split, very hopeful second, I imagined it would be Jonah coming to rescue me. All would be well. I could almost see us, in slow motion, happily embracing, safe at last. But it wasn't Jonah, or even the cops. It was an obviously nervous Spuds, and just behind him, Brad Hernandez carrying what looked to me to be a very big gun.

"Ladies ..." he said grandly. He came down the steps like a king at his coronation; like he'd been waiting a long time for something like this.

In the bathroom, we heard the toilet flush, then Jason stumbled out into the room, still fastening his jeans. He looked stunned. Flabbergasted. Flummoxed.

"I'm not all that interested in seeing the real you," Brad said. "Zip it up." He strolled toward Janet, who got up from where she was sitting, her face like death. He reached out and touched her cheek with one finger, as if testing her skin. "You look remarkably well for somebody who's been dead a couple of months."

"Bite me," she said.

A self-satisfied look spread across his face. "Same old Janet."

He turned to me and smiled a cold smile, if that's possible. "I should thank you, Ms. Brown. If it wasn't for all your idiotic snooping around, I never would have figured out that Janet was still alive. Or had an inkling where to find her." And then to Jason, "What'd you do the other day? Hide her in the closet?"

"I should have told you, Brad," Jason said. "I know that now. I just ... Well, one thing led to another and ..."

"She'll do that to you," Brad said.

"Hold on a minute." It was Spuds, still lingering by the ladder. We all turned to look at him as if we'd forgotten he was there. "I don't get it. What's going on?" He was looking at Brad. "I called you last night because I was worried they were closing in on us and everything was going up in smoke. But now this ..."

"You called him?" Jason sounded mad. "I never even told you his name." He looked at Brad. "I swear to God, Brad, I never even told him who he was working for."

"I noticed one time where you kept the number," Spuds said apologetically. "You told me last night to handle things and I just thought this was something the boss ought to know about."

"My only loyal employee," Brad said.

"But the thing is, Mr. Hernandez, I didn't sign up for ... something like this."

"If you want your share of the profits, you'll do what I say." Brad's eyes flickered back to Jason. "You should have done the deed when you were supposed to, Jason. Now you've got two fish to fry."

I heard a strange little sound. I think it came from me.

"Roger," Brad said. "I want you to go on upstairs and make sure the coast is clear. Can you do that?"

Roger nodded uncertainly.

"You come right back like you're supposed to and I'll make sure you get another gig."

"Another gig?"

Brad nodded. "You do what I say and I'll hook you up with one of my other operations. You know, make sure you get what's coming to you."

Was I the only one who shivered when he said that?

Spuds looked from one to the other of us, his look a question.

"Go on now," Brad said.

He slowly started climbing the ladder.

"Five minutes." Brad called to him, glancing at his Rolex.

Spuds gave us a last look as he disappeared at the top of the ladder. I wondered if he'd have the sense—or the guts, to make a run for it or contact the police.

It was a moment before anyone spoke. "I've been thinking about the best way to do this, Jason," Brad said finally. "Either way, I think it's got to involve fire."

I'm not normally the fainting type, but I had to fight to keep my balance. Since I was a tiny child, nothing has frightened me more than fire. I started gulping air like there was no tomorrow. Well, technically, there might not be.

"Fire?" Jason's voice sounded more like a croak. He crossed his arms, trying to show some backbone but doing a piss poor job of it. "Damn it, Brad. I'm no killer."

"You should have told me that before you took my twenty thou."

Janet gasped. "Twenty?" She looked angrily at Jason. "You said it was ten, Jakes."

He wouldn't look at her, but Brad did and he looked positively gleeful. "Screwed again, huh, babe?"

She launched herself at Brad, furiously trying to slap his face, but he deflected her rather easily, grabbing her by the arm and shoving her back towards me. She slumped against me for a second then forced herself to stand tall. I felt a moment of pity for her, then a moment of pride. I put my arm around her and we hung onto each other for dear life.

"Charming," Brad said. "If only I had a camera."

"Jakes," Janet said. "Do something."

"Yeah, Jason, show some balls," Brad drawled.

The look Jason gave us told me there wasn't much we could count on from him.

"I told you, Brad. I can't do this."

"But it's going to look like you did. Nobody's even going to know I was here." He glanced up the stairs to make sure Roger wasn't there yet. "Wouldn't want to scare the help," he said. "Now where were we? Oh, yeah ... Jason's so distraught over burning you two alive that he turns the gun on himself and dies up there just outside the barn. Imagine the story in the papers—two kidnappings, a major drug operation, a triple homicide. With the cops closing in he was in a corner. What else could he do?"

"Triple homicide?" Jason said.

Brad nodded toward the trap door where Spuds was last seen. "Perfect crimes don't have witnesses," he said, as if we were stupid. He turned his lazy eye on the two of us. "It's the lack of oxygen that will get you first. Trapped underground in a fire. But don't worry. You'll be dead by the time the fire actually reaches you."

I looked at him, searching his eyes for madness, but found only an eerie calm. A sociopath if I'd ever seen one; a sociopath with complete control over us. Silly of me, I know, but in that hopeless moment I decided to try to reason with him. "What about your career, Mr. Hernandez? Your reputation?"

"That's exactly why I have to kill you," he said, all too calmly.

"But you can't possibly think you can get away with ... something like this."

The look he gave me froze me down to my toes.

He looked delighted, as if I'd given him the perfect set up line. "Going to stop me with your psychic powers? I can't wait to see this," he said. "Go on, Ms. Brown. Work your magic."

I was now angry and scared at the same time. "It just isn't ... meant to be." Even as I spit out the words I knew it sounded really lame but saying it felt very important anyway. My inner knowing was kicking in at last and there was a feeling of it ringing in my ears, that it wasn't meant to be. Right along with the heart ripping, ice cold fear. Let's face it, there was as lot of noise ringing in my ears right about then.

"Oh come on now. Is that all you've got? You're going to have to do better than that," he said. He raised his gun almost playfully and took sight at Janet. "Might be more fun to just shoot you first," he said.

I heard two sounds right about then—Janet frantically sucking in her breath, and the sound of running feet above us in the barn.

Spuds appeared at the trap door, looking panicked. "Somebody's coming, Boss." His voice was tight, high. "That warning bell on the gate that rings up at the house just keeps on ringing. Like it's stuck. Like somebody's trying to break through."

"Oh, fuck."

"Happened once before." Spuds looked back over his shoulder. "Remember, Jason? That time the brakes went out on the truck and you just plowed on through? It made the same sound then."

Jason nodded. "Somebody's on their way, for sure. Or will be soon. It's not the Avon lady, Brad."

For the first time Brad looked a bit uncertain. He backed towards the ladder and waved his gun at us wildly, seemingly out of control. As scary as his calm demeanor had been, this one was scarier. He was like an explosion, ready to go off. "You two—over there." He was talking to Janet and Jason, leaving me out. He pointed toward the end of the room where the plants were, the part of the room that was farthest from the ladder. "Move it," he said when they hesitated. "Move it or die." It was pretty obvious by this time that they were going to die anyway, but I wasn't about to point that out to him.

Jason tried for Janet's arm, but she pulled away from him and moved toward the plants on her own. She ripped an especially nice leaf off the nearest plant. "You've got nobody to do your dirty work this time, Brad. For once, you can't just sit back on your lazy ass and ..."

"Shut up."

She tore the leaf in two and threw it down. "Fuck you," she said softly.

"Been there, done that."

They stared at each other like nobody else was in the room.

Jason broke the silence with a loud belch. Janet rolled her eyes in his direction and then started shaking her head. Boyfriends. She really knows how to pick 'em.

Brad ignored her and looked at me instead. The dark, calm, scary look was once again in his eyes. I tried to step away from him, but he reached for my arm. My initial reaction was to struggle but it soon hit me that being out of the underground room, no matter what the consequences, was bound to be a lot better than staying behind.

Brad glanced up at Roger, who was once again looking down from the opening. "Time's a wasting, Roger. Pull her up." He forced me to start climbing, pushing me from behind in ways that made me want to try to speed up just to get away from him. I could hear Janet saying something from below but couldn't quite make out the words. My head was buzzing with fear.

Roger lifted me out onto the barn floor and let me go.

"You let her get away, you'll rue the day," Brad said, climbing out onto the floor.

Roger quickly took hold of me again. "Sorry," he said, low enough so that only I could hear.

When Brad grabbed hold of me again, I felt the horror really beginning to set in. He was leaving Janet and Jason to die in the basement. He was taking me with him wherever he intended to go and that could mean anywhere and anything. The nightmare wasn't going away. It wasn't getting any better. If anything, it was getting worse.

Spuds shut the trap door. As if from a distance I heard Brad order him to move the workbench back into place, heard him refuse. He ordered Spuds to pour kerosene over the trap door, and once again, I heard him refuse. I heard the explosion from Brad's gun and watched, sickened, as Spuds fell back not far from where we stood.

Then we were out the door and Brad was running, forcing me along with him towards the Cessna, though I couldn't see much right about then. My hair was in my eyes and I was gasping to catch my breath. When we got to the plane Brad somehow got me up into it, although I must have been a dead weight right about then. He shoved me into one of the back seats, pulled the door shut behind us and sank into the pilot's seat.

I managed to lean forward in the seat a bit, trying to look out the window, hoping to see something, anything. At first there didn't seem to be anybody about. I wondered if Spuds had given a false alarm in hopes of stalling things. Since he gave up his life, I hoped not. But then I saw it, a flash of color out of the corner of my eye. An SUV—a familiar dark green one. Going breakneck speed up the road and across the field, it was heading straight for the plane. Thank God that Jonah has a four-wheel drive.

And thank God Brad hadn't fastened my seat belt. I guess that when you're in a hurry and you're planning to kill somebody anyway, you don't much care if their seat belt is securely fastened and their seat is in the upright position. Hearing first one of the propellers roar to life and then the second one, I tried to propel myself up from my seat, but just then the plane lurched forward, throwing me back into it again. I struggled on, pulling myself up at last and then swung haphazardly at Brad, delivering a glancing blow against the side of his head. It wasn't a direct hit or even a really hard one, due to the angle I had to work with, but he hadn't seen it coming. It at least served to slow him down. He tried to fight me off, but I kept at him. Anything was better than letting the plane take off because then I'd be done for sure. He finally had to let go of the controls, turning to get hold of me, grabbing one of my wrists so tightly, I though it was going to break. The plane shimmied and slowed to a stop, swinging around almost forty-five degrees as it did so. With more power than I ever thought I had, I managed to wrench myself free from his grip, then fell back against the seat, exhausted.

Swearing, he turned back to the controls, but it was too late. Jonah had pulled his SUV directly in front of us, blocking the plane's path. Strange as it sounds, it wasn't until I saw his car there that the full and awful impact of the situation I'd been dealing with finally became real. I am not brave and I don't do extreme sports—unless you count some of my relationships. Truth is, it's hard to even drag me to an action movie most of the time. They're just too violent. But here I was, in the middle of my own very scary little independent action film, and getting really very worried about the ending.

I couldn't see Jonah, but I could hear his voice and it was strong and certain and sounded like home. "Seems like you've got a problem, Hernandez."

"Fucking bastard," Brad growled. He looked back at me as if he was weighing his options and when I saw him pick up his gun, I half expected him to shoot me point blank. "Come on," he said, waving it in my general direction, "Make yourself useful." He reached back to drag me forward, cursing when I fought him, then opened the door a bit so Jonah could get a look at us both.

Jonah had his gun drawn, held steady with both hands, pointed straight at us. I thought I noticed a slight reaction as he saw who was really in the plane, that I was there, too. But he didn't give himself away.

Brad opened the door all the way, holding me in front of him, using me as the proverbial shield.

"Don't be a fool," Jonah said. "It's over and you know it."

"The hell it is. Put the gun down and move back."

"Let her go."

Brad put the gun to my head. "You want me to kill her?"

A long moment went by during which I thought I saw my life before my eyes. The good parts, anyway. Then, slowly and reluctantly, Jonah lowered his gun.

"Now. Put it on the ground and move back."

Another long moment.

"On the ground." I could now feel the gun against my head.

He was upping the ante and Jonah did what he said.

Brad then jumped to the ground, taking me with him, keeping me in front of him.

Sounds hard to do, but small planes are surprisingly low to the ground. And it seemed almost effortless for him. Must have had a lot of practice.

There was a split second when Jonah looked directly into my eyes and I grabbed onto the strength I saw there and felt its comfort. It was so strong that it felt as if he had actually reached out to me. Then, his expression changed and someone different was there; someone I'd never seen before. Instead of the man I'd come to know so intimately, I saw someone totally focused, ready to pounce. A bystander probably would have been surprised to know we had ever even met.

"You better think twice, Hernandez," he said. "You want a murder charge on top of everything else?"

"They'll have to catch me first. Besides, I've got ... insurance." He illustrated by sliding his hand up disgustingly close to my breasts and pulling me back harder against him. It was your typical swaggering B movie crap. Who writes this stuff, anyway?

I squirmed against him, trying to loosen his grip, which only made it worse. "He killed Spuds," I said.

I was just going to add that Janet was actually still alive, when Brad said, "Shut up. Just shut the fuck up." I saw the anger in Jonah's eyes. And the realization—after one killing, another would be so much easier. Nothing left to lose.

Brad made Jonah move back even further and then, once he was satisfied, he moved us forward like a couple running a sack race, quickly scooped up Jonah's gun, and pocketed it. He glanced at the plane and considered his options. "Guess we're going to have to take your car." He started moving slowly backwards towards the SUV, pulling me with him, his arm tight around my waist, then stopped suddenly, when Jonah started to follow. "Last chance," he said coolly. "Back off, or she dies."

In that surreal moment, something even more surreal—as we got closer to Jonah's car, I could see that the entire right front and side of it was smashed and battered; so smashed and battered that there was no way Brad would be able to open the passenger side door. A glance at Jonah and I was pretty sure he was thinking the same thing.

"You better rethink your options," Jonah said, sounding strangely casual in the midst of the mayhem. "The sheriff's already on his way." He nodded toward the gate, then glanced up at the sky. "They'll be swarming all over this place any minute now."

"They'll let us through," Brad said. "Unless you want her blood on your hands."

"I'll hunt you till my dying day, Hernandez." More B-movie stuff, but it sounded infinitely better coming from the Good Guy.

Brad started moving back with me again, noticing the problem with the car door for the first time. "Shit," he said, "Shit, shit, shit." He switched directions, moving me with him toward the driver's side, and right then, right at that dark, seemingly hopeless moment, something remarkably unexpected happened—I got a very clear vision of Sandy Roget in my somewhat clouded head. She was sitting across from me in my cozy little office, yattering on about some problem or other. It didn't matter what. What mattered was the vision of her big white, pearly teeth. They were practically snapping at me.

I knew exactly what I needed to do. When Brad tried to shift me around so that he'd be able to get us into the driver side door, I saw my opportunity. I wiggled in his grip just enough to get a bead on his ear, and then, I bit him. With a vengeance I never knew I had. It wasn't lethal, but it was enough of a shock to do the trick, shock him, and make him mad.

With an angry groan, he shoved me away from him so hard that I fell to the ground. He grabbed for the door, trying to open it. I thought that Jonah looked almost amused as he went after him. The two men grappled with the gun, then it spun out of Brad's hands, landing a few feet away. They fell to the ground fighting and I could see that Brad was trying hard to reach the gun, but each time he almost got it, Jonah yanked him back out of range, like he was playing with him, cat and mouse. When Brad tried to get the other gun out of his pocket, Jonah was too quick for him, pinning him on the ground, his knee against Brad's back.

Jonah looked up at me. "Handcuffs," he said. "In the glove compartment."

I stood there. A rock. Clueless.

Brad tried to rise up one more time, but Jonah slammed him back down again. "Elizabeth …." He was talking to a child. "There are some handcuffs in the glove compartment. Get them for me, please."

I nodded, trying to break the fog of unreality that was keeping me frozen. I forced myself to the car, went automatically to the passenger door, then, realizing my mistake, reversed direction and opened the driver's door, leaned in across the seats and found the cuffs. By the time I made it back to him, I noticed that Jonah had already reclaimed his own gun from Brad.

The look in his eyes when I handed him the cuffs surprised me—if there was any impatience there, I certainly couldn't see it. "Thanks," he said, giving me an almost smile. He sounded like this was something he did every day. Then again, maybe it was.

I watched, a little awe struck as Jonah did his thing. Everything he did seemed to be an economy of motion. Completely in control, he yanked Brad to his feet, took him over to the Cessna, forced him to sit down, and then handcuffed him to a leg of the small plane. And though I couldn't hear what he was saying very well from where I stood, I think he may have read him his rights.

After that, he came straight to me. He took me by the shoulders and I felt strong energy streaming back into me, like the circulation returning to a leg that's been too long asleep. I put my head against his chest and he held me there for a few blessed moments.

"Damn if I didn't think I'd lost you," he said softly, his mouth against my hair.

I was too choked up to do anything but just hold on. A few more moments of blessed relief and then I woke up. I pulled back to look into his face. "Oh, God, Jonah, Spuds is in the barn. I think he might be dead."

We started towards the barn at a run.

"And Janet ..." I said, trying hard to keep up. "We were in the underground room and ..."

"Underground room?" Jonah glanced back at me. He was several feet ahead of me now, loping towards the barn, and I was losing speed fast and nearly out of breath.

"Oh, and wait! Jonah ..." But he had already disappeared into the barn. I caught up with him at last, blinking my eyes, trying to adjust to the darkness inside. "Jason Jakes is here, too."

"I see that now, " Jonah said quietly. As my vision cleared, I saw that Jason was standing just in front of us, holding Janet back against him, a large knife pressed all too neatly against her throat. The tennis game had taken an ugly turn.

Spuds still lay sprawled out where we'd left him.

"The sheriff will be here any time now," Jonah said quietly. "Make the smart choice and let go her go."

"Like I'm gonna take advice from a cop."

Janet said, rather desperately, "Oh, Jakes, haven't we had enough?"

But Jason was staring at me now, as if he'd seen some kind of ghost. "I can't fucking believe you got away from him," he said.

"I told you," Janet said. "I told you she had powers. You really want to mess with something like that?"

Jonah looked down at me and said, almost playfully, "You haven't been casting spells again, have you, Libby?" What, was he never afraid? Or was this just his way of dealing with a serious situation?

"I ... Uh ..." I desperately wanted to find my way into his relaxed frame of mind, but it was beyond me at the moment. I went for the serious instead. "He refused to kill us even when Brad ordered him to."

"Good to know." Jonah said, reaching out to touch my arm.

"Be quiet," Jason said. "I've heard about enough out of you. First you screw with my relationship, now you're trying to screw with my head."

Jonah gave me a questioning look. "I did some counseling."

"I gather it didn't take." Still light and humorous. Is he even human? And, yes, he is, as it turns out, because he looked at Jason quite seriously then and said, "She can testify that you refused to kill them. They'll go easy on you, maybe even make a deal."

"You've got to listen to him, honey," Janet said. She tried to turn her head to look at him, but stopped as she felt the knife against her throat. I thought I saw tears glistening in her eye.

"He's a cop, Janet. Cops lie."

"But, Sugar Bear ..."

"You're as bad as all the rest of them. If it wasn't for you, none of this would have happened." He shifted her in his grip and said to Jonah, "Give me your gun."

What is it with men and guns anyway? It's a constant hassle. Would Sandy's husband think that whoever had the biggest gun, or was the best shot, should rule the world? As far as I'm concerned, whoever invented guns should have been shot.

When Jonah didn't respond, he pulled Janet more tightly against him and pressed the knife against her throat. "I said, I want your gun."

Under the circumstances, it wasn't long before he had it. Jonah put it on the workbench as ordered and Jason, still hanging on to Janet with one hand, simply picked it up. Checking it out, he seemed pleased. The physically weak man who Brad had so easily brought to his knees was now puffed up and strutting. Apparently Jason feels more himself when he's packing heat.

He pulled Janet around and pushed her in the direction of the trap door, then ordered the two of us to join her. Feeling like I wouldn't be able to breathe if I had to go down there again, I was only mildly comforted when Jonah took my arm and said, "It's going to be alright." He seemed to mean it, though I couldn't begin to see how.

Turns out, Janet and Jonah must have been on the same page. Instead of going down the ladder like a meek little lamb, Janet turned around and headed for Jason, a look of determination on her face. "You can't do this, Jakes," she said. "You can't do something that you can't take back."

"Stay back, Janet," he snarled, but she kept on going.

I stood, frozen, waiting for him to shoot her, but he seemed frozen as well. He stared at her, and the closer she got, the more conflicted he looked. She reached out for him and he reacted as if he'd been burned, looking down at where she'd touched him.

In that brief moment, Jonah made his move. He shoved me in the direction of the workbench and launched himself toward Jason.

Diving behind the bench, I watched in horror as Jason took aim and fired. It was one of those slow motion moments when time seems to almost come to a stop. It was a gift from God that Spuds was able, at that exact moment, to rise up from the dead just far enough to kick Jason in the knee and bring him down, then fall back with a loud groan. The shot went wild, lodging itself somewhere in the roof and we heard a clatter of pigeons as they flew away. Fortunately, I don't think any of the birds were hit, because nothing but a few odd feathers fell to the ground.

It was only seconds before Jonah got hold of the gun. Cursing loudly, Jason raced for the door, Jonah behind him. Janet ran after them, with me in close pursuit. We stood in the doorway, fascinated, as Jonah stretched out his stride, running Jason down, slowly and relentlessly closing in on his prey. When he caught up with him, Jonah swung Jason around. The momentum brought both men down but it was obvious from the beginning, which one was in control.

"Oh, dear, oh God," Janet said, as Jonah brought Jason back towards us. She buried her face against my shoulder, unable to watch any longer. Obviously, their Alice in Wonderland tennis game wasn't quite over yet.

Fortunately, it was right about then that a helicopter arrived and only a few minutes later when the sheriff's vehicles came pouring into the yard. Janet and I stood together without speaking, watching as they spread out to cover the area. An ambulance arrived and EMT's rushed in to examine Spuds, then transferred him to a stretcher. As they brought him past me, I reached out to take his hand. "Thank you so much, Roger," I said. His grip was weak, his face pale, but miraculously enough he was able to smile. Spuds, the man I'd had no respect for at all had suddenly became a VIP (Very Important Potato). He had saved Jonah's life and quite probably, my own.

"Bullet in the chest," the EMT said. "Lucky for him, it missed the mark. He'll need a little work, some recovery time, but he should do just fine."

Looking up, my heart did a back flip. Jonah was heading towards me across the yard and there was something about the way he was walking that made me weak in the knees. I think I could have sunk down and melted right into the ground, it felt so good. He had never, ever looked better to me than he did right then. And I had never wanted so much to run into someone's arms, build a great big nest and stay there.

Janet stepped away from me as he got closer. I have no idea where she went or when she went there. By that time all I could see was him.

He took my hands in his like they were something precious. "Libby," he said. He breathed my name rather than speaking it, looking into my eyes for what felt like forever. He looked weary and wonderful at the same time. He pulled me closer and gently stroked my hair back from my face. "Next time we go somewhere, let's make it a real vacation," he said. Then he wrapped his arms around me and we held on to each other for dear life, ignoring the people swirling around us, busy at their work.

When we finally broke apart, he said, "I wish I could just take you back right now, but I've got to finish up here first."

I nodded, not wanting to stop looking up at him.

"C'mon," he said. "You'll need to give your statement, but we'll do that at the station. Right now, you can sit in my car. You must be exhausted."

I hesitated, seeing that two cops had Janet beside one of their cruisers, questioning her. I felt drawn to go to her, help her somehow. In some ways, I felt like we'd been comrades in arms. We'd very nearly died together.

Jonah followed my gaze. "She's a suspect, Libby."

"She's a kidnap victim."

"You just about died because of her. I think you've done enough."

They were handcuffing her now, putting her into a squad car separate from the one Jason was in. She gave me a frantic glance just before she disappeared.

Jonah caught my look. "I saw her drive by while I was waiting for you at the hotel, Libby. That's where I went. I was looking for her."

I nodded, still staring toward the sheriff's car.

"Libby?"

I finally looked at him.

"How did you find her, anyway?"

"Actually, she sort of found me."

"You mean, kidnapped you."

"No. Not exactly." And to his doubting look. "Well, it's not the whole story."

He went to get the SUV and pulled it up in front of me. Getting out, he ran his hand over the battered front of the car. "Some gate," he said, ruefully. I had to get in the driver's side and climb over the gearshift into the passenger seat, which, once you're past the age of sixteen, is never easy and certainly not graceful. I flopped awkwardly into the passenger seat like a seal landing on the beach, hoping he wouldn't watch too closely.

"Try to relax. I'll be back as soon as I can." He gave me a look that warmed my heart, my toes, and probably some other parts of me if I hadn't been too numb to notice, then shut the door and went back to his work.

With a sudden sense of panic, I pushed the "lock" button, locking all the doors. I rested my head against the back of the seat and closed my eyes. It was a funny thing, though, I kept having to open them. It wasn't that I needed to see what was going on, but I still had such a sense that I needed to watch out for Brad or Jason—like I might have to run away at any time. I was still on alert, still in the experience. I lost it as soon as Jonah got into the car. I didn't even know I was crying until he fished a napkin out of his glove compartment and handed it to me. Then he just sat there quietly and waited, his hand on my shoulder.

When I finally regained some control over myself I began to think what I must look like. Yesterday I had fallen in the mud. Was that only yesterday? Looking down at my clothes, I could see that the evidence was still there. It had been a long time since I'd had either makeup or makeup remover and there had been no mirror in the tiny bathroom in the barn. Thank God Janet had at least let me borrow her brush. I picked anxiously at the dried mud on my jeans until Jonah put his hand over mine to stop me. "It's okay," he said. He pulled something out of his shirt pocket and handed me a little miracle—the silver and malachite pin.

"Last night we came out here, but had nothing to go on. This morning ..." He stopped and I realized he was fighting back his own emotions. "If I hadn't found it ..." He reached out and touched my face. "It was by the gate."

"It was in my pocket." It seemed like such an amazing thing, that it had somehow gotten from my pocket to the open ground. "I guess it fell out in the truck and then, when Janet got out to open the gate ..." It didn't matter, really. It only mattered that it was with me. I held it to my cheek, feeling the calm power of the stone.

Silence while we both imagined what might have happened. As if echoing my thoughts, he said, "I didn't know if you were dead or alive, Libby. Once I found the pin, they were able to go for a search warrant, but I knew I couldn't wait till they got here."

"So you rammed the gate?" And when he nodded, "It was ... excellent timing." I smiled and he leaned over to kiss me.

A sheriff appeared at Jonah's open window, interrupting us. "Detective ..." He bent down to look in at me. "Ma'am." Ma'am? Had it really come to that? "You going to bring her down to the station when you're through here?" He was grinning, so, obviously, he hadn't missed our kiss.

Jonah nodded.

"See you there, then." He looked like he was just about to ma'am me again, but then changed his mind. Must have caught the storm warning in my eyes.

Jonah rolled up his window and started the car, then leaned over to kiss me again. As we broke apart, I said, tightly, "Oh, God, Jonah, I almost got you killed. I should have never let you just walk right into that barn."

"I knew better than to walk right in, Libby. It was my mistake."

"But I didn't tell you what you needed to know."

He stopped me. "Actually, you did. When you told me Jason had refused to kill all of you, I knew it was just a matter of time. Besides," he said, gently, "it turned out okay."

Jonah backed the car up and headed it toward the gate, then looked at me again. "But there is one thing I'm curious about. Who the hell is Spuds?"

The Guardian Angel Does His Thing

Jonah slipped into the room hoping no one would notice him. He went directly to the bar and stood there waiting for the bartender. To his dismay, a woman appeared out of nowhere and settled herself entirely too close to him on the nearest bar stool.

"Hi," she said brightly.

He glanced at her and saw pert—pert blond hair, a pert nose, pert everything. He gave the briefest nod he could manage, then turned back to the bar, grateful the bartender was now approaching. He ordered coffee, to go. The woman ordered a white wine.

"You're Detective Haley, aren't you?" she said.

He looked at her because he had to.

"Caitlin Carter." She plopped her business card in front of him. "Maybe you've seen me on the news?"

She held out her hand.

He shook it reluctantly.

"You were certainly the hero of the day. Wow!" She propped her elbow on the bar, rested her chin on her hand and looked up at him through long lashes that were used to slaying men.

He gave her a measured look.

"And how is Ms. Brown doing?" And when he didn't answer, "She must have had such a terrible ordeal."

"She did," he said shortly.

"I'd love to do an exclusive."

"You'll have to talk to the sheriff," Jonah said.

"Oh, come on, Detective. You know that's not what I want. I want first person. In depth. One on one." She said it like it was a come-on and she was practically batting her eyes at him now. Two other reporters had already accosted him. He had told them nothing and with this one he intended to do the same. Only this one was also trying to flirt with him, which really made him mad.

The bartender was back with his coffee and her drink, as if they had come there together. "Let me get that for you," she said sweetly, putting some bills on the counter.

"No," Jonah said more gruffly than he'd intended. He handed the bartender some money, then poured sugar in his coffee. Too much, because he was so irritated.

"The whole psychic angle," she said. "It's got story written all over it. I want to know how she found that missing woman. And what about you and her? What about the way you had to jump in and save the day. I mean, people will eat this stuff up."

He snapped a plastic lid on his coffee, not even looking at her any more.

"I do hope you'll at least give her my card?"

He left it on the bar.

Back upstairs, he made sure no one was around before unlocking the door. They no doubt already knew what room they were staying in but they weren't going to hear it from him.

Libby was lying on her side, a blanket all the way up to her nose as if she was trying to hide from something. She stirred when he locked the door and he saw that she was looking at him. He set his coffee on the table and went over to her.

"You getting any sleep?"

"Lots," she said happily. "Oh, just lots."

"Good." He moved the blanket off her face so he could lean down and kiss her, then pulled it up again and tucked her back in. She snuggled in and drifted right back to sleep.

Smiling, he settled himself in the chair and started sipping his coffee. Later he'd try to read the paper, but for now he just wanted to sit with her and see that she was safe. He thought about his little girl, the other person in the world who he most needed and wanted to keep safe, and eventually felt such a deep need to hear her voice that he took his cell phone into the bathroom so he could give her a call.

His ex answered the phone. "Oh, God, Jonah," she said. "Are you okay? I just heard about what happened on the news. My God!"

It was already on the news? He assured her he was okay.

"I guess you still can't resist playing Rambo."

Were they back to that again?

"Jonah? Are you there?"

"Yeah."

"That woman you saved ..."

"I think it's more like we did it together," he said softly.

"Is she your ... girlfriend?"

"We came up here together, if that's what you mean."

"I see."

"Look, Ginny, I'm fine. She's ... going to be fine. I actually called up to talk to Amy."

"She's not here," she said shortly. For the first time ever he wondered if she was lying to him about his daughter's whereabouts. "Besides, Jonah, what kind of people are you running around with these days, anyway? I mean, have you even thought about Amy, about how it might affect her?"

"What the hell are you talking about?"

"Psychics," she said darkly.

Jonah had to fight the urge to laugh and then fight harder to resist the urge to get into it with her. "Just tell Amy I called," he said, and hung up.

He went back into the bedroom and sat staring at the newspaper for awhile. He couldn't really say he was enjoying reading it. For that matter, he couldn't really even say he was reading it at all. His mind was somewhere else, going a hundred miles an hour. So much had happened in the last few days, both personally and professionally. Most especially, personally. Sitting there watching Libby sleep, he felt the tenderness rise up in him like he'd never known before and he knew he could no longer deny the strength of his feelings. He had fallen for her in a big way. He just hadn't realized it—or at least accepted it, until today.

What he wanted to do, what he really desperately wanted to do was go over there, wake her up and tell her exactly how he felt. He closed his eyes and considered, then stretched out his legs and leaned his head back against the chair. It wouldn't do to rush into something like that, would it? At least not until he'd thought about it a little more.

It had been such a long day anyway. He had slept very little the night before and now he was stiff and sore and tired from the morning's activities. Adrenaline had made it seem easy at the time, but now ... *Not as young as I used to be*, he thought, smiling. It would have pleased his ex to hear him say that, but she was never going to get the chance. He took one last look at Libby, then closed his eyes again and let his mind drift into welcome sleep.

Manifesting (My) Destiny

I opened my eyes a crack and peeked out at the world, relieved to see that I was still apparently safe. I was lying on top of the bed in the hotel room, in my nightie, a blanket over me. Jonah was sitting in the chair at the end of the bed, reading the paper. I watched him a moment, then closed my eyes tight, wanting to maintain the feeling of comfort I got from having him there, guardian to my sleep.

Other, more painful memories flooded back over me but I tried to push them away. We'd spent way too long at the sheriff's office giving my statement. They of course wanted to go over everything repeatedly, and by the third time through, it seemed like one excruciating detail after the other. I don't know how they felt, but personally, I was sick of hearing about it. Or thinking about it. Not that I could stop.

The next thing I remember I was lying down on the bed. So tired. I had scrubbed my face clean, taken a long, luxurious shower, and washed my hair. Hair still wet, I had decided to lie down just for a few minutes to take a nap. Now, it was how many hours later? Past sunset. The light outside the window was almost gone.

I stretched, catching Jonah's eye as I did so. Suddenly, he was no longer looking at his paper. He smiled the nicest smile.

I turned over and went back to sleep for awhile. When I woke up sometime later, he was still there. I thought I might just stay like that forever, it felt so safe, but this time he noticed right away that I was awake.

"You hungry?"

"I don't know." Right then, nothing seemed settled. Not even that.

"You've been sleeping for hours."

I struggled to sit up, groaning a bit at the stiffness of my back and the ankle that still hurt some when I moved it. I plumped the pillows together and propped myself up against them, still feeling a bit off kilter, like I might be leaning a bit.

He grinned. "You look like you've been rode hard and put away wet," he said, putting that little cowboy twang to it.

"Stop it with the sweet talk."

He put down the paper and came to the bed, sitting beside me. "Actually, you look great. Best thing I've ever seen."

I liked the look in his eyes. Genuine.

When he leaned over to kiss me lightly on the forehead I had the distinct impression he was afraid I would break.

We had those big juicy burgers and streak fries like we had the first night. Turns out I was pretty hungry after all. And besides, as Jonah so lovingly pointed out, it was sort of our third anniversary. As in three days since we, well—finally got together in a big way, I guess you could say. I wasn't sure I could handle him being so romantic like that, but somehow he even got them to deliver the food to our door.

We didn't sleep together that night. Correction—we did share the same bed and he did hold me till I was nearly asleep. And I'll admit it, I clung to him like that last wet noodle you can never get out of the pan. We just didn't do anything about it. I was too tired even for something like that. And who knows what he was feeling.

The morning sun woke me; it was in my eyes. I was halfway through a dream in which Janet and I were at a rock concert where we couldn't seem to push our way through the rowdy crowd. Two cowboys had lifted us over their heads, trying to help us get to the stage. Instead, they were so drunk that the four of us fell flat on the ground, nearly trampled by that same rowdy crowd. I snapped out of a deep sleep with the words to "Gypsies, Tramps and Thieves" indelibly stamped in my head. I'm guessing it was a Cher farewell concert.

Jonah was already awake, lying on his side facing me. Apparently, he'd been watching me sleep, which might have creeped me out with some guys I've known, but with him it just made me feel more ... safe. I was very big on safe right about now. I opened my mouth to speak, though I can't think now what I was going to say. Besides, Jonah took the words right out of my mouth.

Later (much later) he told me about the reporters who were camped outside. Since I was just not up to the challenge we hatched a plan to stay inside all day and then try to sneak out after dark that evening. It occurred to me that staying in the room might be a story in itself. I could just see the headlines at home, "Cop and Psychic Make Hay While the Sun Shines." Well, that would be Lindsay's headline, anyway. I could picture Frank reading the story and shaking his head. "I can't compete with that," he'd say humbly. "I can't compete with that."

Jonah had unplugged our room phone and the office was screening our calls. They were instructed to give out Jonah's cell number, but only to a very small list of people. I took a call from Lindsay, who was crazy with worry and ready to drive up and take care of me. Only Jonah's being there put a stop to it. My mother called from her home in Boston. She had, of course, heard about it on the news. Once she was assured that I was safe, she seemed more interested in talking about the new man in my life than anything else, which was oddly comforting to me. There was a written message from Frank saying he was thinking about me, and there was a stack of messages from God knows where. I stuffed them in my suitcase for later.

The restaurant gladly brought us our breakfast—apparently they were getting a real charge out of all the activity going on, making a lot of money off the media, and more than happy to oblige. The lady at the front desk was having the time of her life just fielding all the calls.

We got into it a little after breakfast.

I was pacing, trying to make a point. "Janet was just as much a victim as I was."

Jonah was having none of it. "She kidnapped you."

"She gave me a ride. She wanted to talk."

"Libby ..."

"It wasn't her. It was her sicko boyfriend. Or, should I say, boyfriends."

Jonah came over to me and turned me to face him. "You're talking about a woman who was planning a life with the guy who was hired to kill her."

"But he never actually did." Good God, I was starting to sound like Janet now.

"Are you listening to yourself?"

I sighed. "So they're an odd couple."

"Were an odd couple. I doubt they'll see much of each other now. They may still have the motive, but not the opportunity."

"You talk like it's a crime."

"Their relationship? What do you think?"

"Love," I said. "There's no explaining it."

That got a smile out of him. "Tell me this, Libby, if she hadn't given you that ride would you have been in danger?"

I avoided answering as long as I could, then shook my head reluctantly.

"You ever hear of the Stockholm Syndrome?"

"I'm a therapist, Jonah, of course I've heard of it. Hostages under threat of being killed bond with their captors, but I really don't think

Janet was in that kind of situation. I just don't think that's what was going on with her."

"I was referring to you."

That almost made me mad. Would have made me mad if I hadn't been so mad for the guy. If he hadn't saved my life. If he wasn't looking at me with such warmth right now. "I wasn't there long enough," I said finally. "It takes three to four days at least." Maybe he had a point, but I wasn't in the mood to concede it. "What's going to happen to her, anyway?"

Jonah shrugged. "That's not my area." And to my worried look, "Chances are she'll make some kind of deal, testify. I doubt she'll do any jail time."

"Like Spuds?"

He nodded. "Your dear couch potato."

"Well, he may have saved your life. If he hadn't ... If I hadn't been such an idiot about sending you into that barn." I sat down on the bed, too mixed up to do anything else.

Jonah sat, putting his arm around me and pulling me against him. "We wouldn't have been in that barn if I hadn't brought you into the case in the first place."

"Okay," I said softly. "Okay."

We left for home that night, hoping to avoid the media blitz, but still got nabbed by a TV crew. Did they never sleep? For that matter, were they even human?

"Ms. Brown? Ms. Brown? How are you holding up?" It was a petite, pert-nosed blonde woman smiling up at me, mike at the ready.

I felt Jonah's hand tighten on my arm.

"Tell us, how did it feel being locked in that barn? Were you quite convinced you were going to die?" Her teeth gleamed unnaturally in the spotlight as she shoved the mike further into my face. "Tell us about it," she said eagerly.

"It was hell. It's over."

I tried to move past her, but she stuck like glue.

"You must have been so scared."

"I was unable to escape," I said shortly. "Kind of like right now."

I saw the shock on her face. It's okay for reporters to be rude as hell to the people they're going after. We've all seen those interviews when they ask somebody who has just lost their entire family in a plane crash, *So, how do you feel?* Then they zoom in hungrily when the person starts to cry. Now that's news you can use.

"Ms. Brown has nothing more to say." Jonah pushed us past the woman towards the car.

"But, what about the two of you?" She called after us, and I'm quite sure I heard her scurrying our way, heard the cameraman lumbering behind her. "How do a psychic and a cop coexist?"

Fortunately, we were in the car by then and didn't have to hear any more of it. I didn't look back but I'm quite sure they were still filming us as we drove away.

Jonah looked over at me and grinned. "So, how do a cop and a psychic coexist?"

He put his hand on my knee and squeezed it.

We ended up driving most of the night, but we got home, something we both seemed to need and want. Jonah suggested I go to his place and it turned out to be a good suggestion. I had been dying to see what it was like.

Jonah lives in this great house near the beach. It's not huge, but it has that rustic but well cared for look only a beach house can have. I expect he and his wife bought the place some years ago when you could still get a cottage three blocks from the beach for under a mil. I doubt he could have afforded it now.

When we stepped into the house I was immediately taken by the quiet. Good energy. There were bookshelves with actual books on them, a used brick fireplace, dark wood trim, and a soft, deep carpet that made the place feel cozy and warm. He served me hot cocoa, not the instant kind, but the real thing that you have to watch and stir, and then we collapsed into his big, comfy bed.

Sometimes being really, really tired really turns me on. This was one of those times. For that matter, just knowing that I was in his bed turned me on. In a way, it felt like the first time that we ever really made love. There was a new depth to touching one another. I had come back from the edge of a very scary place and Jonah was the one who had brought me back. It definitely felt like a new dimension.

"Remember that night we danced at the club?" Jonah was holding me beside him, my head tucked beneath his chin. "What was that, anyway? What happened?"

"Maybe we met before."

"Well, yeah, sure, when you came to the station, but to tell you the truth, I thought you were a total nut case."

"Hmmm ... Flattering," I said. "But I meant maybe we met before in a more intimate way."

"I think I would have remembered something like that."

I mean, past lives."

He was quiet.

"You think that's stupid."

"I don't know," he said, and then, "Who knows?" He thought about it awhile and seemed to warm up to the idea. "Maybe I was a king and you were my consort."

"Maybe I was a queen and you were my willing servant."

"Hmmm, that has definite possibilities." He moved his hand down my back, a soft caress.

I stretched happily so I could look up at him. "I'm not one of those people who think we were all royalty. You and me, we were probably just peasants trying to grub out a living in the forest somewhere. Maybe you were a … woodsman, and I was a …"

"Woodsman's wife?"

Interesting. Now he was talking about a wife. I snuggled in closer, the comfort was so nice. And for once, I wasn't afraid. That thought scared me, though, the fact that I wasn't afraid.

It occurred to me that we could have stayed in Jonah's house—specifically, his bedroom, indefinitely. Maybe it would take days before anyone would notice and, in the meantime, we could be together and not have to face the world and its endless problems and possibilities. I felt like I was experiencing a bridge of connection unlike anything I've ever felt. Each moment seemed to slip into the next like a perfect string of pearls; strong, beautiful, and connected.

We shared breakfast on the little brick patio in his backyard, munching on oranges and toast and pretending that we had all day. He has this wonderful ivy that grows all over the fence, old established rose bushes and a camellia the size of a tree. Small and contained and completely private, the yard felt deliciously like a secret garden to me. I didn't want to leave.

But life was calling. Jonah needed to go in to work for at least part of the day. And Peeps? Well, Peeps was calling, too.

After swinging by the Pet Palace, I was home by eleven. Peeps couldn't seem to get enough of me. His revved his little kitty body up to a super purr like I'd never heard before and insisted on sitting on my chest, my lap, and anywhere else he could find a spot big enough to hang on to.

When I went to the bathroom, he followed me, curling up at my feet on the fluffy white bathroom rug and looking up at me adoringly. It paid off big time—I fed him tuna from a people can, let him lick whipped cream off my fingers, and held on to him as tightly as he seemed to want to hang on to me.

The phone was ringing a lot but I turned it down so I didn't have to hear the damn thing. Lindsay took off work to be with me and played secretary, listening to what the callers had to say, then jotting them down and deleting them so the machine wouldn't get full. It might have been nice, though, if it had gotten full. Then there would be no more calls.

She brought a couple over to me, but I didn't want to look at them. "You'll have to face it eventually," she said.

"News people?"

"Yeah, one or two. But I was thinking more about the whole psychic thing, not the news people. These people here are all calling you for help."

I groaned.

"You can't blame them. Maybe they lost a loved one. They heard about you finding people. Naturally they'd want to call." She waved a slip of paper under my nose.

"This one's about a missing teen."

I hid my face in my hands.

"Seriously, E., you ought to be happy you can help. You know, it's a gift and all that?"

I'd told her that many times. And I believe it. It is a gift. "It makes me anxious."

"What?"

"Being expected to know. You know?"

She rolled her eyes.

"It's not my right to tell other people what they ought to do. Or think."

Lindsay smiled indulgently, looking strangely wise, probably because we'd had this conversation before, on more than one occasion. "But what if you can help them with something they can't possibly do for themselves?"

I sighed. "Some people just don't want to be found."

"Like Janet Packard?"

I nodded.

"But most do," she said. "Besides, maybe the more you resist, the more this thing will—you know, come at you. You know, like it's your destiny or something?"

I didn't tell her out loud that I'd pretty much come to that same conclusion.

Peeps was eyeing her lap and about to leap into it. "Get away, you furry little devil," she said. Seeing she hadn't deterred him in the least, she stood up and started walking around the room, Peeps in hot pursuit. "Rita called," she said, still trying to outrun Peeps. "She says they're getting calls at the office, too."

"Oh, God."

"Actually, from the sound of her message, I think she likes it. Makes her feel important, you know. Where the action is." Lindsay finally picked up Peeps, handling him as if he was contagious, and plopped him on my lap. "She also said something about Jonah."

"Jonah?"

Lindsay went to the table to sort through her message pile, finally pulling one out. "Oh, here it is. She says—and this is a direct quote, *When are you and the detective going to pick out the china?*"

I made a face. "Rita would be ecstatic if I was dating a serial killer."

"Well, when are you? Picking out the china, I mean."

"I don't even know his middle name yet."

"But you want to."

We were grinning at each other now.

Lindsay stayed busy with the messages, sorting them and stacking them. Then she insisted on fixing Peeps and me a light lunch—a toasted cheese sandwich and a bowl of hot Campbell's tomato soup for me (my ultimate comfort lunch) and bits of sharp cheddar for Peeps. When we sat down to eat it felt like I was finally home again.

We ate in companionable silence, with only one brief sarcastic comment from Lindsay when Peeps settled himself on her feet. She looked under the table and gave him a dirty look, but maybe for the first time ever, she didn't try to shove him away.

She drummed her fingers on the table as if building up to something, then finally said, "So, you ever try out a bounce castle?" It seemed an odd way to break the silence.

I hesitated, a spoonful of soup halfway to my lips. "You mean those blow up things kids jump around in?"

She nodded, grinning foolishly.

"At kids parties? You can rent them?"

She nodded again.

"What do you mean, try out?"

"You know." She gave me one of her expressive *I'm talking about sex* faces, but I still didn't know what she was talking about. She dabbed at her mouth with her paper towel/napkin. "I mean it," she said happily. "You should try it sometime."

I suppose I looked stupid. No light had yet dawned.

"There are other things to do than just bounce."

"Ah," I said, the sun finally peeking up over the hill. "You and Officer Byron?"

She made a face. "Ted and I never really ... clicked."

"You were trying too hard."

"Too hard has never been a problem."

We both giggled.

"He was interested in you because you made a fool of yourself at the police station," I said.

"So?"

"Doesn't exactly bode well for a meaningful relationship, does it?"

"Whatever," she said. "Water under the bridge and I'm glad it's gone."

"So, then who ...?"

"Walter."

I almost choked on my sandwich. "You always said Walter wasn't very ..."

"Creative?"

I nodded.

She raised her brows at me and smiled. "You think you know a guy and then he surprises you." She sat back in her chair happily and I thought I detected a slight, though gentle kick under the table. Peeps came out with a frustrated meow, but still gave her a look of adoration before padding off toward the living room and the potted palm.

She leaned forward, putting her arms on the table. "At first, it was like, let's jump around in there, you know? I always wondered what it would be like. It looked fun, but I never got to play in one when I was a kid. Did you?"

I shook my head. "We always had skating parties."

She nodded. "So, anyway, Walter and I were at one of his friend's houses and they had this one in their yard, left from a party they had for their four-year-old. The people who rented it out weren't coming by to pick it up till the next day." She seemed lost for a moment, remembering, then came back to the present. "At first, we just jumped around, but it's hard to keep standing up so pretty soon we were on our backs, flopping and bouncing around. And laughing like idiots. And then, the next thing you know ..." Her eyes almost closed as she thought about it. "Well, I think we both got the idea at the same time."

The doorbell rang. When I started to get up, Lindsay jumped up ahead of me. "Stay put," she said. "You never know who it might be."

She was right. She returned to the kitchen with Jonah in tow. His eyes met mine immediately; like he needed the reassurance of seeing me there, as much as I needed it, too. I went to him and we held on, Lindsay smiling at us from the background.

"You want some lunch?" She asked Jonah when we finally broke apart.

"Yeah," he said. "That would be great."

When she served him the soup, she kissed him on the cheek, which seemed to catch him by surprise. "That's for her," Lindsay said, pointing towards me. "For taking care of her."

So we sat at the table, the three of us, or should I say four. Peeps was now dogging Jonah, insisting on his attention. There was a nice feeling about it, somehow, Jonah looking from Peeps who was now standing with his front paws on Jonah's lap to me who would definitely have her paws on Jonah's lap if we'd been alone in that kitchen right about then.

Still, Peeps and I spent the night alone. It seemed important somehow to be back on track, back in my own little house with my own not so little cat sleeping on the end of my comfortable queen sized bed. It was not normal, but almost. Because the truth was, nothing would ever be normal—or the same, again.

The next morning the phone rang early enough that I figured it had to be a friend. When I picked it up, however, it was Janet. Lord knows I'd wanted to go see her, but as Jonah had patiently explained, seeing her—or even talking to her, was not a good idea. The case was ongoing. I might have to testify. And having any connection with her at all could certainly mess things up for the DA.

She wouldn't take no for an answer when I told her I couldn't talk. 'But I'm out of jail," she said. "My ex bailed me out."

Mr. Old Leather Watch had come through for her, poor sucker that he must be.

"My lawyer says I'll be able to make a deal."

"Good," I said. "Now I really ought to hang up."

"Wait." She sounded pained. "You know yourself that Jakes would never have killed anybody."

"Janet, I can't talk about this."

"Brad's the real problem. The DA just has it out for Jakes."

Maybe because he's such a repeat offender, I wanted to yell, but I said nothing. I had thought I wanted to see Janet because I cared about what happened to her. Hearing her now, I just wanted to scream her away.

"They actually wanted to charge me with kidnapping." She sounded incredulous. "I mean, you know as well as I do. I didn't really do anything. I didn't do a damn thing."

She was almost right, and earlier, I would have stuck up for her. Now I just wanted to get the hell out of Dodge. "Don't call me again, Janet," I said, and then hung up with her still talking into the phone.

I'd have to tell Jonah about the conversation, but not right now. I went to the beach instead, sat on the sand for a long time, talked to God and talked to my guides. Prayed that I'd never need to go through anything like that again and asked for guidance in how to find ways to help people that didn't involve risking my life. Life felt sweet and good and precious again and there wasn't much that could bother me right about then.

Except maybe for Sandy Roget. She popped her head in my office door looking heavily made up and inquisitive. "You okay for a session, Elizabeth?" She flounced in dressed in black leather pants, tight ones, and a white halter top that made no attempt to hide the fact that she wasn't wearing a bra. Her shoes were black leather, high heeled, with tiny straps just over the toes. CFM shoes, if you know what I mean. I imagine Rita was in the lobby right about then, coveting them.

Sandy sat down, started to pull out her cigarettes, then laughed. "Old habits. Actually, I'm trying to quit. Haven't had one since ..." She checked the clock, which read 10:21. "Well, since 8:35." Her gold bracelet jangled against her wrist as she put the cigarettes away.

"Good for you, Sandy." I sat opposite her, my note pad in my hands. I was well aware she was staring at me. And she hadn't said an odd word yet.

"I'm just so ... flabbergasted," she said.

Ah, there it was.

"All this time I was going on about my spousal dilemmas and here you were, out playing Charlie's Angels with a good looking cop. And getting shot at!"

"I wasn't shot at."

"Well, you know what I mean. Looking for innocents in the dark bowels of hell."

I had to smile.

"I so admire that, Doctor."

"Sandy, I'm not a doctor. I'm an LCSW."

She waved my response away. "You're worth ten psychiatrists. Trust me, I know." She and her halter-top settled back into the couch luxuriously. She stretched and smiled a sly cat smile. "Jimmy thinks this outfit is hot."

"It certainly is."

She looked pleased. "Well, as you know the teeth thing wasn't working for me. So now I'm into the clothes thing."

"The ... clothes thing?"

She nodded. "Oh, yeah. It's from that same book I told you about. Number ninety-five. "Dress for Sexess." With the right ensemble, even a lackadaisical lothario can't resist handling the merchandise, you know?" She laughed. "Jimmy's got no idea how much I spent on the new clothes, but, trust me, he's not about to complain."

"But are you … comfortable with your new look?" Since I'd last seen her, she'd somehow gone all the way from Maria in *The Sound of Music* to a high-class whore.

She glanced down at her low cut top. "I do worry about falling out."

We shared a smile.

Okay, so Sandy Roget still had a long way to go. I would always be grateful to her for those big white teeth and the courage they had given me to use my own.

After work, I knew I had to see Frank. It was telling that he hadn't called me since I got back home. I called him at lunch, but talked only briefly. He was late to a church budget meeting. They seem to have a lot of those.

Tilly and I pulled up in front of the rectory, feeling like I hadn't seen it for a long, long time. It even looked different. Smaller somehow, like when you come back as an adult and see a place differently than you did as a child. It took me a minute or so to work up the courage to get out.

The only light I saw was in the kitchen window, so I went around to the side door and knocked. He called to me to come in and I stepped into a room smelling of ginger and cinnamon.

He was standing at the counter spooning cookie dough onto a baking sheet. There was something so wrong about seeing him like that. I needed for him to look manly and untouchable, to be working on a report or a speech or, better yet, rebuilding a carburetor.

Seeing him like that, all soft around the edges, I couldn't handle it. He was vulnerable, easy to destroy. It was just too much.

"Elizabeth." He dropped the spoon and came toward me. Our eyes met as he went in for the hug and I could see the knowing there.

"Thank God you're okay."

We broke apart slowly. He pulled out a chair for me at the table and I sat, remembering immediately the dreams I'd had about his kitchen window and the times we'd shared a meal, as well as other rather tasty things.

He sat down across from me, putting his hands together on the table in front of him. Almost a praying stance. "Guess I won't be seeing much of you at church."

"It's just not me. It never was, Frank."

He nodded. We sat there for a few moments uneasy, uncertain of what to do or say. "It was a shock to hear what happened," he said at last.

"It was … difficult."

"I hope you aren't going to make a habit of it."

Of what? Jonah?

He seemed to realize. "I mean, getting into danger like that."

"God, I hope not."

The timer went off on his oven and he had to get up to remove a batch of cookies. As he deposited them neatly onto the cooling rack I thought my heart would break. It was wrong, wasn't it, to discard such a wonderful man? A man who makes cookies?

"Want one?" He was offering me a particularly large oatmeal raisin cookie.

I shook my head. It would have been tantamount to treason.

Frank lined up neat little spoonfuls of dough on the empty cookie sheet, then slipped it into the oven. He leaned his back against the sink and said, "Now you're going to say we need to talk, right?"

When I didn't speak, he said, "Okay, then I'll start. I just need to know what's going on."

I looked around the room awhile before I answered.

"I think you owe me that much," Frank said, sitting back at the table.

I took a mental deep breath. "I may have lied to you."

"About the detective?"

I nodded.

"Then you were together before the trip?"

I shook my head.

"Then it wasn't a lie."

Was the bastard trying to kill me with kindness?

"You know I'll always love you, Frank."

He smiled sadly. "The kiss of death, when a woman says it to you like that." He sighed, then sat back in his chair, looking almost nonchalant. "Are you sure about this, Elizabeth? Sometimes when you've been through something intense like you just went through …"

"I'm a therapist. I know about that."

"Somebody saves your life, it probably makes you feel all kinds of things."

I nodded reluctantly.

"Elizabeth?"

"Of course. I'm … grateful to him."

"More than that."

"I was feeling it before the trip," I said softly. "I was feeling it before."

He got up and started fussing with the cookies again, checking the ones in the oven, and piling the cooled ones into a vintage Pillsbury Doughboy cookie jar.

He's going to be all right, I thought, but then I wondered if I was just making something up to make myself feel better.

He looked up at me and said tightly, "Well, we can't ever go back to the past, can we? Lord knows, I tried." He washed his hands, then came toward me as he dried them on a dishtowel. He sat next to me. "I'd already figured it out, Elizabeth. Did you really think I wouldn't notice?"

"I know. I'm sorry."

"The handwriting was on the wall, " he said, with a dramatic sweep of the hand.

Was that an actual feeling starting to show? I was starting to sweat.

The last batch of cookies was beeping at him from the oven. He got up to take care of them and I could see a new stiffness in his movements as he almost threw the cookies on the cooling rack. "Maybe you'd better go," he said.

I stood, trying to think of something to say.

"Damn it, Elizabeth. Would you just go?"

I picked up my purse and slipped out the door. Even then, the smell of cookies followed me hopefully to the car.

* * *

After Janet got out on bail the papers said she had cut a deal and would testify for the prosecution, but I'm not so sure. After my front row seat at the tennis match, I think the final game is yet to be played. The trial is a ways off and I may have to testify, but I'll bear that cross when I come to it. More and more information has come out about Brad Hernandez. Turns out he had five different "growing grounds"—Rancho Park was only one of them. And they were all run by former clients of his, the sleazier the better.

It has become increasingly clear to me that my life has changed in some very big ways. I now regularly get requests from people looking for lost loved ones. I've had to turn down interview requests from places like People Magazine, and I've been stopped on the street by people asking for readings and everything else people think a psychic could or should do. God knows, the list is strange and long. After trying so carefully for so long to avoid being known as psychic, it happened anyway. People can now paint a target on my back and take their pot shots. I'll be the brunt of jokes at parties. Office workers gossiping at bars and water coolers will know my name.

And then again I meet so many people who don't feel that way at all. They, too, have realized that there is a lot more to life when we allow ourselves to experience it. Statistics show that a surprising number of Americans say they've had some kind of contact with departed relatives or some other kind of psychic experience. I'd like to suggest that those experiences are also spiritual, that we ought to broaden our definition to include not just departed relatives, but guides and angels, and most of all, God. Opening up doesn't have to be limited to knowing that the spirit of your dear, departed Aunt Jeannette is in the building. It can also lead to so much more—those beautiful and powerful moments when we can truly feel our own intimate connection with All That Is.

***

How is it that a person can suddenly become so indispensable? I mean, you go along living your life alone and think nothing of it and then somebody like Jonah comes along. You don't even realize it when it's happening, but all of a sudden not seeing him daily feels like a punishment. Just a few weeks ago, not seeing him was just a normal part of life. Now, it's unacceptable.

It had been way too long—two days, since we'd seen each other. The phone calls had been flying hot and heavy between us but our separate commitments had kept us apart since the lunch we shared with Lindsay and Peeps that first day back. Now, though, tonight, we were finally going to get together. It was all I could do to wait.

I got home from work and was standing in the kitchen sorting my mail when I noticed something decidedly odd in my back yard. I went to the window and peered out. Smack dab in the middle of the lawn was something really strange. Peeps and I went out to examine it, and sure enough, it was a bounce castle. I darted back into the house when I heard the phone ring.

"So, what do you think?" It was Lindsay, and Walter was on her other line.

"We thought you might be due for a little distraction," he said, his deep voice welcome to my ears.

"You shouldn't have." But I was smiling broadly. And remembering that there is certainly a lot more to Walter than he usually lets on.

"You've got it till tomorrow afternoon," he said.

Lindsay chimed in. "So, you know …"

"Make hay?"

"Exactly."

I hung up just as my doorbell rang.

Jonah looked like heaven to me and it took us awhile to make it out into the kitchen because we were quite naturally unable to separate ourselves for some time. But when we did finally find our way there, I had already turned on the back yard light. It was just enough light to show that the bounce house was out there, but not enough to shine into the inside of the thing. That would still be dark and private. In other words, it was just the right amount of light.

"What the hell?" Jonah had stopped to stare out the window. "Is that one of those ... bounce houses?"

I nodded, trying to look mysterious.

"Having a birthday party for your niece?"

I just smiled.

Jonah looked a bit disappointed. "I was kind of hoping it would be just you and me tonight," he said, running a hand through his hair.

"No parties?"

"No." He was looking a bit puzzled.

"Not even if it's a private party?"

"Private ...?" Our eyes met and I saw the realization start to hit him.

"Very, very private," I said.

A slow smile spread across his face. He took hold of my hand, lifted it to his lips and slowly and deliberately kissed my palm. "As always, Elizabeth, you surprise me," he said softly. The old fashioned kissing of the hand thing had certainly surprised me. And the way he was looking into my eyes ... Well, there was nothing old fashioned about that, but I think I understand now why women used to faint so much.

When we were finally able to stop looking at each other, I took his hand and led him out the back door into the night. The funny thing is, just before we climbed into our castle, I glanced back at the house and caught Peeps watching us through the sliding glass door. I could have sworn I saw him wink.

Libby's Common Sense Guide to Metaphysics

1. Everybody has psychic abilities. You just don't know it yet.

2. If you think you don't have spirit guides, try paying more attention.

3. Anybody desperate to define reality for you is probably still desperately trying to define if for themselves. Stop paying them so much money.

4. The only way to teach peace is to *be* peace. What are you teaching by the way you drive your car?

5. Jesus absolutely would never have picked up an Uzi.

6. Love once created never dies.

Printed in the United States
116679LV00003B/200/P